IAN
QUICKSILVER

THE WARRIOR'S
RETURN

IAN
QUICKSILVER
THE WARRIOR'S
RETURN

ALYSON
PETERSON

SWEETWATER
BOOKS
AN IMPRINT OF CEDAR FORT, INC.
SPRINGVILLE, UTAH

ISBN 13: 978-1-4621-1629-4

Published by Sweetwater Books, an imprint of Cedar Fort, Inc.
2373 W. 700 S., Springville, UT, 84663
Distributed by Cedar Fort, Inc., www.cedarfort.com

Library of Congress Cataloging-in-Publication Data

Peterson, Alyson, 1979- author.
Ian Quicksilver : the warrior's return / Alyson Peterson.
    pages cm
Fifteen-year-old Ian Quicksilver has discovered the unsettling truth that he is not a scraggly cast-off, bouncing around in the Nevada foster care system like an unpicked lottery ball, but the Last Warrior Prince of a distant planet threatened by a sociopathic magician.
ISBN 978-1-4621-1629-4 (perfect : alk. paper)
[1. Magic--Fiction. 2. Magicians--Fiction. 3. Princes--Fiction. 4. Princesses--Fiction.] I. Title. II. Title: Warrior's return.

PZ7.1.P45Ian 2015
[Fic]--dc23

                                    2014042683

Cover design by Michelle May
Cover design © 2015 by Lyle Mortimer
Edited and typeset by Justin Greer

Printed in the United States of America

10 9 8 7 6 5 4 3 2 1

Printed on acid-free paper

For my warriors: Tanner, Brooks, Allison, Amy, and Ami.
And for Aaron, my biggest fan,
who has never read a word I've written.

ACKNOWLEDGMENTS

I'd like to thank Amy Milligan, the very first person I trusted to read and edit my books. I strive every day to live up to her faith in my abilities. A super special thank you to Ami Hendrickson and her unhealthy devotion to my writing despite my adverb overuse. Ami knows all my dirty secrets and surprisingly still loves me for it. I pray that doesn't someday bite her in the butt.

Thank you to Alissa Voss for plucking Ian out of the slush-pile. An even larger thanks to my editor, Emma Parker, who never fails to make me feel like a million bucks. Thank you to the most understanding publicist in publishing, Kelly Martinez, who puts up with my abject stupidity and manages to make me look good regardless. Of course, I must thank my copyeditor, Justin Greer, who gets the importance of character linguistics, the Oxford comma, and binge-watching *Chuck* reruns (not in that order).

Thank you to KJN Andy, BKJN Moses, and SBN Jin at World Class Martial Arts for teaching me the ins and outs of fighting and weapons.

A hearty thank you to my family (all eight of us and Mom and Dad). It would be impossible to be subject to our brand of crazy and not have a sense of humor, no matter how twisted and noir the humor is.

A heartfelt you-freaking-rock to my sons who supply me with ample writing material. Their sarcasm, personality, and unfailing courage have won them the enviable title of Honorable Bankhir Warrior. This book is all about you two. Of course, if I mention them, I have to mention Allison Timberlake, who is my lady warrior with true southern sass. I love you.

And finally, an enormous thank you to my husband, Aaron. He is my cheerleader, ringleader, and book pimp for all of my novels (none of which has he read). For that, his seat in the Hall of Awesome is secure. After all, it was his idea to camp at the base of an active volcano where the concept for the Warriors of Bankhir was born.

–A. Peterson

P.S. JEFFSTER! 4EVER!!

1

Flushed.

First memories are dangerous things. I can remember all sorts of stuff down to the slightest detail. My memory is that good. But the memory I would love to forget is the one where I got flushed down a massive obsidian cosmic toilet. Go figure.

There was this huge, roundish black basin filled with swirling who-knows-what that looked like sparkling star sludge. How, exactly, a toilet could be filled with weird universe goo was beyond me, but I was dangling over it. The dangling part was fine. It was the getting flushed part that sucked.

So, really, it was no surprise that, fifteen years later, I was on the verge of stopping another kid's flushing. I stood at the door of the one (and only sometimes working) bathroom in our drafty trailer, where my evil twin foster brothers were trying to give the new girl a swirly.

"No! Please don't!" Carrie, the new kid, gasped as she tried to brace her feet on the slippery linoleum. She was nine years old with long brown hair—and scruffy, like we all were.

"Oh come on," Jim cajoled. Or it could have been John. The ham-fisted brothers looked so much alike I could never tell them apart. "This is our way of saying 'welcome to the family.' You should feel honored."

With a heavy sigh, I shucked off my pack and set my

breakfast on the zipper. It wasn't my intention to make a career out of rescuing little kids from the clutches of the Evil Twins, but this was the one clear exception.

"Okay," I said, turning back to the twins, ready for a full-on brawl. Considering I was about half their size, it was more likely that I would get squashed like a bug. "That's enough. Let her go."

It was as if I hadn't been there at all. Carrie's progress continued to the grubby porcelain throne undeterred. Not that I was surprised. It was normal that I got ignored, which was probably why I was the foster kid who had been here the longest.

"Hello? Anyone listening?" I said over the top of Jim and John's dim-witted identical guffaws. "Fine. I'll just come in and get her out."

I sized up the situation. I was scrawny, barely a hundred pounds with my shoes on, and runty. I may have looked like a stunted skeleton, but I had massive oversized feet and hands that would make an NBA scout cry. The demonic twins were twice my size and leaned a little toward the sadistic side of mean. I may not have had bulk on my side, but I was scrappy. Speed was going to be my ally.

Not thinking twice about it, I lurched into the bathroom, hooked an arm around Carrie's waist, and spun her out of the twin's clutches. That was the easy part. Shoving Carrie out into the hall behind me, I came face to face with the twins who . . . uh, didn't look all that happy. I gate-crashed their party, and now I was going to pay.

"What do you think you're doing, Weenie Boy?" John growled.

Weenie Boy? I may have been skinny and too short for

my age, but *weenie*? That rankled. The Evil Twins sized me up with matching sneers.

"Hilarious," I muttered. Jim (or John, I really didn't care) made a lunge for me. I ducked and grabbed the towel rack bar. Everything in this slapped-together dump was cheap junk, but for once I was glad the bar easily popped off the wall. I clocked John in the shin with it and leaped out into the hall to slam the sliding door shut. For the final touch, I wedged the bar into the doorjamb.

"Not bad, eh?" I said with a grin, but nobody was around. Carrie had run off. I stood in the hall, alone, listening to the twins swear at me through the door. Not only had Carrie busted a move out of there, but she had taken my Pop-Tart too. Figures. My empty stomach growled in protest. Down the hall, I caught a glimpse of brown scraggly hair flying behind Carrie as she ran out the front.

"You're welcome!" I hollered. "Not that you noticed or anything."

I hiked my pack over my shoulder and left the twins banging on the bathroom door. They'd find a way out sooner or later.

As far as mornings went, that was pretty typical.

Phil and Janet Barfus were my foster parents. They were the proud owners of Puckerbush's Home for Displaced Children, which was really just a fancy name for the town trailer dump. Complete with at least a dozen dirty cast-off kids.

Phil was tall and thin everywhere except his gut. I didn't think Phil Barfus owned another tool besides his trusty roll of fix-all duct tape. He never went anywhere without it. He wore the same three variations of T-shirt that said 'Unlock the magic of Nevada' on them with a faded picture of the Las Vegas Strip and jeans that smelled like he'd soaked them in beer and dirt.

Janet looked about the same, except she smelled like cigarette smoke. A trail of ash followed her wherever she went. I don't think she or Phil had jobs. However, they did get a check from the government for taking in foster kids. That all got spent on the slot machines at the town casino.

I guess my living situation sounds pretty bad, but it wasn't horrible all of the time. Phil and Janet minded their own business and expected us to do the same.

Heading for the front door, I braced myself for yet another day of school at Puckerbush High. I did a quick once-over at the door. Blond hair still a tangled mess? Check. Blue eyes, squashed nose, and scrawnier than a chicken? Check, check, and, unfortunately . . . check. I was ready for school. On my way out, I did a sound test to make sure I was indeed in existence as a human being. I didn't expect resounding results, but I had to try.

"So," I said with my hand on the door. "I'm going to school now."

Phil leaned back in his La-Z-Boy and turned up the volume on the TV. He scratched at his potbelly with a dwindling roll of duct tape, and Janet flicked a bit of ash in someone's sandwich before closing it.

"Have a great day, Ian," I said to myself, and responded with "Thanks! I will. I'm going to ace my math quiz today. Then maybe I'll wheeze around a few laps in gym class and cheat my way through chemistry."

Still nothing.

"Right," I said and shoved my way out the door. "Good to know nothing has changed."

I could have announced I was going to start a riot with pencil erasers and no one I lived with would hear it. However, there were advantages to being practically invisible. I never got told what to do or asked where I was going. I could go anywhere and do whatever I wanted. And yet, the Barfuses still had the upper hand because it's really hard to get into trouble in Puckerbush. There was absolutely nothing to do in town. Outside of town was only dirt and rocks for miles in every direction.

Halfway to school I was wheezing. I don't know about air in other places, but the air in Nevada is dry and thin. No matter how hard I huffed it in, I never got enough. I took a deep drag from my asthma inhaler to open up my lungs. Chemicals: the breakfast of champions.

Coughing up half a lung, I turned down a quiet street in the dead center of town. It sounds lame, but I had to walk down that same street every day. Which was odd because on that street was a house that most people avoided: The Hernfelds'.

Now, I'm not going to go all spooky on you and say the place was haunted. There was nothing unusual about it. It was a normal two-story rambler as ugly and slapped together as every other house in town. Mr. and Mrs. Hernfeld were a regular couple that worked for the casino (like everyone else in town). They had a kid too. I think.

But that's not the point. The point is, for years I walked the same route to school that took me past the same house. Every day, I stopped for half a second to look at it and then moved on. Don't you dare call me crazy. We all have weird habits. Maybe you have to eat the inside of your Pop-Tart first before eating the outside, or you have a pair of lucky shoes you have to lace up counterclockwise. For me there was something about that house . . .

I did my half-second gawk at the sagging roof and lonely windows and walked on. That was when I saw *him*. A massive hulking shadow of a man hiding behind the Hernfelds' shed. I only got a brief glance before he was gone. The hair on the back of my neck prickled. Not that I had much experience with this sort of thing, but it felt like I was being watched.

For a full minute, the street was empty. Then kids straggled out of houses and slogged to school. The desert sun beat down on beat-up trailers and burned into browned lawns. But there was no sign of the fleeting dude-shadow.

It creeped me out. I was never watched. Heck, everyone I knew barely acknowledged my existence. To have someone actually look at me, let alone hide and watch me at a distance, was downright disturbing. I ran the rest of the way to school. Bad idea. By the time I made it to my locker, it felt like I was threatening to hack up both lungs and maybe a kidney.

And yet, even with a deafening cough to announce I was there, I still got knocked into. The kid who bowled me over on my back turned around to see who he'd tripped over. He looked straight over my head. When he didn't see me, he shrugged and kept on going. It was always like that.

"Don't mind me," I said, scrambling to my feet. "I wanted to hang out on the floor anyway."

Dusting myself off, I headed toward first period math. I had my hand on the doorknob when I saw the dude-shadow again lurking around the corner. He was head-and-shoulders taller than everyone else. At least I thought so.

He moved fast. All it took was a blink, and he was gone again. An uneasy feeling welled up in my gut. I could have sworn I could feel his glowing, lamp-like eyes right on me. Weird.

I shook myself. Glowing eyes? That couldn't happen though, right? Maybe living with the Barfuses was finally getting to me and I was starting to cook up imaginary friends. Though, if I were going to do that, you'd think I'd imagine one who didn't freak me out. I headed into Calculus and tried not to think about it. I was fine for most of the day. The freaky-eyes guy didn't show up again.

Until I hit fifth period gym class.

Ever get the feeling that things are about to go seriously wrong? Yeah. Despite the lack of ominous music, there was an unnatural hush in the boys' locker room. Everyone was whispering and throwing furtive glances at the Coach's office at the end of the hall. Something was going down.

The class filed outside for an hour of physical torture. For the millionth time since first grade, I didn't bother to line up for teams. I headed for the bench along the sun-baked brown football field to watch. Coach Yonk wanted to win. Kids like me didn't create winning teams. All my life I had been benched for being undersized. My asthma didn't help much either. It's hard to get out and play sports huffing on an inhaler every five minutes. I hated sitting on the bench. Hated it.

"Kid," a deep voice barked. "Hey, kid!"

I looked up and squinted at a towering figure who came out of nowhere. He looked vaguely familiar. I could have sworn that in the glare of the afternoon sun his eyes glowed slightly.

I jumped off the bench. This couldn't be happening. Nobody had eyes that glowed—and if they did, I didn't want them for a gym teacher. "Yeah?"

"Get out onto the field, Nancy," he said.

A few of the other boys snickered.

"You want me to play?"

"Do you need a hearing aid too, Nancy? Get out there!"

I didn't need to be told a third time. I grabbed a helmet and shoved it down on my knotted blond hair.

"What happened to Coach Yonk?" I asked. I didn't want to accuse this guy of stalking, but it was uncanny that the new coach showed up the very same day the watching shadow did.

"He retired," the coach said, smirking. "Suddenly."

The new coach pushed me out onto the field. Judging by the force applied, I would bet that Coach Yonk got shoved off a cliff by his replacement. It was supposed to be gym, but since half the varsity football team was in my class, touch football got upgraded to making meat paste out of each other. My team had the ball first.

"I'm going to fake the handoff and throw to the left," said Bryce, the quarterback. I don't think he saw me, because I was on his left. It was the only position open.

Everyone yelled "Break!" and spread on the line. Bryce hiked the ball, and the field erupted into chaos. I'd seen football played before, but this was nothing like what I saw on TV. This was a death match. I ran left and down the field, wide open. Bryce had no choice but to throw it to me. As my fingers closed on the leather, I was broadsided by a bullet train.

Or at least, that was what it felt like when I skidded ten

feet into the grass under a heap of human bodies. I hung on to the ball to the bitter end. It took the new coach five minutes to unearth me where I lay flattened into the ground.

A hand waved in front of my face.

"Hey, kid, how many fingers do you see?"

"Five."

"And who am I?"

If he was checking for cognitive clarity to rule out concussion, he was asking the wrong questions.

"The new Nazi who just made me play with a bunch of meat grinders," I said, coughing some air into my lungs.

"The name is Coach Corbin, kid," he said, grabbing me by the front of the shirt and lifting me clean off the ground. "Don't forget it. Go run five laps."

And that was how I got my personal sadistic stalker.

For the next couple of weeks, when I walked to school, Coach Corbin followed. At school, it was "Hey Nancy, your shirt is untucked. Go run five laps." Every time I dropped my books, Coach Corbin was there to kick them over to me and say, "I don't deal with butterfingers, Nancy. Five laps." The worst was when I had to pee and he cut me off at the bathroom. Ever had to run five laps on a full bladder? It sucks.

If I didn't do something soon, my lungs were going to explode. After the five millionth lap, I'd had enough.

It was high time I devised a plan to get rid of the coach.

2

The plan was simple. I needed to get out of gym class. Pronto.

In the days of Coach Yonk, I could have asked to get out of gym class, and he would have signed off on an excuse form faster than he could make the track team sprint. Corbin was a whole other matter entirely. Asking to get out of gym class would cost me more laps than I could count.

I forged a pretty convincing doctor's note; now all I needed was the principal's signature. Maybe he could deal with Coach Corbin for me. It was a long shot, but it was worth a try.

The halls were relatively empty. Most kids waited until the last minute to get to class. I went for stealth, skimming down the hall, checking in all directions for the Coach. You'd think that a man of his size would stick out like a linebacker in a ballet class. But I never knew where he was until it was too late and he had already pounced on me. However, this morning I made it all the way to the main office without seeing him at all.

Mr. Alred, the science teacher, threw the door of the office open wide and burst out into the hall like he did in every room he entered or exited. I can't tell you how many times he'd crashed the door into my face, but this time his explosive exit was to my advantage. I slipped in behind him, unseen and unheard. The office was empty, thank goodness, excluding Miss Reeder, the school secretary who also doubled as the school nurse.

I tiptoed to her desk and leaned in close. I wasn't trying to be creepy or anything, but Coach Corbin could pick up my scent a mile off, I was sure of it.

"Miss Reeder," I whispered. "I need to get out of gym class. I've got a doctor's note."

She leaned forward with a curious blank expression on her face. Crud. She hadn't heard me.

"What was that?"

"Gym class," I said, only marginally louder. "I need to . . ."

Like an eerie horror movie, the office door opened and blew my hair into my eyes. I didn't need to turn to see who it was. I could feel his glowing eyes boring into the back of my head. He'd found me.

"You need more time in the weight room if you ask me." A wide, heavy hand slapped down on my back, making me career forward into Miss Reeder's desk. My ribs smacked into the Formica desktop and smarted like crazy. I was doomed. I had to admit, Corbin was good. Just seconds ago he was nowhere to be seen. I straightened and rubbed at my banged-up torso.

"I don't need time in the weight room," I wheezed. What I needed was to get away from the man who had a personal vendetta against living and breathing like a normal human being. I looked to Miss Reeder for support, but that was a lost hope. Her cheeks flushed a bright pink and she fingered her long brown hair. I gagged. How could anyone have gaga eyes for Corbin? Nasty.

"What this boy needs is a few good laps around the track," Corbin boomed, gripping my shoulder in a way I was sure would cut off the blood supply to my arm. He picked me up and physically steered me around. "Good morning to you, Miss Reeder. I'll take it from here."

Miss Reeder simpered a reply as Corbin's hulking mass shoved me out the door and deposited me in the hallway. I desperately wanted to rub the feeling back into my arm, but I figured doing so would gain me an extra lap or two on the track during lunch.

"Trying to get out of my class, are you?" Corbin asked, dangerously soft.

In times like these, it was wise to shut my mouth, but Corbin had gotten under my skin, and I'd never been all that wise anyway. "No, I'm trying to get out of a trip to the emergency room."

Corbin's face didn't change expression, aside from a minimal lift to his eyebrow.

"Are you giving me lip, boy?"

Squaring off with a man ten times my size was never a smart move. Like an idiot, I said, "Lip and two lungs. What more do you want?"

Corbin's other eyebrow lifted to match the first. My bet was that his overmuscled brain was working double time on how many push-ups and sit-ups I was going to do and laps I was going to run to pay for the comment. He grinned in the sadistic way he always did when pronouncing my doom. I braced myself.

"Finally," he said nodding in approval. "You show a little spirit. It's about time."

I couldn't have been more shocked.

"Right then. I'll just go to class now," I said, skirting around his mass and not believing my luck. His hand shot out and clotheslined me in the chest.

"Not so fast, Nancy."

Ah, that was the other thing I hated about Corbin. He never called me by name. It was always 'Nancy, do this' and 'Nancy, do that.' My bony shoulders tensed. Corbin's eyes glinted. No, they outright glowed under the fluorescent lights, brighter than I'd ever seen before. If he was sizing me up, he must have been using radioactive X-rays. Not only that, but I could have sworn that out of his hand came a wisp of silvery smoke. I should have freaked out, right then and there. Between the glowing eyes and the smoking hand, I should have screamed like a girl and run for my life. But I didn't. There was something familiar about that silvery stuff. It felt like warm milk and lazy afternoons.

It made me remember things.

Deep in the back of my mind an image shuffled forward and played like a movie in my head. I was in an ethereal stone room where a massive sword, with a fat emerald sunk into the hilt, was being presented to me. A horse was there too. At least, I thought it was. I could recall a big white head and hot, smelly horse breath blowing on my face from its hairy muzzle. My shoulder hurt like someone had pressed hot coals or a branding iron into it. Weird.

How could I remember something I'd never seen before? I'd been at the foster home practically since birth. And yet, the vision was as familiar to me as my own current memories. My heart pounded in my throat and I backed up a few hasty steps. I gripped my shoulder. It didn't hurt in reality; it had only hurt in my memory. Under the thin T-shirt I could feel my skin heat up where the pain had been. I had a birthmark there. At least, that is what I thought it was. Though no birthmark I knew of burned.

The second Corbin's hand left my chest, the memories

faded. If he had any idea what he'd just done to me, he didn't give any indication. I tried to breathe and shake off the jumbled mess of images in my head.

"I want five laps after school, and be quick about it. I want to see effort, kid!"

We were back to normal. I gave him a curt nod and ran to Calculus. I skirted along the back of the class and took a desk in the farthest corner, unnoticed, as the bell rang. I didn't mind blending in and disappearing in school. Being friendless had its advantages, like not having to explain why my gym teacher just reached into my head and shuffled through my memories.

I couldn't lose it. I was already a misfit foster kid, and I didn't need to add 'mental case' to it. A deep sigh escaped me as Mr. Fenske started the class and droned on about an upcoming test. Ice-cold gusts of air blew down from the vents in the ceiling, a stark contrast from the rippling horizon beyond the window, baking under waves of sweltering desert heat. I zoned out.

In my mind I could see every detail of a land unlike anything I'd seen on Earth. It had great leafy trees resembling Earth's tropical palms, but with fatter and thicker fronds that cast deep shadows on the pebbled, white sandy beaches. From what I saw, the weather was perfect: warm with a cool ocean breeze. I found I missed it so much a deep ache rumbled in the pit of my stomach. I felt homesick. As if I didn't come from Earth in the first place.

I had to shake that out of my head. Just the thought of being from another planet kind of freaked me out.

Puckerbush, Nevada, was starkly different to the tropical palm planet place. Here it was life-suckingly hot during the day and bitter cold at night. Nothing grew here except scattered and stunted grass. I could count the trees in the entire town on one hand. The air smelled like dirt. That was reality.

One class melded into the next. Occasionally I would get knocked into in the hall. Not on purpose, mind you. That would mean that I was seen and noticed, which never happened. I ate my peanut butter sandwich on sickly white bread alone, sat through all my classes, and got a perfect score on my test in English studies. I'd be proud of it, if it weren't so easy. Then the final bell rang.

When the exit bell rings in Puckerbush High, it triggers a mass exodus of stampeding teenagers. Everyone was eager to leave, but I headed the opposite direction. I had a date with the track.

I tossed my bag and shucked my shirt in a locker in the empty locker room. The overpowering smell of sweat and unwashed gym shorts didn't bother me. What bothered me was that in the big mirror at the end of the row I could count every rib sticking out under my goose-pimpled, pasty white skin. My stomach caved inward, even. Depressing. I was the scrawniest kid in tenth grade.

"Stupid delayed growth spurt," I muttered to what I thought was an empty room. It wasn't. Coach Corbin was standing in the doorway, waiting for me.

"Stop your whining, Nancy, and get out to the track," he bellowed.

"I'm going. I'm going," I said as I struggled into a white T-shirt, popping my head through the hole, making my hair stick up on end. I caught a side glimpse of Corbin giving me a calculating look. He paused before moving on, as if he was caught between wanting to say something or remain silent.

The first couple of laps weren't too bad. I think I was getting accustomed to my lungs burning and gasping for air like I was trying to breathe through a clogged straw. One day, I was sure I was going to pass flat out from lack of oxygen, but it hadn't happened yet. Until then, I was going to live off sucking in bitter-tasting chemicals through my inhaler.

Dry heat pressed in around me, baking off every drop of sweat I put out. I cursed Corbin under my breath. He sat under a wide umbrella gulping down ice water like it was nectar and watching my progress through dark sunglasses.

I rounded the quarter-mile track for the umpteenth time—I'd lost count—and staggered to a wheezing halt.

"I think—I think that's five," I said through gasps of air. I was probably off by a lap or two, but my legs were on fire and my feet couldn't possibly take one more step. My lungs hurt. Bad.

"It's five. Go clean up."

There it was again: pity. I stopped breathing for a full second. Was Corbin actually growing a heart? I wasn't going to stick around and ask. I got back to the locker room and dressed in record time. My chest hurt. I knew the pain wouldn't ease when I got home and around Janet's secondhand smoke. I grabbed my books and was about to bolt when a glint of something shiny caught my eye.

Call me stupid—anything you like—I'd agree with you, but I was curious. And my curiosity took me right into Coach Corbin's half-empty office. What I saw made my jaw drop.

The desk and chair were pushed against the wall, leaving a wide-open space. Big, hulking Corbin stood in the middle of the tiled floor, up on one leg, swinging a colossal broadsword that looked strikingly similar to the one he'd drummed up in my memory. The only difference was the hilt of his sword had no emerald. That same silvery smoke that wrapped around his hand earlier was laced up his arms. His eyes were like two bright automobile headlights.

"Whoa" was all I could mutter. That was when I was discovered. Corbin's face turned from deep tan to an angry puce. Crud.

Any other kid would have bolted, but both of us seemed to be having a hard time finding our voices. Corbin recovered first.

"Get out!" he bellowed.

All I could do was stand like a statue and stutter, "You . . . You have . . . a-a . . ." I wanted to say "sword," or anything for that matter, but all I could do was gape. Corbin shoved the sword out of sight in the equipment locker, slammed it shut, and locked it.

"You didn't see anything, kid. Go home!" Corbin shouted. When he started pounding toward where I stood, my escape senses overcame shock, and I ran.

I ran out of the school and through the parking lot. I ran through yards and over fences to the edge of town; I didn't slow down until I staggered, heaving, up the rickety front steps of the first of four trailers of the foster home. I clung to the broken metal banister and coughed until my stomach ached. I couldn't get enough air, and spots swam in my blurred vision. I scrambled for my inhaler, but chemicals gave me no relief. I wheezed air into my lungs, hardly believing what I had seen.

But it was unmistakable.

Coach Corbin was not human.

3

The next morning, I wondered if I could attend school and act like nothing had happened.

Fat chance.

Young, dirty kids scurried around my scrawny legs in a maze of arms, legs, and noise. I passed out lunches, making do with what little was left in the cupboards. It was payday today, which meant Janet and Phil were at the casino playing the slot machines. Groceries would come from whatever was left over. Most kids didn't last long in Puckerbush before getting adopted or moving on to another foster home. I was the oldest. I'd been there the longest: that odd kid who blended in with the peeling wallpaper.

"Hey! No pushing," I said as a shoving match between a kid named Andrew and one called Ryan got heated. I could have shouted, but they wouldn't have listened. Everyone got a lunch and filed out of the main trailer at a run. I usually followed close behind to make sure everyone got to school in one piece. Today, I lagged behind. I was not looking forward to a meeting with the coach.

Though I was distracted by my impending doom, I made my usual run by the Hernfelds'. The house had changed. I couldn't explain how (frankly, I was too preoccupied), but the odd loneliness that hung over the structure was gone. Though how I could know that by looking at a totally normal house, identical to all the other ones on the block, was unexplainable. I shook that thought out of my head. Corbin must have really rattled me. I was losing it.

How else could I describe thinking that a regular house could be less lonely than normal?

I dragged my feet and slowed to a crawl as the school came into view, wondering—not for the first time that morning—if I could hide behind someone tall in my classes and disappear for the entire day. I skipped going to my locker and went straight to Calculus. There wasn't anyone particularly big or wide in my class, but this was Corbin I was dealing with. I could roll in mud and hide on the roof, and he would sniff me out like a bloodhound.

I made it to lunch without seeing him once. Which, instead of giving me a false sense of confidence, worried me. Corbin never, and I mean *never*, missed an opportunity to slap his meaty hand on my back and demand laps. By the time fifth period gym class rolled around, I was jittery. Mr. Alred took over as substitute for Coach Corbin. Despite my name on the roll, it was as if I wasn't there at all. I sat out the entire basketball tournament. Not a word was said to me.

Afterward, I packed up my bag, said good-bye to Mr. Alred, and headed to the library—where my luck ran out. For the most part, the library was deserted. I was able to toss my backpack on a table and settle down in front of the single school computer for a little game time or harmless hack.

I should have known it wouldn't last.

"Have you found her yet?" a hoarse whisper asked over my shoulder. I jumped a good foot out of the chair and took in more air than my lungs could handle. The library had been empty not seconds before, and now none other than Coach Corbin was standing over me, trying unsuccessfully to hunch behind my chair to diminish his bulk.

Thanks to Corbin's sudden appearance, I about coughed out my tonsils.

"Wh-what?" I wheezed. "What did you just say?"

Corbin's steely blue eyes scanned the library.

"We can't talk here. Too many listening ears," he hissed. I looked around us, a little incredulous. There was a first grader poring over picture books in the corner and the ancient librarian, Ms. Pettis, bent over a pile of returned books. I was sure the kid wouldn't care, and Ms. Pettis was pushing eighty and moved about as fast as a deaf geriatric snail.

"Like who?" I said. "Besides, since when do you play hooky from your own class?"

A flicker of the old Coach Corbin returned. "Talk to me like that again, Nancy, and I'll—"

"Make me run a billion laps," I said. "I know the drill." I don't know what got into me, but seeing Coach Corbin nervous leveled the battlefield. That, and I had a boatload of questions. "Where did you get that sword?"

I barely got out the last word when Corbin clapped his hand over my mouth. "Shut it! What is wrong with you? Do you think it's safe to talk so openly like that?" he said. He pulled up a chair and sat down next to me.

"Why not? Who do you think is listening in?" I said, but to avoid Corbin slapping his hand on my face again, I whispered, "It's not like I'm going to go around telling people you're not human."

Really, all I wanted to do was spur the guy a little into spilling the beans. I didn't expect Corbin to snort incredulously and look down his nose at me like I was off my rocker. "You think I'm not human?" he said. "Ever take a good look at yourself in the mirror?"

"Why would I do that?"

"Because you'd see that neither are you."

I had to bite down on my bottom lip to cut off an all-out laugh. "Me? Not human? Uh, I don't want to state the obvious or anything, but you are five times my size and your eyes glow—in broad daylight."

Corbin shook his head, his face never faltering. "You've been away for too long. Haven't you ever felt like you didn't belong here?"

"Sure I do, but what does that have to do with anything? I'm just a scrawny foster kid. If that was the requirement for being alien, then every kid at the foster home is from another world."

"So you're saying you don't remember anything?"

"Like what?"

"Like why you're here. Your quest. The princess?"

Okay, it was official. Coach Corbin was hopped up on goofballs. I already thought he'd lost it when I caught him fending off invisible foes Chuck Norris–style with a sword from the Crusades, but in just a few words he cemented it. The guy was nuts.

"I don't know what you're taking about, but I think your meds are a little on the strong side. You should get the dose adjusted," I said. I grabbed my backpack and made to leave, but Corbin caught me by the wrist.

In one blow, I was back on the weird planet with the funky palms and lapping ocean. Images flooded in of a huge man who looked just like me: tangled blond hair, blue eyes, standing crooked the way I do when I'm irritated. The man handed me off to a freaky guy who was totally goth-obsessed. He wore all black. Even his eyes and hair were black. I shuddered. His eyes were creepy. He had no colored irises, just soulless ebony pupils.

They were discussing me and how I was to be sent away. My oversized body double kept insisting that my sword and horse must go with me, wherever I was being sent off to. Another kid was there, an infant wrapped in a fluffy green blanket with a silver half-moon pendant strung around her neck. I couldn't explain it, but I wanted to help her. The reason became apparent when we were taken to a dark room with an altar. A basin on the obsidian altar opened up into a whirlpool of universe stuff and stars. The freaky-eyes dude dropped the girl into the swirl and the memory-me screamed. Heck, the real version of me watching the memory wanted to scream *Help! The black-eyed guy flushed a baby down a gigantic cosmic toilet!*

I was next. Flusher Man picked me up. We had a mini stare-down at first. Then he pronounced a curse and dropped me. Down I went.

I yanked my wrist out of Corbin's hand. Remember that memory I had of being flushed? The one on incessant and irritating repeat? Yeah. It happened. For real.

"What the heck was that?" I said, sitting down hard in my chair. "Forget that question. Who was that guy and why did he just drown me in a cosmic toilet?"

"You didn't drown," Corbin said. "You traveled from one end of the galaxy to the other."

"Is that supposed to make me feel better?" I said, trying hard not to panic. "Couldn't I have traveled by spaceship or something? There's nothing cool about being flushed."

"For the last time, you weren't flushed. Besides, spaceships are a human invention. Humans always need something tangible so they can wrap their half-wit minds around interplanetary travel."

"Awesome," I said, totally out of my element. "So, all I need is to find a big whirlpool and hop in to get to Jupiter?"

"Now you're just talking garbage," Corbin said. "Everyone knows Jupiter is uninhabitable."

"Stupid me," I muttered. "Okay, fine. Look, for some reason I have these weird things going on in my head . . ."

"Memories. You were seeing what happened to you before you came here."

"You're kidding, right?"

"You want further proof? Then I'll give you proof. Does this look familiar?" Corbin lifted his sleeve over his shoulder and showed me a mark on his skin. "It's the Bankhir symbol for warrior. You have one too. In fact, we were all branded with the same mark at birth. We *are* the Warriors of Bankhir."

Yeah, I should explain that one. I'd had what I called a birthmark on my shoulder since forever. Though it didn't look like a birthmark. It looked like I had been branded with a hot iron. The scar tissue was two circles looped within each other and a diagonal sword dashed through the middle of them. Corbin had one on his broad shoulder and so did I. I stared at his mark. Unconsciously, I scratched at my shoulder where the brand pulsed.

"It's the brand I got when I was presented my sword and horse," I said. "Whoa! How did I know that?"

"Your memories are coming back," Corbin said with a satisfied smirk as he lowered his sleeve. "Though I don't think they were ever really gone. We warriors have perfect photographic memories. I'm sure that being an infant when you were sent away didn't help much for recollection."

I wished he'd stop talking. I was trying to sort things out, and throwing more information at me didn't help.

"So this place, you called it Bankhir?"

"Our home."

"And the big guy? The one who looks like me?"

"Your father."

"The King," I blurted. What the heck! I was getting a headache. Memories were flooding in so fast I could hardly keep track of them all. "The funky-eyed guy, the one who's a total goth and creepy, he sent me here. He took me from my home."

Corbin nodded.

"Are there more of us here?" I said. "Do I know any . . . ?"

"No, dingus. It's just you and me, as far as I know."

I could barely feel the burn in my lungs for all the hope jumping around in my stomach. I finally had something to look forward to. A free pass, if you will, to get out of Puckerbush. No more Phil and Janet, no more dry, sweltering Nevada desert, and no more foster home. It was too good. From what I could remember of the place called Bankhir with the wide palms and beaches, it looked amazing. Which meant there had to be a catch.

"Did my father send you?"

Corbin's eyes narrowed. "In a sense, I guess you could say that. How much do you remember?"

"Not as much as I should, apparently. Are you really an alien?" I said, waiting for this brief reality to shatter.

"Am I really a . . . ? Seriously, kid?" Corbin said caustically. "Do I *look* human to you?"

I looked him over. He was a solid six-foot eight, wide, well muscled, with a bent nose and blue steel eyes with permanently dilated pupils. I could hardly forget how those eyes glowed.

"Okay, fine. That was a stupid question," I conceded. "But what are you doing here?

Corbin's eyes slipped off my face and a muscle pulsed at his temple.

"That's not the problem right now," he said shiftily. "The problem is that you have two months until the Great End."

"The great what?"

"End, bean brain, the deadline to your quest. The one that if you fail, we all die."

"I might need a refresher course on that one. I don't remember a quest."

Corbin leaned forward, skewering me with his eyes. "You must remember. The quest is why you are here. If you don't complete it, you can't go back to Bankhir."

There was the catch. I knew it! I knew that my free pass out of Puckerbush was too good to be true. I wasn't too sure what I was supposed to recall. Yet there *was* one thing. I had buried it deep, way down and out of sight. When I was five, Janet took me to a shrink in Reno to get my head checked out. I had spouted on and on for months about finding a princess. I had to find her or the world would be destroyed. The shrink passed me off as having an overactive imagination, but only after making me endure an hour of abject humiliation.

"Right. That quest," I said, and the muscle under Corbin's eye started doing somersaults.

"This isn't playtime, Nancy."

"Ian," I corrected. "And according to all the stuff swimming around in my head, I am a prince." I added that just to irk him. It wasn't every day I had the upper hand over a man who had made my life a living hell.

"Don't push it," Corbin warned. "You haven't earned your crown yet."

I should have figured as much.

"Tell me you've found the princess," Corbin said, leaning in close. "We don't have much time to work with here."

"Hold on to your gym shorts," I said. "Just so I've got this straight. I have a quest to find a princess, right?"

"The Princess of Garfel."

"And Garfel is . . . ?"

"Our sister planet," Corbin said. "At the center of this galaxy are two planets: Garfel and Bankhir. One produces magic and the other wields it. You must find the Princess who was sent with you here to Earth. Don't you remember?"

Drumming up that memory was hard. I could remember more of the sneering shrink's face than the details of the actual quest. "There was something about a princess and sixteen years to find her? I blocked out most of the details."

Corbin's face fell and the annoyed tic under his eye had a heyday, dancing around like crazy. "You're kidding, right? Or is that human sarcasm? Your sixteen years are almost up. You can't forget the most important reason why you are here!"

I got a little irritated. I'll admit it. Janet and Phil didn't exactly make life easy growing up. Not for me, at least, when I was spouting crazy talk.

"I didn't exactly have the best childhood. I blocked a few things out. I wanted to forget."

"You can't forget. You're a Bankhir Warrior."

"Look, here on Earth, most folks don't take it well when a kid starts talking about quests and princesses like his head got dropped off at a geeky Renaissance Fair. Besides, at five years old, how was I supposed to know it was real? It wasn't as if I quit the quest on purpose!"

"A real warrior would have found a way. We never fail and we never give up."

"Who said I've given up?"

"Well, you obviously haven't grasped the enormity of what is at stake here."

"I grasp it," I said, but I didn't. Not really. It looked as if Corbin was going to burst a blood vessel. His eyes bulged.

"Grasp this, then," he said in a hoarse whisper. "Our world is bound to Garfel, our sister planet. Bound by Deep Magic that is starting to crumble. The Magic Keepers of Garfel have been fighting with the Warriors of Bankhir for centuries, and if we don't find peace, both our worlds will implode. Do you get my meaning, Nancy? Implode. As in the end of life as we know it."

"I got that part," I said, nodding stiffly. Corbin may be one of my kin, but he hadn't changed with familiarity at all. "You made that perfectly clear. But you weren't there when I got flushed by that creep in black."

Corbin clamped his mouth shut and chewed on my reply for a full minute as he studied me.

"That . . . creep"—his voice dropped to a strangled whisper—"is the magician named Silivus, and trust me when I say don't get on his bad side. I wouldn't be calling him names if I were you."

"I take it you've had a run-in with the . . ."

"Don't! No insults. And whether I did or did not have an . . . *issue*," he said, biting the word off with a snap of his white teeth, "with him is not the topic of discussion."

"Did he get under your skin?" I said with a half grin. Finally, the mighty coach had fallen. Corbin's fingers flexed and his face clouded over. I wondered if he was considering clamping his hands around my scrawny neck.

"Have you found the princess or not?" he said.

I hated to say it, but I had to admit the truth. "Not."

Corbin spat out a curse I'd never heard before.

"Come again?" I said. "Did you just swear in Bankhirian?"

Corbin waved me off with an irritated swipe of his hand. "Haven't you been searching?"

"Not really. But in case you didn't know, Mr. Mysterious Magician didn't introduce us," I said. "I have nothing to go on. I don't even know her name, let alone what she looks like."

"Holy birthing banfis!" Corbin ran his hands through his peppered gray hair and his eyes bulged.

"Is that another cuss word? because I'd like to learn a few," I said, trying to lighten his darkening mood. Corbin ignored me.

"This is worse than I thought," he said as he rubbed his cheeks wearily. "Look, you have to understand that there is more to this than you were told. Silivus came to your parents and told them that our war with Garfel was going to be our doom. We've been fighting for so long that it has drained the Deep Magic from our worlds. Silivus asked them to either make peace or die, but Bankhir warriors forgive as good as they forget."

"Which is not at all," I said.

Corbin nodded grimly. "The only way we could find peace was to take one of our own away from Bankhir and let him grow up away from all the fighting and politics. The same was done with a child from Garfel. It was our last hope."

That much I had concluded from my brief meeting with that baby-flushing lunatic magician.

"So I was picked," I said.

"You were picked, mostly because you are the king's only son. Not to put more pressure on you or anything, but yes, it's that big of a deal. The Garfelians did the same and gave up their firstborn daughter."

"Why not another prince?" I asked. Judging by the shifty look on Corbin's face, there was a reason for that, and I wasn't going to like the answer.

"Because the idea was that you two would co-rule both worlds."

"Co-rule?" I didn't like where this was headed.

"To put a finer point on it: marry."

And then my head exploded. "What?!" I shouted as I bolted to my feet. "You've got to be kidding me! I'm just a kid."

"*Shhhh!*" Ms. Pettis joined the fray, shuffling to where we sat when the volume of our conversation was too much for her to handle.

Corbin stood and grinned apologetically to Ms. Pettis. "Terribly sorry, ma'am. I'll take this noisemaking miscreant out to the hall," he said, clamping a heavy hand on my shoulder so I couldn't escape. Out in the deserted hall, I wriggled out from under his grip. My quest had taken on a whole different light. Not one I was particularly pleased with.

"This is insane," I said. Despite the flood of memories that confirmed everything Corbin said as true, I was struggling. Heck, I just found out I had to marry a girl I'd never met to save a bunch of people I barely knew. It was a lot to adjust to. In fact, hyperventilating seemed like a perfect next course of action.

"I agree, but you have little choice in the matter. Your bride was picked, but that's not everything. Silivus gave you until your sixteenth birthday to find one girl—your betrothed—and fall in love with her."

My head had already exploded once. Now I was just numb.

"Fall in love? As if marrying me off to a total stranger wasn't bad enough?" I grumbled.

"If marriage were all it took, then this little excursion to Earth would have never happened. Our planets need to heal, and healing doesn't come through a politically slapped-together union. It needs the power of an ancient magic that can only be unlocked by the bond of two completely different kinds of magic. How is that done? Through love, kid. Real, tangible love," Corbin said, and the more he repeated it, the more panicked I got.

"How do you expect me to do that? I don't even know the girl!"

"Then we find her," Corbin said, as if it were as simple as that.

"We . . . find her?" I said, half dazed. "Billions of people on Earth and we're just going to walk out there and 'find' her? And in five months, no less."

"Five months?"

"Yeah. You said I had until my sixteenth birthday. That's not until March."

"By whose account? Your birthday is December 20. You were sent to Earth in March at three months old. So, we're talking two months to track this girl down. How hard could it be?"

How hard? The air left my already-struggling lungs and I bent and gripped my knees to catch my breath. My brain went blank. How hard could it be? Hard! I couldn't get my own foster parents to acknowledge I existed, let alone a girl! And then do it in two months?

If I had truly known how difficult it would be, I might have blacked out flat on the ground. So it was a good thing I didn't. Being sprawled out on the ground with drool on your chin isn't attractive. Corbin whacked me on the back a few times as I struggled for air.

Then, the unthinkable happened.

4

A burst of hot, dry air gusted in from the desert through an open door. It blew in not the scent of dirt but the briny smell of ocean air and salt. I had an oddly familiar feeling in my gut, like I had experienced this before. It felt like home. As I straightened up, both Corbin and I froze.

In walked a tall, raven-haired girl with olive skin and the most brilliant green eyes I'd ever seen. I'd say she was beautiful, but I'd be lying. She was exotic.

And she looked lost.

The halls were empty except for us. She searched down one hall and then the other, uncertain which she would go down first. When she saw us, she figured we must have known what we were doing.

"Hi, I'm new here," she said, her voice sweet. Corbin recovered quicker than I did and held out his hand.

"Welcome to Puckerbush High," he said. The girl stared at Corbin's hand for a long time, chewing on her bottom lip. *To shake or not to shake*, that was the question of the day.

"Thanks. I, uh, am looking for the main office," she said, digging her hands into her pockets. Not to shake.

"Down the hall, second door to the right," Corbin said, jabbing a thumb over his shoulder.

"Great," she said brightly and skirted around us, giving wide berth even though we made no move to step closer to her. "Well, thanks again."

Corbin grabbed the front of my shirt and pushed me,

staring like an idiot, out of her path to the main office. His jaw was just as unhinged as mine was.

"Paint me green and call me a grippah," he muttered in awe. It must have been another one of those Bankhir cuss phrases he was using, because I had no clue what he was blathering on about. Neither of us said much until she passed us with a friendly smile and entered the main office. One thing I barely computed through the shock was the distinct feeling of my lungs opening and the unusual ability to breathe without help of an inhaler. The farther away she got, the more the feeling subsided.

"Well, she was nice," I said still gaping at the door swinging shut behind her. By 'nice' I meant 'way too good for this institution.' "Call me crazy, but that girl is not human."

"Spot on, Einstein," Corbin said. "She's not."

"I was kidding," I said. "Are you sure?"

"I've been killing Garfelians since I was twelve, and they all have the same black hair and olive skin. Besides, I've met the Queen of Garfel, and that girl is the spitting image of her mother."

I didn't know a good enough cuss word to express the sinking feeling in the pit of my stomach. That magician sure knew how to ruin a guy's life.

"That girl is the Princess?"

"The one and only," Corbin said. "Couldn't you feel it? She was practically radioactive with Deep Magic."

"I felt something alright," I muttered.

"How can you possibly complain? We're saved! I thought I'd have to bust you out of the foster system and hunt her down, but here she is! Dropped right into your lap."

"I wasn't complaining," I said. "I just had a reality check and 'completely out of my league' comes to mind."

"In your league or not, you'd better get busy," Corbin said. "We're talking two months and counting to get that girl to think you are the best thing since Bankhir steel."

"How am I," I said, pointing to my bony chest, "supposed to get *that* to fall in love with me?" I ended up jabbing my finger impolitely at the closed office door that the Garfelian Princess had disappeared behind.

Corbin must have been reading my thoughts, because he tore his eyes away from the door to rake me over, from the top of my tangled blond hair down to my scrawny legs and oversized feet.

"We're screwed," he said.

I didn't have to look down at myself to know he was right. I was doomed to blend in and disappear, and I was sure that by the end of the school day, I wasn't going to be the only guy vying for her attention. There would be bigger, healthier, and better-looking guys.

I. Was. Screwed.

I wasn't far off the mark about my prediction.

The Princess of Garfel was Arianna Hernfeld. Turns out the boring and dead-normal Hernfelds had a kid after all. I had been house-stalking the Princess's home and didn't even know it. Arianna had been homeschooled for years. It was almost as if she had been locked in a dungeon and recently escaped. Nobody knew anything about her. With a girl like that walking around Puckerbush, you'd think she'd stop traffic daily. If she wasn't already beautiful and friendly, kind to a fault and so blasted nice, she just had to add intriguing to the mix.

She was the main attraction and I didn't stand a chance. I was as uninteresting as they got. By the end of the week, Arianna was swarming with friends. Everyone wanted to gawk at the new girl, Corbin included.

We stood together in the far corner of the dingy orange linoleum cafeteria, observing from a distance. Corbin studied her intently, scratching his chin, deep in thought. We looked idiotic. I barely came to his elbow and was about as wide as his thigh, but he insisted.

"I have a plan," he said. "I say we divide and conquer. We should strike high and fast. That way we can limit the damage."

"And carry her off like a prize cow? I don't think so," I said. "This isn't war."

"Says you. You've been around humans too much. It's made you soft."

"Thanks," I said acidly. "It's not like this entire quest isn't a total crock anyway."

"What's so bad about it? The last quest I was sent on, I was given one hundred of the King's greenest warriors and sent to keep the peace in Grenick. Getting a princess to fall for you is cupcakes compared to that."

"Grenick?"

"An outer planet. It's not far from Earth, actually. The place was infested with scorpions the size of horses and the people were lawless. On a good day it was as calm as the running of the bulls in Barcelona. It was, hands down, the worst quest ever."

"Call me crazy, but I think I'd trade."

"Don't even joke," Corbin grumbled. "You know what is at stake here."

"Yeah, yeah," I said. "Bankhir will do a massive space kablooie if I don't get together with some girl."

"Not just any girl," Corbin said and nodded in Arianna's direction. "That girl."

"Who just so happens to be the hottest girl in the whole school," I grumbled. "I know. Besides, who says I'm going to go through with this anyway?"

Corbin's eyes took on a glow of menacing light. "Why wouldn't you?"

The human answer would be to say that I had no interest in a planet that played host to a magician who threw me off like yesterday's garbage. But I wasn't human. It was obvious because my heart burned with unwavering allegiance to a planet and a King I hadn't seen since birth. Either it was stupidity or it came with the brand seared into my arm, but I was going to complete this quest even if it killed me. It was in my blood.

"Fine," I conceded at last. "I'll still do the quest, but it's not going to be easy."

"Deal with it, kid," Corbin said. "If it were easy, it wouldn't be a quest."

"Of course not," I said. I took one bite of my limp sandwich and chomped off the end of a cigarette butt. Janet was at it again. Cooking was not her forte. I spat it out and threw the rest of it away.

Corbin took notice. "You can't afford to skip a meal, kid. You already look like fetter legs."

"Dude, speak English. I only spent three months on Bankhir. I don't know what a fetter is."

"They resemble a chicken. Taste like one too, if you ask me."

"Right," I muttered. "Clarification makes it so much better."

"No, it makes you a skinny wimp," he said. "Keep skipping lunch and I'll add laps to your run."

"Because nothing is more of a turn-on to a girl than a sweaty guy straight off the track."

Corbin gave a short huff of a laugh and got a dreamy look in his hard eyes. "Got my second wife that way. That woman definitely liked a man worked into a lather before—"

"Stop! I don't need to know," I interrupted before my imagination went haywire. I turned back to Arianna and her lunch table teeming with eager faces. I had to hand it to the girl; she wasn't cocky about the attention. She was genuinely interested in everyone talking at her. I noticed she did a funky thing where she would lean away quickly if anyone tried to touch her. That was easily accepted, though. No one seemed to notice or care. Arianna was the "it" girl at school.

"Have you noticed she dresses funny?" Corbin asked.

"Don't tell me you're into fashion," I said.

"No, it's called basic recon. You need to learn a few things about being a warrior. The biggest part of winning hand-to-hand combat is noticing the details. Now, look at that girl and tell me what you see."

I tried. Corbin put me in a funk by grouping relationship advice in with war tactics, but I took a closer look. Arianna's face was flushed and she kept tugging at her collar to let in air through her clothing.

"She looks warm."

"Good. Why would that be?"

"It's Nevada and it's over a hundred degrees outside?"

"Look closer."

I did, and that was when I noticed. "Is she wearing gloves?"

"Gloves, compression sleeves, and long pants. Don't you think that is a little odd for the weather today?"

"Yeah," I mused. I hoped that didn't mean it made her crazy, because I was already in a time crunch and the less drama the better. "But it's not exactly a conversation starter."

"It's a beginning. I'd like to know why she is sweating it out in the middle of the desert."

"Really, I think it would be easier if I could just get her alone," I muttered under my breath. I didn't expect Corbin to be listening, but he stiffened. "What? What did I say?"

"Plenty," he said and clapped me on the back. My skin stung where he struck, and I stumbled forward under the force of the blow. "I have to go look into something. Stick around and keep your schedule open."

"I live in Puckerbush," I said to his retreating back. "Where would I go?"

Corbin didn't reply. He disappeared before the cafeteria door swung shut. I gave up on lunch and headed out to my next class: Advanced English. So far, I had completely struck out landing a class with Arianna in it. I was zero for seven classes. Our lockers were at opposite ends of the school. The closest I got to her was once when I passed her on my way to the bathroom. It wasn't exactly a prime time to introduce myself.

I got through the end of school with my stomach in knots. I didn't want to be a part of the groupies that followed Arianna, but it was hard not to linger on the fringe of the crowd. Everyone wanted to know her, talk to her. The closest I got was nerd distance, twenty feet away.

I made it home to find Phil in front of the TV and the house in chaos. Janet was at the helm at the stove, smoking and tapping ash into a soup pot.

"I'm home," I said. I swear I only added to the noise. When no one replied, or even acknowledged I was in the door, I added, "I had a great day at school. Thanks for asking."

I nicked a flat roll from the counter and cold meat from the fridge and disappeared into the back room. My room was the size of a closet in the farthest trailer out. Everywhere else in the house smelled dirty, like an unwashed gym bag that had been forgotten for years. I couldn't escape it.

My room was the one exception. It was military clean with my sleeping bag rolled up and stored in the corner. I did everything I needed in a five-foot by four-foot space. On my wall hung a calendar that had 'Welcome to Nevada: *Catch the Fever!*' plastered on the cover with a photo of the Las Vegas Strip at night.

Flipping forward to December, I marked the twentieth: my birthday/doomsday. Then I let the pages flip back to October, where I marked off today's date. One day closer to sixteen, and my heart did a flip-flop in my chest.

The details of my quest were still a little foggy. However, there was one memory that flashed forward, clearly as if it had happened yesterday. It was the moments before the flushing incident. The creep magician picked up the baby version of Arianna and doused her in a plume of sickly looking, dirty blue magic. She coughed on the cloud as he muttered a curse, damning her to lose her memory. Laughing, he also cursed her with incredible power, more than she could handle or explain.

I remembered being angry. Who curses babies anyway? It was just wrong, and when the magician turned to me, I felt like kicking him. He picked me up and tendrils of tainted Deep Magic curled around my body. The stuff hurt, like it was sucking away my soul bit by bit. That's when I heard it, magnified and echoing in my ears: the curse.

"Remember what you have lost, Warrior Prince, and know that I took it from you," the magician had said. Instantly, I knew what he meant. I lost my parents, my planet, my sword and horse, and my strength. I was flushed to Earth with nothing but my name and a pile of memories.

And a quest.

If I wanted my life back, Arianna had to like me. Fat chance *that* was ever going to happen. I couldn't for the life of me figure out how I was going to get Arianna to acknowledge I existed, let alone . . .

I couldn't finish the thought. Instead, I started in on my homework, putting more effort into it than necessary. Nobody noticed I was a no-show at dinner. I didn't care. Finishing well after dark, I settled in for the night. I figured if I didn't at least talk to Arianna by tomorrow, I would start trying Corbin's battle strategies.

I was stuck in a haze, halfway between asleep and awake, with my eyes three-quarters closed, when a hand shot through the window above my head. Thick fingers grabbed the front of my shirt, yanking me out of my ratty sleeping bag. I was pulled upward so fast, my face smacked into the windowpane and stuck there. In the dark I could see the outline of broad shoulders and two light blue eyes glowing brightly.

"I told you to keep your schedule open," Corbin hissed. He forced the rusted window fully open. I almost complained, but I was too excited to snap back at him.

"What did you find out?" I said.

"Plenty," Corbin said as he pulled me, head first, through the window and deposited me on the dirt. "None of it useful."

"Like what?" I said, dusting myself off. Corbin put his finger to his lips and pointed to the only cluster of bushes in sight, a good quarter mile away from the trailer. It was a short walk, but I was busting with questions. In my desire to not think too closely about my quest, I was impatient to know more about Bankhir, my family, and a million other things.

"So, aside from running, what do you like to do?" Corbin said once we were out of earshot of the trailers.

"Like hobbies? And for your information, I hate running."

Corbin waved off my argument. "Exactly like hobbies. Do you read? Ride horses? Paint?"

"None of the above," I said. "Why?"

"I spent the afternoon spying on your little girlfriend—"

"She's not my girlfr—wait a sec, what do you mean by 'spy'? You didn't do anything creepy, did you?"

"Not at all," Corbin said with a shrug. "I merely scouted out her house. I retrieved enough information from her room to get a pretty good idea of what we are up against."

"You went into her room?" I yelled at him, louder than

I intended. "That qualifies as beyond disturbing. What is wrong with you?"

"Scouting enemy territory isn't disturbing. Get back to the problem at hand," Corbin said. "Have you done anything unusual or particularly cultured?"

"I live in Puckerbush. The most exciting thing I've ever done is help Phil smoke out prairie dogs," I said.

Corbin laughed weakly, oozing sarcasm. "We're doomed."

"No, we're not," I said, unwilling to see the facts. "I'm sure I could find something in common with her."

"You don't understand," Corbin said. "This girl is classy. She could wipe the floor with you if she wanted to and her parents are strict. No friends over, period. And they keep an annoyingly close eye on her."

"That's weird," I said. "How did you find that out?"

"I listened in on a few phone conversations."

I shook my head. "This is great. You bug her phone and the next thing I know we are in jail for aggravated stalking."

"You're still hung up on human ethics," Corbin said testily. "Think like a Bankhir Warrior and maybe we can figure this out."

I was trying. Trust me. "The only chance we have is to get her alone at school," I said glumly. "Though getting through the horde that follows her around is going to be a trick. I'd have to get into her classes, maybe find a subject she really likes and then strike up a conversation."

Corbin still looked skeptical. "What makes you so sure that will work?"

"Haven't you ever heard the saying that the good guy always wins?"

"No."

"Well, he does."

"I think that is the dumbest thing I've heard since I've been on this planet. Trust me, I've seen enough of this world to make that a fairly degrading statement."

"What else do I have? I am a decent guy. Which means I can make this work."

"By being decent?"

I hated it when he sounded so skeptical. "Well, for humans on Earth, that's saying something."

Corbin snorted. "Sure it is when you have nothing else going for you. For the record, Nancy, just because you grew up among weakling humans doesn't mean that Bankhir Warriors are the same. At six years old we already are well versed in battle strategy. We start weapons training at seven."

I kept quiet, hoping he'd get the hint that the discussion was over. But Corbin couldn't resist the urge to rub it in.

"By ten we're at full height and at twelve are fully muscled," he said conversationally. "Though it takes until fourteen to get hair on our—"

"Would you shut up?" I interjected, not wanting to hear where I should be having hair, and probably didn't.

"Why? I was going to say chest," he said. "Just pointing out the differences between us and humans."

"I am well aware of the differences." And the fact that I was woefully behind, even by human standards. "Besides, having a big hairy chest isn't going to get the girl."

"Couldn't hurt."

I lost my patience. "What's the plan? Can you get into

the computers at school and change around my schedule or not?"

"I'm just a gym teacher," Corbin said. "Only the school counselor, vice principal, and principal have access to the schedules."

"I guess we'll have to hack the system," I said.

"I was hoping you might say that," Corbin said. He grabbed me by the arm and started to drag me toward the school. I had to jog to keep up. I could have protested a little harder, but I had questions and I needed answers.

"So," I said, trying to sound casual. "What is Bankhir like?"

"I thought you remembered everything."

"I remember about three months' worth. When you're a baby, that's not much."

"It's not a bad place," Corbin shrugged, but the look on his face told a different story. He missed it, bad. He released my arm. "Most of the cites are destroyed except for the capital and a few nearby towns."

"Why?"

"It doesn't take brains, Nancy," Corbin said. "When you are at war for nearly five centuries, destruction happens."

"Who started the war?"

Corbin stopped short. In the dim light of a half moon I could see his glowing eyes narrow. "I don't think I should be telling you that. You are supposed to be free of politics."

I squared off with him. "I think I can handle it. Besides, if I fail my quest, I'd like to know what I lost."

"Fair enough," he said and started walking again. "Though, I'm going to edit out most of the details. I will not fail your father a second time."

"What happened the first time?"

"None of your business!" Corbin snapped irritably. "Do you want to know the history of Bankhir or not?"

"I do! I won't ask about your massive betrayal again," I said placidly.

"I. Did not. *Betray* . . . anyone," Corbin huffed. "It was the smallest of misunderstandings. It's not my fault that ruddy magician is such a . . ."

"Yes?" I said when Corbin stopped and clamped his mouth shut.

"Bankhir history," he said in a strangled voice.

I let it drop.

"Bankhir and Garfel are sister planets. They are identical in every way, and they orbit each other, bound together by Deep Magic."

"Or gravity," I said.

"An explanation cooked up by blind humans who wouldn't recognize magic if it hit them in the face. Gravity," he snorted. "Stupidest thing I've heard of since the infamous battle of Cerlid."

"What happened?"

"Nothing that concerns you. Too steeped in politics. Back to history," Corbin said. "Deep Magic has always been cultured by the Garfelians. They cultivate it and we warriors wield it. We also protect other peaceful planets in the galaxy. We gain our strength from the Deep Magic Garfelians put out. The more magic, the stronger we get. Without it we are weak, like humans."

"But what about us? We have magic too, right? What was that silvery stuff you were putting out earlier?"

"Warrior Magic. Bankhirians have our own brand of magic. Not nearly as strong as Deep Magic, mind you. It's used only for minor things like tracking, communication, and fighting."

"Oh good," I said. "For a second there I was worried you were messing with my head when you drummed up all my memories."

"I didn't *mess* with anything. I merely helped you recall who you are."

"And when you say 'help,' you actually mean *force*," I said. Corbin glared at me. I obviously irritated him, even in the dark.

"Not that it matters," I amended quickly.

"No, it doesn't," he said crisply. "Now, where was I?"

"Sister planets and two different kinds of magic."

"Right. That brings me to the magicians. We were fairly simple people, but when the magicians came they brought with them an age of enlightenment."

"Sounds tedious," I muttered. "Like school."

"It is, but they meant well."

I was getting a little lost. "Where did the magicians come from?"

"They were born of the stars and can live for hundreds of years. It wasn't all book learning. They made tools and created objects to make life easier. Over time, they died out, leaving only one behind: Silivus. It was around this time that the Garfelians began hoarding the magic, claiming that it was running out.

"But, you see, we Bankhirians need magic to live. We were slowly getting weaker, and what little magic came from Garfel was not enough."

"So, it was Bankhir that started the war," I said.

"The first war was a long time ago, nobody remembers," Corbin said, but he didn't sound convincing.

"Liar."

Corbin sighed deeply. "I've spent more years fighting than in peace. It's not my place to tell you what really happened and do it objectively."

"Right," I said, and kicked a clod of dirt off the road. "I'm supposed to grow up in neutral territory."

"And get the Princess to fall for you," Corbin added.

I flinched. "About that," I said. "How important is the love thing? Is there any way I can skirt around it? Couldn't we be hand-shaking friends and call it good?"

"No," Corbin said flatly. "That was the one stipulation everyone could agree on. The Garfelians knew of an ancient magic that was very powerful, almost uncontrollable. It would require both Deep Magic and Warrior Magic. To bind the two takes more than an agreement of peace between kings. It takes a permanent bond, which means the only thing that can heal our worlds is . . ."

"Love," I spat. "I know, but have you taken a good look at Arianna?"

"I have. She is a very beautiful princess," Corbin said. "I don't see why you couldn't fall for her. Now, if she were an ogre, I might sympathize."

"If it were only about her looks, my end of the quest would be a done deal, but it's not. She's out of my league," I said.

"You got that right," Corbin said. "Can't you comb your hair or something? Eat a few extra meals? A few added pounds wouldn't hurt any."

"I'll be fine."

"What you really need is a growth spurt."

"Alright already!" I shouted in frustration.

"No really, you're an entire head shorter than she is. I've seen seven-year-old Bankhirians taller than you."

"Would you shut up? I already know this quest is going to be plenty difficult without you adding to it."

"I haven't added anything to your situation. I was just pointing out that you are going to have to really pull something miraculous off to get this girl to fall in love with you."

"She could fake it," I said, hopeful.

"You can't fool Deep Magic, ancient or otherwise. Heck, even weak Warrior Magic can detect a lie."

"Of course," I mumbled under my breath. "What was I thinking?" I didn't have long to mull in my own misery. Corbin stopped on the school lawn and surveyed the dark brick building. "We're here," he said. "Now all we have to do is break in."

"Phase two is to break into my high school?"

"No, phase two is to break into the school computers and find out all of the Princess's classes. Priorities, Nancy! Get your head on straight."

"Right," I said as I followed Corbin around the back where the dumpsters lined the alley. "Because when you spell it out like that, it doesn't quite sound like breaking the law."

He pointed up to the third floor where one window had been left wide open.

"I left the window to my office open and jammed it so the janitor couldn't shut it," he said. "You never know when you need to get into your place of work."

"Don't you have a key to the school?"

"I have a key, but no code to the alarm. Now get up there."

"This is so illegal," I muttered. "You want me to climb?"

"Would you rather fly up?" Corbin snapped. His bright eyes got a crazy glint to them, like he had gotten a magnificently insane idea. "How much do you weigh?"

"A hundred pounds with clothes on," I said.

"Perfect," he said, and grabbed the waist of my jeans. "Just don't forget to grab the windowsill if I don't get you all the way in."

"What?! No!" I cried out, but it was too late. Corbin wound up and chucked me upward like a javelin. Cool air bit at my eyes and made them tear up. Amazing how quickly my vision could blur in three short stories of a building.

In a haze, I could see the open window I was speeding toward. I could also see that I was going to fall short of shooting through it. I scrambled for a hold on the windowsill and got a skin-ripping grip on the metal edge. My legs kicked and flailed, but I was stuck.

"Move it, Nancy!" Corbin hissed from below. "We don't have all night."

"Easy for you to say," I grunted as I tried to get my elbows up over the ledge. I hated it when he called me names. "I'm sure you could crawl up the wall like an over-muscled maggot."

"Watch it, kid," Corbin said. "I have excellent hearing."

Was there anything he couldn't do? It was irritating.

It took more effort than I had muscle on me to get in the window. Once inside, I collapsed on the floor, coughing and wheezing. Rubbing at the sore spots on my chest where the sill had scraped me, I got a good look around Corbin's office. It wasn't much. Just a desk, a computer, a chair, and the cabinet where I'd seen him shove his sword out of sight. The office was the size of a closet with a door that afforded a clear look out into the school gym.

"I'm in."

"Good, now hack into my computer. All the teachers' computers are linked into the same system; all you need is the correct password."

"Easy," I said and sat down at his desk. I was pretty decent around computers. It took me five minutes to bypass Principal Bertolio's password and find Arianna's file. One minute more and I was in all her classes. Starting tomorrow, I was going to be stuck to her like a fly on flypaper.

"Are you done yet?" Corbin called up impatiently.

I shut off his computer and leaned out the window.

"Keep your shirt on," I said and swung a leg over the ledge. "How am I going to get down?"

"Jump."

"You'll catch me?"

"No, I'll let you fall and break your neck and then we'll all be screwed," he said. "Of course I'll catch you, numb-nuts!"

"That makes me feel all warm and fuzzy inside," I said and looked down. "You know, it looks a lot worse going down than up. Maybe I'll just wait it out here in your office until morning."

"You'll jump down or I'll . . ."

I never got to find out what kind of exercise-related torture he was going to threaten me with. The arrival of the night deputy shining his floodlights into every building on the street shut Corbin up. The patrol car turned the corner of the drugstore and headed our way. The next checkpoint was the school.

"Jump!"

I aimed for the reflector-like shine of Corbin's eyes in the dark and pushed off from the window. It was a long way down, a trip that went by too fast. My heart thumped in my ears. Then my spine smacked against something unforgiving and hard.

"Oof! You need to get some meat on you, kid," Corbin grunted as he dropped me to the asphalt. "That was like catching a bag of dorfin bones."

"Let me guess, a doofus is some kind of animal?" I groaned, rubbing gingerly at my cracked ribs and back.

"It's called a dorfin," Corbin said. "Big bird. Has nothing edible on it. You really need to get back home. I don't like talking to a dumb human."

"I'm not dumb," I protested. Corbin grabbed me and hid both of us behind a clump of bushes as the patrol car passed and shined a light down the alley. We didn't come out until the car rounded the block and sped off.

"Well, that was a successful mission," Corbin said, dusting dry leaves of his shirt. "Good night."

Then he walked off down the street and disappeared around a row of houses. Just like that, I was left standing on school property to limp home clutching my ribs.

5

In my haste to get into all of Arianna's classes, I failed to pay attention to exactly what I was getting myself into. Drama, for one, was not going to be fun. Art was a close second. Biology was livable, but the true torture was Remedial Algebra. I was about to step foot into the easiest class I had ever attended in the entire school. The class was populated by a majority of sixth graders. The only other sophomores there were Arianna and a massive football player from the varsity team who deemed me worthy of an acknowledging grunt. If ever there was a chance to talk to Arianna, it was here.

I sat in the back—my usual place in any classroom—but today I was joined by the totally gorgeous Arianna. Since my schedule change last night, the closest I'd gotten to her was a glimpse of the top of her head as her friends mobbed her in every class. Sun shone through the window, refracting a sheen of blue off her jet-black hair. She wore artfully ripped jeans, a brown T-shirt that had a pink storm trooper from Star Wars on it, and running shoes. Did I mention she looked amazing? She did, even if she was wearing a long-sleeved shirt and gloves. Just sitting next to her made me want to yank the hem of my shorts over my bony knees and wish that I had given my T-shirt an extra wash. It's not like I looked like I was homeless or anything, but I knew I smelled like Janet's secondhand smoke. That, and it didn't help that my feet were busting out of worn-out sneakers.

Arianna leaned back in her seat and shook out her hair. I about passed out. Waves of warmth radiated off of her, like an afternoon on the beaches of Bankhir.

I racked my brain for a conversation starter but decided that her aura was not a good opening line. *Hey, you remind me of a distant planet* wouldn't work. No girl likes a guy sniffing at her. But I couldn't help it. I took a deep breath, reminded once again that asthma stunts life. It was glorious relief when she was around and my lungs cleared. Another uncool one liner: *By the way, thanks for helping me breathe.*

I shook myself back into reality. I caught sight of Corbin in the hallway trying to get my attention. He was miming something. It looked like he was threatening to pound me as he ground his massive fist into his palm and then pointed at me.

Yeah, yeah. I know. I rolled my eyes at him, which made his mouth form a thin angry line and his nostrils flare. If I didn't talk to the girl, he'd blow a blood vessel.

I had a 4.0 GPA. How hard could this be? "So," I said, tearing my eyes off Corbin's beet-red face. I should mention here that my voice broke. Yeah, talk about sounding manly. "You're new?"

Arianna straightened and turned slowly to look at me like I was born yesterday and it amused her. "Yes."

"Cool."

Brains? Check! Charm? Not quite. Apparently brains were not going to help me break the ice. I looked out the door for Corbin and mouthed *help!* However, instead of helping, he jabbed a finger at me, jabbed his other finger at Arianna and then smacked them together. Then, if that wasn't obvious enough, he slid his finger across his throat.

I got the point. Here goes attempt number two.

I studied her for a minute, trying to look for the things nobody else would notice. There was no way I was going to mention the weird gloves. Looking at her was distracting. It was hard to find words when the girl I was trying to talk to was a walking piece of visual perfection. But I couldn't sit there and stare at her. That was rude.

I cleared my throat and said, "Do you like Star Wars?"

"Star Wars?"

"Yeah," I said pointing to her shirt. "You have a storm trooper on your . . ." It hit me that I was pointing at her chest. Not. Smooth. "Not that I was looking at your . . ." I fumbled and shoved my hand under my knee. I was screwing up, big time. "You know what? Never mind."

Arianna frowned at me for a moment. "Good idea," she said, and turned back to her algebra book.

I avoided looking out into the hall, where I was sure Corbin was having a coronary. The bell rang and class started. It seemed as if that was going to be the end of my conversation attempts. Arianna was a good student who took notes and paid attention. I fiddled with my pencil and tried to block out most of the boring droning from the teacher that was just review for me anyway. I had this class in fourth grade. It was going to be another easy A.

When the bell rang, Arianna was out of there. I couldn't blame her for not wanting to risk another chance encounter with the boy who couldn't say two sentences without being offensive.

I exhaled heavily. Another class down and two more to go. I headed toward the gym, knowing that for the next hour, Corbin was going to pound me. Yay.

Oddly enough, the boys' locker room was empty. I dressed alone. Corbin stalked out of his office at the end of the row, stalling when he saw me.

"Kid, what are you doing?"

"Attending gym class," I said.

"This is girls' gym class."

I halted mid-pull of my shirt over my head. Think fast!

"I'm your assistant?" I said hopefully. The static from my gym shirt made my tangled blond hair stick up and the fabric clung to my scrawny ribs. From the incredulous look on Corbin's face, I thought for sure he was going to make me do laps.

"You couldn't assist a fly, but get on with it, Nancy," Corbin said. I ran to the gym only to be greeted by a flock of girls with Arianna at the center. Why did they have to giggle? It was totally disturbing.

"Listen up, class!" Corbin barked. "This here is my assistant."

If he called me Nancy, I was going to brain him.

"If you need anything, ask *Ian*." He really put the punch into my name and he pointed to me in case the girls didn't know it was me he was talking about. Maybe he was going to play nice after all. "Today we are playing flag football. Ian will get the ball and help you with your flags."

Never mind. I was going to kill him instead.

Corbin shoved a ratty box of colored belts with yellow and blue flags Velcroed to them in my arms. I started handing them out. The girls grabbed what they needed and treated me as if I wasn't there at all. I was the robot, doing his job.

"I do like Star Wars," a voice said. I had to look up a

good five inches, but it was Arianna. She didn't look at me as she picked out a blue belt. She had on the assigned gym shorts and shirt, but she still wore a full body compression suit and gloves. Fully covered for gym class? Insane, but she still managed to look unbelievably beautiful. I about dropped the box.

"Yeah? Me too," I said. I wish my voice hadn't spiked an octave. Arianna smiled, and then she was gone.

The class filed out to the soccer fields, and Corbin came up behind me. "Please tell me you actually talked to her?"

"I did." Surprise, surprise.

"Good," he said and thrust a football into my gut, knocking the wind out of me. "You're on defense."

I had to run to catch up with him.

"I'm not going to play. I'm the assistant," I puffed as we got out to the field.

"The assistant who will die a mysterious and violent death if he doesn't get out there and play defense," Corbin said, shoving me out in the middle of all the girls.

Arianna was blue. I was yellow, and there were barely enough sophomores in the class to make two teams. A hefty girl from the blue team took point, snatching the ball out of my hands. I think her name was Jenny; she could pass for a linebacker any day.

"We'll start," she smirked, and lined up the girls for a play.

There was something surreal about playing football with twenty girls. I was thinner than half of them, which wasn't encouraging. Jenny snapped the ball, and then it was chaos. Girls ran everywhere, colliding with each other and laughing. The only one who seemed to mean business was Jenny and a wide-open Arianna. Jenny threw a perfect spiral—no surprise there—and Arianna caught it.

I wasn't sure if it was the Bankhir Warrior in me or what, but I gave chase. It wasn't easy. Arianna was fast, but thanks to Corbin and his endless hours of running, I was too. Not that I'd ever tell him that. He might gloat himself sick. I kept up a few paces behind Arianna and my wheezing asthmatic lungs cleared. There was something about her that made me feel stronger, like I could finally take a full breath and not cough up a lung. It made me want to whoop a victory war cry.

We were closing in on the end zone, which was when I figured it was time to take her flag and stop messing around. I made a leap for it and grabbed the fluttering blue cloth—or at least, I thought I did.

Rip!

I tripped and fell to the ground and did a tight roll onto my back. There were shrieks. I thought they were of victory, but I wasn't that lucky. Air filled my lungs, but not for long. The clogging feeling crept back and soon I was gasping. Coughing out a lung, I sat up slowly to a field full of laughing and pointing girls.

What the?

In my hand was not the flag. It was Arianna's gym shorts. I had missed my intended target and ripped them right off. Leaping to my feet, I spun around to look for her. I got a glimpse of Arianna as she flung open the back doors to the school and disappeared inside.

The score was *My Doom: 1; Me: 0.*

6

I can't say that once you've ripped the shorts off a girl it gets any easier to talk to her.

To Arianna, I was pond scum. No, make that the larva that feeds on the slime under the pond scum. Or the parasite that feeds on the larva that eats the slime. Whatever. I was the lowest of low in her book. Completely ignoring me seemed to be her mode of punishment for the shorts incident.

"It's been two days," I said as I tossed a baseball into a bucket. Corbin had me separating baseballs from softballs in his office. It was mind numbing. "I feel like I'm counting down to my execution."

"That is, if the Princess doesn't kill you first," Corbin muttered as he leaned out the equipment room door to check on a volleyball game taking place in the gym. "Pick up the pace, you lazy pile of couch potatoes!" he yelled down at them. "I want to see sweat. Real, genuine sweat!"

"She's not going to kill me," I said, tossing a handful of softballs into a bin. "It wasn't that bad."

"Wasn't that bad?" Corbin snorted. "You pantsed the reigning Princess of Puckerbush High in front of all her friends. I'm surprised you haven't been lynched."

"It's probably a good thing she forgot my name then," I said and sighed. "What haven't I tried? There has to be another way to get close to this girl."

"Does she have a favorite subject?"

"I pay attention to her in class, but she doesn't exactly

show any excitement for one subject over another."

Corbin interlaced his fingers and rested them on his head, deep in thought. He stared down into the gym, but I don't think he saw anything.

"You know, she's failing Algebra," he said. I dropped a softball on my foot. I didn't feel it crunch into my toes. "And not just kind of failing it. I'm talking flat-out flunking. Not that I can blame her. I always hated mathematics."

"How did you find that out?" I said, bending to grab the ball before it rolled under the desk.

"I thought you knew."

"Uh, no."

"Well, I overheard Mr. Fenske talking about it to Mr. Alred. You were there with me."

I knew vaguely what he was talking about. "They were clear across the room from us at lunch," I said.

"Right," Corbin said, nodding. "I keep forgetting that you are damaged."

Damaged? "I am not."

"What other word do you have for it? I have a mile range on my hearing. Would you rather I called you handicapped?"

Add one more thing to the list of what I was missing. "I bet you can see around the curvature of the Earth," I said sarcastically.

"No, but I can see in the dark," he tapped his temple with his finger and grinned. "Twenty–twenty vision on a moonless night. I can see better detail than infrared."

So that was why his eyes glowed. Pompous, bragging . . .

"Watch the insults," Corbin warned. "I can still make you run laps, assistant or not."

60

"Don't tell me you can read minds too?"

"No, but the look on your face said plenty."

I took a deep breath, ready to say something snappy, when Corbin put his fingers to his lips and whistled hard and shrill.

"Pack it up, Nancys," he shouted. "I want everyone cleaned up and out of here in five!"

He turned back to me as I finished sorting. His face was serious. "You're running out of time, so I suggest you go to Mr. Fenske and lie your face off that you are a whiz at math."

"I *am* a whiz at math," I said under my breath.

"I could care less if you were an astronaut," he spat. "Get in good with the math teacher and volunteer to be a tutor. *Her* tutor."

"Yes, sir," I muttered, and left to get dressed.

A tutor? I could ace any subject just by sitting in class, but I'd never tutored. I cleaned up, ran a hand through my messy hair, and grabbed my bag on the way out of the locker room. Corbin wasn't around, so I made my escape to my next class. I should have guessed I wasn't lucky enough to get away.

Corbin plucked me out of the hall crowd a few doors away from History 101 and dragged me into the teachers' lounge. For all the eyes that snapped up and stared at me like I was something nasty, I might have entered the Forbidden City.

"Hey, Fenske," Corbin said. The math teacher flinched. Good to see I wasn't the only one the coach rattled. "I hear that the new student will need a tutor for your class."

"I think I'll be fine finding my own tutor," he said. "Thank—"

"Good," Corbin barked and held me up like a slab of meat. With no real effort, mind you. "This kid will report first thing tomorrow. Glad I could help."

The last image I had of Mr. Fenske was of him with his mouth hanging open. Corbin tossed me out into the hall and slammed the door in my face. If all Bankhir Warriors were like the coach, then I had a sinking feeling I came from a planet of jerks.

By the next morning, I was dreading school. Well, not *dreading* it, exactly. More like nerves coupled with sweating—a lot of sweating—and my heart pounding in my ears. I was going to be one-on-one tutoring with my betrothed. That thought alone made me feel ill.

I showed up to Remedial Algebra with one hand holding my book and the other trying to flatten down my mass of tangled blond hair. If I owned a comb, it didn't show. Mr. Fenske looked up to greet me, but it was obvious he couldn't place a name with my face.

"Thank you . . . uh . . ."

"Ian," I reminded him for what felt like the millionth time over the years.

"Thank you, Ian, for volunteering," Mr. Fenske said, and pointed to the back corner, where Arianna was already waiting for me.

"Any time," I said, and made my way to the back of the class. It was like walking through a slow-motion dream . . . or nightmare.

I plopped my books down on the table next to Arianna.

"Morning," I said to the back of her head. "I am your tutor."

"I really apprecia—" was as far as she got when she turned around and saw it was me. "Oh."

I guess it was better than "get lost, you pervert!" I sat down and tried to act casual.

"I take it you were expecting someone else?" I said. "I get that a lot. No worries. I'm sure you didn't want to be tutored in the first place."

"Um, no," she said. The olive skin on her cheeks flushed pink. "It's fine that I have a tutor. I just didn't think it would be you."

Again, it wasn't a full-on "beat it, loser," so I held on to what little hope I had left.

"So, you're flunking math, huh?" I said. I did a mental dope slap. Way to state the obvious!

"Well, yeah," she said to her gloved hands. "I'm not very good at it. Please don't make fun of me."

Holy crap, she was nice as well as beautiful. I was stinking it up. I should have said "it's okay" or "we all are, don't worry about it," but I didn't. Like a pea-brain I said, "Well, I am really good at math, which is why I'm your tutor."

If she had smacked me, I would have deserved it.

"Then why are you in Remedial Algebra?" Arianna said, a little irked.

I shrugged. "I liked the view better in here over College Calculus," I said.

Arianna snorted out a half laugh, like she wasn't sure if I was being serious. "Who are you?"

I was right. She did forget my name.

"Ian," I said, keeping it to that. But then I blurted, "And you don't like to be touched."

Her smile disappeared. "How did you know?"

"It was easy; you're sitting as far away as you can without being rude, and you wouldn't shake Coach Corbin's hand on your first day here," I said.

"That was you with him?"

Geez, I was invisible. Not that it was hard to imagine that the most beautiful girl in school saw right through me like I wasn't there at all.

"Yeah, that was me." I must have sounded irritated because she smiled, apologetic.

"Look, it's nothing personal. I'm a little OCD about getting close to people," she said. "But, to make up for starting out on the wrong foot, I have to tell you, I really hate it when people call me Arianna. It's so old-school."

"So you prefer Anna or . . . ?"

"Ari," she said.

"So why don't you correct them?"

"I don't want to be rude," she said—shy, like I was going to judge her for having an opinion.

"Well, I don't think you'll have a problem with that here," I said, feeling out of my depth. How she could function without blowing off steam once in a while was beyond me. "So, uh, where do you want to get started? We can skip a lot if you hate the basics."

"I'm good with the basics, and really, I do like math," Ari said as she opened her book. "I just think it would be easier to understand if I had a better teacher."

"Because of the homeschool thing?"

"Yeah. Neither of my parents were all that good with it."

"If it makes you feel any better, the teachers here aren't that great either."

"I don't think they are all that bad," Ari said. I had to

stifle an incredulous snort. This girl was way too nice.

"So, how come I've never seen you before?" I said. Contrary to everything coming out of my mouth up to this point, I have to say that I was not completely stupid. I made a mental note to never mention that I had been house-stalking the Hernfelds for years. I was curious, though. "I've lived in Puckerbush my entire life and I never knew the Hernfelds had a kid."

"I don't get out much."

"That's an understatement," I said. "What did they do, lock you up in the basement? You don't turn into a hideous beast or anything, do you?"

Okay, I redact the comment on my intelligence. When it came to sarcasm, I was an idiot. Ari didn't laugh. She did, however, give me a long, calculating look.

"It's just better that way," Ari said, and that was the end of the explanation. She flipped the pages of her book to the fourth chapter. She didn't seem upset, which made me feel like a jerk. I wanted to clear the air with her.

Which meant that it was a good time to insert my foot into my mouth. "I'm really sorry about what happened in gym class, uh, on Monday," I said. "Totally not what I intended to do."

"Do what?"

"You know, uh, grab your shorts, and uh . . ." I was sweating again. I could feel a bead of it roll down the back of my neck.

"Oh my gosh. That was you?" she said as her eyes widened in mortification.

"Good gravy," I blurted. "It's like I'm invisible to the world!"

"You should have stayed that way," Ari said, glaring. "I

didn't even look back to see who had ripped my shorts off!"

"I'm sorry." I would have loved to smack myself hard across the face right about then. "I have really bad aim . . . a-and your shorts were a lot bigger than the flag."

"So, you're saying I'm fat?"

"No . . ."

"Or that my butt is too big. Is that it?"

"Not that either. Heck, I've never even looked at you . . . like that," I said. I could feel my ears redden and heat up like an inferno. "Look, it wasn't that bad . . . right?"

"You are so not helping your case right now," she said.

"I'm not trying to make you feel worse," I fumbled. "But I wanted you to know it wasn't on purpose."

"I should hate you."

"That's right, you should," I said. "You have every right. But, I'm still sorry."

"You're sorry. That's it?"

I exhaled in exasperation. "That's all I've got."

She was killing me. I looked up to see that Ari was half grinning.

"You're making me pay for it, aren't you?" I said, and she laughed. It was musical, and the motion made her hair shimmer.

"Yes, I am," she said.

"I'm sure I deserve it."

"No, you don't. I was fully covered, so it wasn't that bad," she said and reddened. "Never mind, it was that bad. I'll just try to forget it was you who did it."

"Thanks. Are you always this nice?"

"I try to be, but you are different," she said, cocking her head to the side.

A dormant engine of hope kick-started in the pit of my stomach.

"Good different?"

"Maybe," she said with a note of finality.

Idle chat was over. I flipped open my book to the right lesson and got started.

The tutoring thing didn't go as bad as I thought. I explained the lesson and Ari seemed to get it. Really, it felt like I was only parroting back what was on the pages of the book, but Ari picked it up. Which was a good thing because I kept getting distracted. I wasn't sure if it was the familiar warmth coming off of her, but it was a rerun of gym class all over again. My lungs cleared and I sat up straight to fill them to full capacity. Something I'd never been able to do pre-Ari.

Weird. I tried to place why it affected me so much. Corbin said she was practically radioactive with Deep Magic, but it had been so long since I knew what that felt like, I had no idea what that entailed. I stared out the window, tapping the eraser of my pencil on the word problem she was working on as I slipped deep into thought.

The last clear memory I had of Bankhir was at dusk, when the sun's dying rays reflected off the blade of my sword. The sky would light up with waves of rippling color, seeping into every living thing. It felt like comfort food filling me up from the inside out, but without the eating part.

"Hellooo? Earth to Tutor Guy," Ari said, waving her hand in front of my eyes.

"The name is Ian," I said, half awake. "And you feel weird."

"I what?"

I snapped out of it. "I mean, you feel fine. Not that I was touching you or anything. It's just distracting."

"Uh . . . I don't know what to say to that," she said. I expected her to get up and leave. Or at least lean away from me like I was contagious. But she didn't.

"Sorry. I'm sure you get a lot of weirdos saying dumb stuff to you," I said. Me included. It was that beautiful girl thing that brought out the stupid in every hormonal guy.

"No, I don't," she said. "Most people don't like to get near me after a while, let alone talk about how I feel to them."

"Yeah, sorry about that. What I said came out totally wrong. Just forget it, okay?"

"It's okay," she said. She tried to scoot away from me and make it look casual. "It was an unusual comment, is all. I don't usually talk this much to one person."

"But you have tons of friends."

"Not really. I'm not like any of them, so it's hard to, you know . . . have an actual conversation." Ari dropped her gaze. I thought my eyes were tricking me, but for a second she looked sad. Her lower lip shot between her teeth and she turned away. Maybe she thought she said too much.

"I, uh, think you're doing pretty great," I said. For once, I actually succeeded in saying something complimentary instead of obnoxiously offensive.

"Thanks." Ari's whispered reply could barely be heard over the end-of-period bell. I started packing up my things, at a loss for anything else normal to say. No sense jinxing a good thing.

"See you in class," Ari said as she tossed her bag over her shoulder and stood up. She was a solid five inches taller than me. Stupid delayed growth spurt.

Ari left me with my jaw swinging open. By the time I got out to the hall, I was semi-numb. I didn't see Coach Corbin coming from the direction of the gym.

"How did it go, lover boy?" he said, looking everything anxious and expectant and nothing kidding in his forced light tone.

I couldn't deny it. I had my first successful conversation with Ari that didn't end with me looking like an idiot. I was going to milk it!

"Lover boy is in," I said.

7

It'd be great to say that this was the beginning. It wasn't.

I still had to contend with Ari's horde of followers that trailed after her everywhere. But after another week, I noticed something else. The crowd was thinning out. People would come to Ari to talk at her, but it was as if they were being repelled. They'd walk over, get within two feet, and then walk away as if they forgot something. Another odd happening was that she cowered away from them as if any person closer than a two-foot distance freaked her out.

Ari stood alone at her locker with a wide berth of space around her. The closer I got, the more it felt like walking into an electrically charged room. Weird.

"Is it just me, or did half the school decide to take a vacation at the same time?" I said, scanning the half empty hall.

"It's just you," Ari said and dug a brush out of her bag. She ran it quickly through black hair that floated with static and crackled when she brushed it. She rubbed wearily at her eyes.

"Tired?"

"I had a rough night," Ari said, and stuffed everything back into her locker. Babe though she was, her locker was a total mess. Junk fell out everywhere as she tried to cram some of it into her bag.

"I must be missing something," I said. I picked up a pen that rolled out the bottom of her locker and tossed it on the top shelf before she slammed her locker shut. "We live in Puckerbush. Last I checked it's pretty low on excitement."

"Maybe for you it is," she said darkly.

Odd.

"Care to explain that?" I said, leaning up against the wall and taking a deep breath. Hanging out with Ari had its benefits, like being able to breathe normally. Sometimes it was distracting. Today, for example. I'd spent most the night hacking because Janet was up to two packs a day and a permanent cloud of cigarette smoke lingered in the trailer. I couldn't get to school fast enough to escape it to be around Ari and fill my lungs with air. It was like drinking from the cup of life. It also made me zone out. Not good when you're supposed to be listening.

"My parents and I had another argument last night. It's just the usual stuff: why can't I be normal and all that."

"Yeah," I said in zombie mode.

"Are you even listening?"

Corbin edged around the corner and glared. His dimly lit eyes were freaky-looking, like a wolf stalking prey at night. I snapped back to attention. He motioned for me to nod and made an exaggerated sad face. I mimicked him. "I'm sorry, Ari," I said, blinking a few times.

"Oh, it'll be fine, I guess," she said, giving me a calculating look. "I just wish my parents would ease up a bit."

"I wish mine would acknowledge I existed," I said.

"They don't run your life like every other parent?"

"Not really, but I think that's the crux of being in a foster home."

Corbin smacked his forehead so hard I could hear it down the hall. I could also clearly read his lips when he mouthed "you idiot!" Luckily, Ari wasn't looking.

"Not to change the subject from my lame family life, but we have that Nevada's History project due on Friday," I said. "We should do it together."

"I don't think that's such a good idea," Ari said, swinging her bag over her shoulder.

"Why not?"

"Weren't you listening to what I was just telling you?"

I opted for honesty. "Sort of."

"Wow, that was blunt," she said. "Do you ever listen to me?"

"All the time," I said as we headed to Art. "Just not this morning."

Yep. I was a total clod. I was going to smooth over the offense, but Corbin burst out around the corner. We were on friendly terms. Ish. But that didn't stop him from hounding me everywhere I went.

"Hernfeld!" he barked at Ari. This was a change from his usual yelling at me and it caught me off guard. "Gym locker inspection today. It'd better be clean."

"Yes, sir," she said, squaring her shoulders. Anyone else would have cowered under Corbin's ferocious glare as he stalked past us.

"Oh great," Ari said and her shoulders drooped. "I'm screwed. I bet he'll make me run laps. I've got junk accumulating in there since I got here."

"He won't make you run," I said.

"How do you know?"

If I knew Corbin, he was playing matchmaker. I opened the door to Art class for Ari and followed her in.

"If it's a mess, you'll probably be stuck with me cleaning gum off the bleachers."

"I think I'd rather run."

Ouch. Though I couldn't blame her. We took a table in the back. Today it was all about expressing emotion through color. Honestly, I thought it was a load of hippie hot air. Mrs. Wiberg lost me when she started going off on how we needed to feel the passion of red. If there were a color for sarcasm, I'd be home free.

"So," I said, slopping a load of brown on a plastic sheet and running a brush through it. "This color thing is weird. When I look at red, the only thing I feel is that I'd like to kick something."

"Violence is a feeling. So, I guess that means this class isn't a total loss. Though I'm not a big fan of red." Ari squeezed out copious amounts of blue and green onto her sheet and began mixing them. I watched her closely for a second. The color she was mixing reminded of something.

"Back to my mad listening skills," I said. Ari snort-laughed. "I was listening when you said in Drama yesterday that you liked aquamarine."

"Not blue and not green," she nodded and spread color on the canvas with a perfect swipe of her brush. "It's right in the middle."

"Because the middle is so much better," I said. The best I could do was to slap paint on the canvas in big lumps and smear it around.

"It's a pretty color."

"Like gangrene," I kidded.

Ari snorted out another muffled laugh. "That's horrible! And it doesn't look like gangrene. It looks more like the ocean."

"Which I've never seen," I lied. I'd seen the ocean, just

not the one on Earth. "What else am I supposed to compare it to?"

Ari studied me for a moment. "Your eyes are pretty close."

I stopped short. My stomach engine did a roller coaster thing and crashed into my navel. "My eyes?"

"Yeah. They're kind of like Coach Corbin's."

Boy, she really knew how to kill it. I couldn't believe I was being compared to that meathead.

"In fact, you guys look a lot alike. Are you related?"

Sure, if you consider that we were two male warriors from the same planet. We didn't look like anybody else in Puckerbush. We both had yellow blond hair, blue eyes that glowed slightly in broad daylight, and the same square face. Even our noses were bent the same way, though Corbin's was a bit more bashed up than mine. For as much as I resembled any other human on Earth, Corbin could be my uncle.

"Related? Yeah, I guess you could say that," I said. "In a very distant, he's-the-crazy-psycho-uncle-everyone-tries-to-avoid sort of way."

Ari laughed loud enough to catch Mrs. Wiberg's attention. She shushed us. It was only natural that we put our heads closer and went on talking in lower voices. Ari kept a stern barrier of space between us, but I didn't care. I could breathe, and it felt good.

"I swear the coach follows me," Ari whispered. "He pops up everywhere I go."

"I know how that feels, though I've known him longer," I said. "Trust me, it can get creepier."

"What is his deal anyway?"

I was going to answer that he was just plain nuts and it was normal, but I didn't get the chance. Ari went to push her hair behind her ear at the same time I reached out for a new color and we bonked arms. Once, when I was three, I touched a bare wire on Janet's ancient hair dryer and sent volts of electricity firing up my arm. This was like that, except multiplied by a hundred. I could feel my hair lift off my head, and my arm tensed into a cramp.

I bit back a yelp. With a sharp gasp, Ari leapt to her feet and backed away from me as fast as she could. Despite my numb and throbbing arm, I reached out to stop her before she stumbled over a chair.

"I didn't mean to do that," she said, cringing away from me. "I'm so sorry!"

I coughed and a puff of bluish smoke burst out my mouth.

"No worries," I said, and coughed again. "Static electricity. Happens all the time."

Ari stared at me for a long time. I resisted the urge to rub my arm where she'd zapped me and started cleaning out my brush in a water dish. Ari took a long time to sit back down again, and when she finally did, she fixed me with an unblinking stare. It was weird to be under a short-distance spotlight. She couldn't stop gaping, like she expected me to drop dead or something. She wouldn't talk and kept up the silent treatment until gym class.

By then I was getting worried. The only person who kept that close of an eye on me was Corbin. It made me wonder if I had something dangling out my nose. The feeling was coming back into my arm too, so it wasn't as if she needed to worry or anything.

I was in the boys' locker room getting changed when I heard Corbin through several brick walls, yelling. I forgot about the locker inspection. If I had remembered, I would have asked Corbin to ease up on Ari a bit. But, according to the racket I was sure the entire school could hear, the beast had lost it.

"What kind of mess is this?" Corbin bellowed. "I want this locker gutted out. Then you will spend the rest of the hour cleaning out the equipment room with Ian!"

Figured as much. I stuffed my backpack into my locker and slammed it shut. On the way out to the gym I high-fived Corbin, who smiled smugly.

"You're welcome," he said.

"Yep."

But Corbin's matchmaking attempt didn't pay off. Ari stayed silent through all of class. It was only yes and no answers through cleaning grimy mouth guards and ripe-smelling cleats.

Defeated? Not yet. I'd been ignored my entire life. Instead of going home after the final bell, I trudged into Corbin's office, slumped into his chair, and told him everything.

"Now repeat what happened again?" Corbin said as he leaned forward with his forehead furrowed.

"I'm telling you, it was just a shock and then she wrote me off for the rest of the day," I said.

"How big of a shock?"

I thought about it. "I suppose if I gripped the wrong end of a cattle prod, it would feel the same. I wrote it off as static, but she wasn't convinced."

"Because it wasn't," Corbin said excitedly. "Garfelians

have this weird way they control the energy that comes off of Deep Magic. If they haven't released it in a while and keep it bottled up, it's like lightning. At night I would watch them spray the sky of both our planets with the excess energy. Makes the northern lights here on Earth look dim in comparison."

"So she shocked me with Deep Magic?"

"No, the energy that Deep Magic generates. There is a difference."

That made sense, but I was still confused.

"But why would it make her so upset?"

"Frankly, I'm surprised it didn't kill you," Corbin said. "Depending on how much she had stored up inside her, she could have blown your head off."

No wonder she was staring at me like I was going to keel over and die. Which gave me an idea. "I've got to go," I said and bolted to my feet.

"Don't screw this up worse, kid," Corbin yelled at me as I ran down the hall. "We've got less than two months left."

I hated the countdown, but I couldn't ignore it either. My lungs were back to normal, so I didn't get far before I had to stop and cough them clear.

Two months. Or less, the way my luck ran.

Ari was nice, but she was nice to everyone. She seemed to like me, though it was more like as a distant friend. If I was honest, it was more like a brother–sister relationship. I shook off the implication.

My feet took me automatically to the Hernfelds' in the center of town. I still walked by nearly every day. A habit was a habit, even if it was a little weird. It didn't look as if anyone was home.

I ran up the front step and rang the bell. I waited for what felt like an age with no answer. I tried knocking, but when my knuckles hit the wood, the door swung open.

Now what?

"Hello?" I called. "Ari?"

Nothing. I kept it up out of sheer desperation.

"The door was open," I said to nobody. "I, uh, just wanted to see if Ari and I could get started on our History project."

I was grasping at air here. Ari wanted to do the project solo. Though, now that I thought about it, I needed a good excuse to give to the police if the Hernfelds called them. When I heard crackling like electricity on a Tesla coil, all thoughts of what I'd hypothetically say to the authorities fled. Shucking my backpack, I took the stairs two at a time. On the landing I could see lights flashing under a closed door.

"Ari?" I pressed my hand on the door and it swung open easily. Technically, I'd never been in a girl's room. I don't know what I expected, but it wasn't this.

Everything in Ari's room was a different color—a dizzying clash of violent, vibrant hues, as if she couldn't decide what she liked best and went for a little of everything. Not only that, but it looked as if the Princess of Garfel was a pack rat.

Ari knelt in the center of her cluttered room, clutching her hands into fists under her chin. I would have guessed it was a weird form of meditation if it weren't for the whimpering gasps of air she took, like whatever she was doing hurt. On second thought, it wasn't as much suffering as it was struggling for control. She was covered head to toe with dark tights, but up the back of her bare neck came a glowing light that snaked around her hair. The bright arcs moved fluidly and shone a bright, vibrant aquamarine.

"What the—?" I muttered.

Ari stirred and broke concentration for less than a second. Apparently that was all it took for her to explode in a mini atom bomb of rippling light. It blew me off my feet. I skidded on my butt across the hall and slammed into the wall. It should have hurt. When she shocked me in Art class, my arm ached for an hour, but the ocean-colored stuff felt amazing.

"Ian!" Ari gasped, and the flashing lights shut off. "Oh my gosh, I didn't mean to hit you like that. I lost control!"

She rushed over and put her hands out as if to help me up, but stopped. Frantically, she dove for her gloves and snapped them on. Either way, I didn't care if she wore them or not. I was flying high and my chest was smoking slightly. It was a faint silvery smoke, almost identical to the stuff I'd seen come out of Corbin's hands.

"Woohoo! That was awesome!" I said and shook my head like a wet dog. My nerves were zinging all over the place.

"Not awesome," Ari groaned. "What are you doing here?"

"Why? You didn't hurt me," I said as she pulled me to my feet.

"With a blast like that, you should be in the hospital."

"Are you kidding? I feel great!"

"You'd be the first," she muttered.

"You've done this before? When? To who?"

Just then, we both could hear the garage door opener kick on and labor to get the door up.

"Crap! That'll be my mom. You've got to get out of

here!" Ari said. In a rush, she pushed me to the stairs. I was halfway down and picking up my backpack when the back door opened.

"Arianna? Honey, are you home?"

We froze on the stairs. The front door to freedom seemed a mile away and Mrs. Hernfeld sounded too close for comfort.

"Holy fright! Not out the front door!" Ari hissed. She grabbed the back of my T-shirt and dragged me back upstairs. "Get in my room, now!"

Hiding out in a hot girl's bedroom wasn't as great as I'd thought it would be.

Ari shoved me through the door and glared at me with wide, frightened eyes.

"Say one word or make one noise and I will end you," she warned.

"Not one word." I meant it. I wasn't going to get Ari in trouble. The door shut behind her as she bounded down the stairs.

"Hey, Mom," she said brightly. "How was work?"

Mrs. Hernfeld's reply was low and muffled. I didn't move. I'd been in houses like this; they weren't exactly quality-built. If one foot was out of place, I was sure the floorboards would creak. I didn't even shift my weight.

I stayed like that for what felt like an eternity. Not that I minded much. The bluish stuff she'd blasted me with still coursed around in my veins. I took deep breaths to try to calm the jittery feeling. I felt irrational and on edge, but at the same time *full*, though I couldn't understand why. My stomach was empty. It was the same feeling I had when I was around Ari and my asthma went away, except multiplied by a million.

Suddenly, it became crystal clear why I had singled out Ari's house. Yeah, I know. This was a weird situation to have an epiphany, but abrupt leaps in understanding rarely happen in reasonable places, like during a test, for example. Epiphanies prefer to hit you in weird places like bathtubs or when you're hanging upside down. Regardless, what I had thought was a funky habit of walking by the same house day in and day out wasn't so funky after all. If I had known how awesome Deep Magic felt, I would have made far more excuses to drop by the Hernfelds'. Like Corbin, I could feel it, and dang, it felt good.

I grinned. It was nice to know that I hadn't completely lost it.

"Okay, Mom," Ari said, louder and closer than before. I stiffened, ready to bolt if needs be. "I'm going to go do my homework now."

The knob turned. Ari slipped in the door and shut it. She leaned on the frame and gasped, clutching her chest like she was about to have a heart attack.

"You okay?" I whispered.

"I'm fine," she whispered back. "Though I don't think I've ever lied to my mom that much in my life."

"You shouldn't have to. I'm totally good with meeting your parents."

"I'm not," she said flatly.

"Talk about cutting a guy off at the knees," I said. I wasn't that bad, was I?

"Look, it's not you, though I want to know why you're not in an ambulance right now. Are you sure you're okay?"

"Totally fine," I said waving her off. "Besides, I want to know what those bolts of whatever that was shooting out of you were."

Ari gulped hard, like she was trying to swallow something bigger than she could handle.

"Fine," she said through clenched teeth. "But not now."

"When?"

Ari grabbed my arm and led me to the window. "Just later, okay? I need to think."

"That explains a lot," I grumbled, but Ari ignored me.

"You've got to get out of here. I'm not allowed to have anyone over, ever."

"Isn't that a little strict?"

"It's safe. You saw what happened. People get hurt around me."

"Except I'm still standing."

Ari stared, wide eyed, at me. "That's the part I don't get. Now get out."

"Sure," I muttered as I climbed out the window and stepped onto the roof of the garage. "Kick out the guy who isn't dead."

I slid down the roof and crawled over the edge to hang off the gutter, willing myself to fall the remaining seven feet.

"Ian?" Ari whispered hoarsely.

"Yeah?"

"I'm glad you aren't dead," she said, then she shut the window.

Me too, come to think of it. I dropped to the lawn and got out of there.

8

Normally, I am not an adrenaline junkie, but that stuff Ari was putting out was addictive. I vaulted over the Hernfelds' fence and ran home. You heard me. I ran and it felt good, like I could go on for miles and not be out of breath. Corbin would have been proud. When I got to my jumble of trailers at the edge of town, my energy was beginning to fade. I was winding down as the last of the bluish stuff she blasted me with dissipated. The adjustment back to having asthma and being weak was torture. I staggered up the front steps and opened the door.

A cloud of cigarette smoke blew out above my head. Through the haze I could see Janet at the sink puffing away over green mush in a bowl. The last of Ari's weird magic left me. I coughed.

My chest hurt, but it wasn't the same as before. It was worse. Or maybe it just felt worse because I got a good feel for what life would be like as a functioning being without asthma. Make me pick between the two, and I'd pick Ari hands down, every time.

"You," Janet said in her low smoker voice. "Get washed up and come eat."

"Yes ma'am," I said, stepping over a toddler. I wasn't sure if she was really talking to me. There were three other kids nearby and I just happened to be one of them. However, I was the only one who obeyed.

Dinner was always a noisy affair. Nobody cared if more

fighting than eating went on, and the younger ones crawled around on top of the table to get at what they wanted. It was utter chaos.

I wasn't sure if it was the inborn military exactness in me, but I could barely stand it. I showered and cleaned up after myself when nobody else bothered to. Then I barricaded myself in my room and tried to get some homework done.

"Boy?" Phil shouted from the front trailer. They were all connected by rectangles cut in the metal walls. "Boy! You got a lady caller."

Seeing as Phil never learned any of our names, that could have applied to about half of us. The volume in the trailers magnified a few billion decibels. I pulled on a pair of clean shorts and tugged a shirt over my head. They felt different. My shorts fell a good inch above my knee and if I lifted my arms I felt a draft. Weird.

Blam! Blam! Blam!

"Hey, Ian!" Phil bellowed as he pounded on my door. It wasn't quite dark out, so it wasn't as if he was tucking me in for the night. Not that he had ever done something like that before. I swung open the door, shocked he got my name right for the first time in years.

"There's a girl at the door for you," he said, jabbing a dirty thumb over his shoulder.

"Say what?"

"A girl," Phil said slowly, like I was stupid. "At the door."

"Ari?" I said, not computing what was happening.

"How the hell'm I spose t'know?"

Kill me now. Who else could it be? I bent to shove on my shoes and rammed my head into the wall. Funny.

That had never happened before. I usually had room to move. I waded through a sea of gawking heads to the door. Everyone wanted to get a look at the exotically beautiful girl standing under the front porch light. Ari waved and winked at a few of the younger ones, causing a wave of nervous giggling.

"Hi," she said, flashing a perfectly even and white-toothed smile. The roller coaster in my gut roared to life and ran loops in my stomach.

"Ari," I said, trying to get my face to cooperate with an answering smile. "I didn't know you were coming."

"Neither did I, but I felt like going for a walk," she said, pointedly. "Like right now."

A surge of eager bodies pressed against my back and legs.

"That sounds like a very good idea," I said, pushing a few kids back out of the way. "Alone."

Everyone wanted to go. The chorus of protests and begging was deafening. I barely got out the door and shouldered it shut.

"I thought a walk would be a good idea," Ari said apologetically. "Maybe not."

"No, a walk is great," I said holding the door closed until the pounding stopped.

Ari took a step off the busted porch and read the lopsided sign above the door.

"Puckerbush Home for Displaced Children? That sounds . . . um, nice."

"Nicer than it's cracked up to be," I said, slowly releasing the door and praying it wouldn't bust open. "We should get going while we have the chance."

I steered us in the same direction as the clump of bushes Corbin and I talked at weeks before. It was quieter there, except for the bugs.

"Did you make it home okay?" Ari asked once the coast was clear.

"Yeah. It was fine," I said. "Hopefully none of your neighbors saw me crawling out of your house like a thief."

"Sorry," Ari flinched. "I've never had a boy in my room before. I kind of panicked."

"It was a day for firsts all around," I said. "I've never had a girl blast me off my feet and then shove me out a window."

"About that," Ari said, dropping the small talk. "You can't tell anyone what you saw, okay?"

"I wasn't planning on it," I said. "But do you mind explaining why?"

"This is bigger than just a quick little explanation. I should be locked up. I knew this would happen, and now it did and my parents are going to kill me. I swore to them I could control it."

"Slow down," I said holding up my hands. "I don't mind. Really. I don't."

Ari's green eyes were almost wild. I thought she might cry.

"What do you want? Money? I'll pay anything you ask."

"I don't want money." I wanted her to like me enough to break the curse, but I didn't say that out loud.

She began to pace, scrubbing her hands through her static-ridden hair and tangling it. "What am I going to do?" she said, mostly to herself. "I've been so good. It's been ages since I last lost control."

"I don't—"

"My parents are going to kill me!" Ari moaned miserably. "They get so mad. But it's not like I try to be this way. I hate it. I hate hurting people."

I felt like a total dunce. It all made sense. The reason why Ari felt so alone when crowded by people. Why she freaked out when we touched and why she kept everyone at arm's distance.

"Your parents aren't going to kill you," I said.

"Why not? They always find out, and then it'll be back to hanging out with myself all over again. No phone, no people, not even pets are allowed because they are so scared I'll end up killing someone. I'm just so tired of . . ."

"Of being alone," I said when Ari fell silent. She didn't answer, but I got it. "Well, you don't have to, because I'm not going to tell."

Ari opened her mouth ready for another argument, but nothing came out. Her forehead furrowed, confused.

"You aren't?"

"Nope."

"Why?"

I could think of a million reasons why. First of all, I knew who she was. I knew that we weren't human. I had a duty to my people and a quest to fulfill. And also because, since I'd remembered how the stupid magician flushed us down to Earth, I wanted payback. But, more important, now that I finally knew her, I couldn't imagine betraying her trust.

Of course, for an alien girl who thought she was human, telling her she was an exiled princess from another planet wouldn't exactly be productive. Instead I opted for:

"Because you're my friend."

In my head it sounded lame, but coming out my mouth was totally different. I couldn't have sealed a promise of loyalty with more finality if I had written it out in my own blood.

"Are you insane? Being friends with me is dangerous." Ari glanced down at her gloved hands, where a faint glow was emanating through the fabric. "Oh no. Not again."

Ari started backing away, her eyes darting around for an escape.

"Don't go," I said hastily. "It's not that bad. You don't have to worry . . ."

"Worry?" Ari said. "I'm *panicking*. This is bad. Very bad."

Ari looked about ready to bolt. Normally I wasn't the grabby kind, but I caught her by the wrist and stopped her before she could run off. The warmth of Deep Magic radiated over my hand and up my arm.

"No!" Ari gasped in fear. "I'm not in control . . . yet." She stopped struggling to get away and stared open-mouthed at me.

"I think you're doing fine," I said as I slowly let her wrist go. "See?"

I held up my undamaged hands and waggled my fingers at her.

"Look, I think it's obvious that I can handle being friends with you," I said. I was skinny and shorter than her and looked like I needed to eat non-stop for a month. I prayed she could see past all that.

"Okay, maybe you can," she said at last. "Though if I didn't just see you get beaned by my magic and live to see another day, I might have changed my mind. How did you do that, anyway?"

"Do what? Live?"

"Something like that."

I rubbed absently at a residual itch on my chest where my nerve endings were still jangling from the influx of magic. How did I survive?

"I'm not sure, but it didn't hurt," I said then back-tracked. "Scratch that; when you shocked me, it hurt like you zapped me with a bolt of lightning. The colored stuff doesn't hurt at all. I just kind of"—I struggled for the right word—"absorbed it."

"Really? You're probably the only guy on Earth that can handle it." Ari reached out and cautiously touched my arm. When that didn't do any harm she began poking around my puny bicep. "The last time I lost control, I put a girl in the hospital for a week."

Corbin was right, annoyingly enough. Humans were weak.

"Well, I wouldn't mind being in the way the next time you feel like exploding," I said, trying to mask my eager-ness. Feeling alive after years of being pathetically ill and scrawny was addictive. I wanted more.

"I can't lose it like that again," she said. "I just can't."

"Ari," I said when she started panic-breathing again. "I can handle it."

It took a minute, but Ari calmed down ever so slightly. "You're sure you're okay?"

"Healthy as a horse," I said. "Granted, I'm more like a half-starved horse, but . . ."

At last, Ari snorted out a tentative laugh. "Friends, huh?" she said. "It might be worth a try."

"Your vote of confidence is inspiring," I said. Ari's smile widened.

"I've never had friends before. It has always been forbidden until I could get my . . . my . . . whatever this is under control," she said. "But I think I'd like it."

Perfect. I was counting down the days to dual planet destruction and she just sent me to the "Friend Zone." Call me crazy, but I was going to take it.

"So, what all can you do with that bluish stuff?" I said, hungry for answers. "How long have you been this way?"

"For as long as I can remember, really. My dad says I was born like this. They had a hard time picking me up because I'd shock them. I just started controlling the other stuff. It feels different. I've studied electricity, but the bluish arcs behave totally different. It doesn't feel electric and I can do things with it that I never thought possible. I know it sounds lame, but it's like . . . like . . ."

"Magic?" I said.

Ari shook her head. "It can't be. There has to be a logical reason why I'm like this."

"Like what?" I said. "Outside of a comic book, there isn't anyone on Earth that can throw off energy like you can. Why not call it what it is? It's magic."

"That sounds totally lame."

"It's not lame," I said, deadpan serious. "I wouldn't know what else to call it."

Ari sighed heavily. "I just wish I could control it."

"You can't? It looked like you were doing a pretty good job of it earlier."

Ari lifted her arms and wiggled her gloved fingers. "That's because I have these on," she said. "They're lined with rubber. My dad had them special made."

"Does it work?"

"Not all the time. It acts like an extra layer of skin, so

the magic doesn't burst out of me. It gives me time to mask it and make it go away."

"So you can go to school and not glow," I said and held out my hand. "May I?"

Really, all I wanted to do was to rip the gloves off her. It was hovering in the high nineties in the evening and it made me sweat to look at them. Ari clutched her arms to her chest and shied away from me.

"Look, you're not going to hurt me," I said. I waited and she slowly held out her arms. I peeled off the right glove that extended to her elbow and then took off the left. Her olive skin was glowing.

It was so tempting to touch her. She had all that Deep Magic stored up inside her. I physically ached for it, to feel whole again and to feel like I was home. I barely knew this girl, but I took her hand and stroked my fingers over her arm. The effect was startling. The feeling of being a loner on Earth drained out, replaced by things I remembered, made sharp with the aid of magic. I could hear the rush of the ocean in my ears, and when I took a breath, my lungs filled with sea brine and salt.

Ari sighed. I snapped out of it and dropped her hand. "Sorry."

"Don't be. I can't remember the last time I felt another person's skin," she said. "I don't think I've ever been touched before now."

"Not even by your parents?"

"Especially not them. They handle me with rubber gloves and insist I wear my compression suit at all times."

"Well, you probably won't need it anymore," I said pointing to her bare arms. "You're back to normal."

Ari jumped back, splaying her fingers as she inspected

her regular, non-glowing skin. "Whoa," she murmured. "Though, I wonder . . . Give me your hand."

She grabbed me by the wrist. Her forehead furrowed as she stared unblinking at the palm of my hand.

"Think of something," she demanded.

"Like what?"

"Anything!"

The first thing that popped into my head was that Corbin was going to flip when I told him about Ari. The thought had barely formed when a miniature version of Corbin's head and shoulders grew out of my palm. This tinier model wasn't nearly as intimidating as the full-sized one, but he looked up at me and glared.

I ripped my hand away before she could look farther into my head.

"That was interesting," I said, trying to slow my heart rate. Ari didn't seem to notice.

"A couple months ago, I learned how to form objects that I was thinking about," she said. "I've always wanted to try it on someone else and see if I could do the same."

"As long as you warn me before making your guinea pig," I said as I flexed my hand and watched the bluish-green magic seep into my skin.

"I promise," she said, then added, "I know this sounds weird, but it's the first time I've shared my secret with anyone."

"You should get out more." I was joking, but Ari only responded with a morose shake of her head. She stuffed her gloves in her back pocket and inspected her arms that were a pale olive tone and weren't glowing.

"I should get going," she said and started walking toward town. "It's getting dark. My dad thinks I'm out for a walk by myself."

"I'll see you tomorrow," I said.

Ari turned and waved. "Bye, Ian."

Ian. She actually remembered my name. The roller coaster in my stomach was going haywire. I watched Ari until she disappeared around the neighbor's trailer.

"Well, hello *Ian*," a sneering voice said from behind me. I about jumped out of my skin. I spun around to find Corbin lurking behind the bushes, smiling smugly.

"What is wrong with you?" I sputtered.

"Just checking up on the lovebirds," he said, his smile widening.

"Can't a guy have any private conversations around here?" I said. I rubbed at the tips of my burning ears, where I was sure they were turning bright red.

"As a Prince of Bankhir, you should be chaperoned at all times when in the presence of your intended."

"Augh!" Why did he have to put it like that? "You do realize that I am still a sophomore in high school, right?"

Corbin shrugged. "Human rules," he said, "don't apply."

"Well, they apply plenty when the Princess thinks she is a human," I said. "Which complicates things. A lot."

"It shouldn't. Besides, it sounded like you were making progress. What are you worried about?"

I got irked. Mainly because I didn't like that I was being eavesdropped on.

"I am making progress," I snapped, then cringed. "Sort of. She wants to be friends."

"Friends? The fate of our worlds is on the line and she wants to be friends?"

"Well, I can't exactly tell her who she is and why I'm hounding her like a stalker. Last I checked, psychopaths don't get the girl."

"Telling her the truth isn't going to help things along, kid," he said. "Just don't waste too much time beating around the friend bush."

"I won't." I hope. I turned to walk back to my trailer. It was full dark out, and the moon was rising over the mountains.

"Hey, kid," Corbin called.

"Yeah?"

"Turn your eyes off. They're glowing."

Corbin dashed off into the night, speeding like a freight train. I could see him even though it should have been too dark to see anything. I looked down at my hands and a beam of blue light shone over my fingers, illuminating such detail that I could see every curve of my fingerprints. It was seriously cool.

"Wow." I stared for another minute until the light began to flicker, fade, and then go out altogether. I was pitched into darkness to trip my way back to the trailers in the dark.

9

Another day closer to sixteen.

Corbin, the meathead, broke into my locker and super-glued a calendar on the door. Every morning before I got to school, he had marked off a day. As if I didn't already know what kind of a bind we were in.

"Hey, Ian!" Ari said from behind me. I slammed the door shut to hide my infernal Almanac of Doom.

"Ari," I said, stuffing my books into my pack. "Hey, you ready for today's test?"

"I think so," she said, then waved me closer. Not that I needed much prompting to stick our heads together. She peeled back her glove to show a section of glowing dim bluish-green skin. Scrawled all over her palm, in her own handwriting, were all the notes from Math class written in Deep Magic.

"A cheat sheet?" I said. "You know that's against school rules."

"You are such a Boy Scout," she said, and sucked the glowing math formulas back into her skin. "And it's not cheating. Technically, all of that came from my memory."

"Technically?"

"Well, some of it I was able to get by magicking it into my skin. I almost pulled the ink right off the page."

I held up my hand to shush her when a few guys from the basketball team walked by. Then I grabbed her hand and covered it with my own so it wouldn't put off suspicious light.

"Just because you can throw off your magic when I am around, doesn't mean you shouldn't be careful about it," I hissed.

"Don't worry so much," Ari said. "I can always make them forget. I just figured out how to do it."

"How do you . . . ?"

A bright light blinded my eyes like the flash of a light bulb on a camera. My brain went blank. I blinked a few times, disoriented. For some odd reason I was holding Ari's hand. I quickly dropped it and tried to put on my backpack upside down.

"Hey, Ari," I said. "You ready for the math test?"

"Yes, Ian," she said around a giggle. "I am going to cheat my way through it and get expelled."

"You . . . are?" What was she talking about? Ari poked me in the arm and jolted me with a quick zap of Deep Magic. My memory flooded back, including what I had missed when she wiped my memory clean.

"Hey! That's not funny," I said as Ari laughed out loud. "You could do brain damage."

"Don't worry, I didn't get you that bad," she said. "I've been practicing that one on myself and trust me, I can do worse."

"I thought you were trying to suppress it?"

"No, my parents want me to suppress it, but I can't help wanting to use it. Well, as long as I don't hurt anyone. When I suppress it all of the time, then it busts out of me when I least expect it, and that's not good. Besides, it's easier to control now that you can handle some of the excess for me."

Ari held her hand out to me. I gripped her bare wrist and let the magic flow up my arm. Breakfast at the

Barfuses' consisted of sickly toast and Kool-Aid. Having Deep Magic course around my insides made me feel full, like I'd snarfed down eggs and bacon. However, it was way better than food. It took less than a second and the glow was gone off her skin.

Ari sighed with relief. "You have no idea how good that feels," she said.

"You're welcome," I said. "And do me a favor and take off the gloves. It's going to be a hundred and five out today."

"Gladly," Ari said, peeling them off and stuffing them in her back pocket. The gloves slapped off her fingers with a snap of electricity. An arc of excess energy struck the back of my hand and zinged up the back of my neck to my head.

"Watch it!" I said, not really complaining. Gut reaction.

"Sorry!"

"Don't be. This time wasn't nearly as bad as yesterday's shock."

I rubbed at my head where my scalp tingled and static electricity clung to my tangled hair. "Uh, we have a big biology exam coming up. It's a team test, so . . ." I hated this part. I always felt so dumb asking her to hang out with me. It sounded too much like begging. "Uh, we should probably study together."

"No can do," she said.

"We don't have to study at your house. We could hang out at my . . . house," I offered, again sounding like a beggar.

"I'd still have to explain to my parents where I am. Saying I'm with a boy will open up a whole can of insanity I don't want to deal with."

And again, she totally shut me down. It was like

watching a slow-motion film of an auto crash test over and over and over. Plastic dummies and all. I was that horrible at this.

"You know, one of these days you are going to realize that I can take the heat."

"We're just friends, Ian," she reminded me. As if I needed it.

Down the hallway, I caught sight of Corbin walking past Miss Reeder, who was blushing furiously and flirting. He made eye contact and glared at me irritably before heading upstairs to his office. I was sure his irritation wasn't directed at Miss Reeder.

I responded with a smirk and turned back to Ari who was staring at me.

"Have you grown?" she asked. "I swear you were shorter than me, but now we're almost eye level."

I hadn't noticed, but now that she mentioned it, I didn't have to look up to talk to her anymore. I was still skin and bone, but at least I had grown into my hands and feet a bit.

I shrugged and said, "It beats being the shortest kid in the tenth grade."

Whatever Ari said next, it fell on deaf ears. Over her shoulder a tall, sallow-faced man stepped out of the principal's office, shaking Mr. Bertolio's hand. He wore a dark suit, pinstriped shirt, and silky black tie. Aside from looking like he belonged on Wall Street in New York and not the Nevada desert, he was strangely familiar. He was balding slightly and he kept his wavy black hair clean-cropped with sideburns. He also wore thick glasses that sat on a hooked nose. When he turned in my direction, his eyes were jet black, like he had no irises and was all pupil.

Holy smokes, it was Silivus. I couldn't mistake those

eyes staring at me with pure, undiluted hatred. The magician was in my school.

I grabbed Ari and, not thinking twice, pushed her behind my back. I gripped her arms, half protectively, half needing support. If he thought he was going to do anything to her, he had another thing coming.

"Ow! Ian!" Ari complained when I blocked her from Silivus's sight.

"We need to get to class," I said, anxious to get where there was a crowd. "Like right now." There was safety in numbers, and the halls were emptying fast after the second bell rang. Besides, the back of my neck was tingling—not in a good way. I'd have to ask Corbin if it was one of those warrior things. I tried shifting toward class with everyone else, but Silivus was closing in. He didn't run, but he seemed to cover ground wicked fast. My hand flew to my left side where a sword should have been and grabbed air. It came as a natural reflex, yet another inborn reaction that must have been a warrior thing.

"What has gotten into you?" Ari said as she tried to pull out of my grasp.

"Nothing," I said over my shoulder. My eyes fixed on the magician who had blocked me in so close, I was forced to put my back up against the wall. Ari was still behind me and she got squashed.

"Good morning, student," Silivus articulated around a sneer.

"Morning," I said through gritted teeth. At the greeting, Ari stopped struggling and gripped the back of my shirt.

"Is there a reason why you are in the hall when you should be in class?"

"I was on my way," I said. Half of my reflexes screamed

to fight and the other half spoke reason. It was confusing to know which I was going to go with. It was clear that Silivus was in disguise as a human, and if he was going to play games, I would play human too, for now.

The magician locked eyes with me for a long time, almost as if he was waiting for me to morph into a killing machine. Weird.

"Then get to it," Silivus snapped. "I have my morning rounds to make in this cesspool of cut-rate learning."

I bit my tongue and stopped myself from saying a snide "you first." Silivus glided off. I say 'glide' because he moved too fast for normal human speeds. Good gravy, I was surrounded: first Corbin, then Ari, and now the magician who flushed me through the cosmos. Forget Area 51. Puckerbush was the new hotspot for aliens. I finally uncrushed Ari. I kept her blocked, my eyes never leaving the magician's back as he disappeared down the hall.

"I hope that isn't who I think it is," Ari said, tugging on my arm.

"I don't know who he is to you, but . . ." I couldn't finish, at a loss for words to explain why the magician was suddenly in my school. "We'd better get to class."

Early morning is never a good time to deal with a drama class, but add Silivus into the mix and I had little patience for being over-expressive. The electrifying tingle in my neck had eased and the knots in my shoulders unwound. Give me five more minutes and I might be able to handle the morning announcements.

"Good morning, Puckerbush High!" Mr. Bertolio sang over the intercom. I don't know why teachers did the pump-you-up routine. This was high school. It was supposed to suck. "I just wanted to say, happy Tuesday. We have a great week in sports as our very own Coach Corbin will lead our football team to another win this weekend against Reno West High."

"Yay for Corbin," I said dully.

"In other news, I'd like to extend a hearty welcome to our new superintendent, Mister Gregory Churchill."

There was clapping over the intercom, but nobody joined in. Ari, on the other hand, had turned white as a sheet.

The mic was handed over and a silky voice said, "Good morning, students." There was no false bravado, only barely harnessed contempt. "I feel compelled to say that this school is the worst excuse for an educational establishment I have ever stumbled upon. Be warned that changes will be made. That is all."

Uh, okay. That was different. There was a long pause, then:

"And that's it for today's news," Mr. Bertolio said cheerily, and added in his usual stern voice, "Will Arianna Hernfeld and Ian Quicksilver please come to the office, thank you."

Ari sprang to her feet at the mention of her name, breathing faster than necessary for someone called to the office. Something was up. She nearly bolted out the classroom door; I had to jog to keep up with her.

"Whoa, Ari!" I said. "It's just a call to the office. They probably need us to sign a waiver or something."

"Sure," she said, her voice spiking unnaturally high. "Nothing serious, right?"

"Yeah. Don't worry."

Ari was so jumpy, her fingers crackled like static when she rubbed her sweaty palms over her jeans. We sat in the main office facing the principal's door. Every so often I'd reach over and tap her on the arm just so she didn't have noticeable arcs of light snapping from her hands. The electric jolts made my arm ache.

The door flung open, and Mr. Bertolio stepped to the side to let us enter.

"Ms. Hernfeld," he said solemnly. "Mr. Quicksilver."

I didn't want to go into the office. Everything about it screamed danger, mostly because Silivus was sitting behind the desk. He looked different, more human, but fifteen years hadn't dimmed my memory of him in the least. I kept rubbing at my left hip, wishing I had a weapon. If meeting for the first time in fifteen years in the hall was bad, sitting in an enclosed room with him was torture. My sense of reasoning dimmed and the urge to fight took over. It was all I could do to sit down and stay there.

"Ah," he said as he looked up at us and smiled in greeting. Sort of like when a lion smiles at a gazelle and thinks 'dinner.' "Ian Quicksilver, you're looking . . . flushed."

Nice one. Leave it to an evil magician to bring up my infamous intergalactic toilet travel. My hackles rose. "What's it to you?" I said.

"Now, Ian," Mr. Bertolio said. "I think our new superintendent only wants to help you."

"I bet he does," I said flatly, my gaze unwavering on his face. I felt unexplainably on edge, like the magician was going to spring out from behind the desk and attack.

Silivus's eyes dropped to a file he was flipping through—mine, probably.

"You have quite the interesting record," he said silkily. "Now how does the only valedictorian in school have a psych evaluation from a trained professional in Reno?"

I think my jaw unhinged and dropped into my lap.

"Those records are confidential," I said.

"Not for me they aren't," he said. "It says here that they found you delusional. That you kept telling your foster parent you were from another world."

It felt like he punched me in the gut. I did not need Ari to hear the blathering of my five-year-old self. I remember that year as clear as if it were yesterday. I wasn't as smart then. I wanted to complete my quest and had turned to Janet for help and a ride. I didn't understand that humans had no direct contact with other races from distant planets. It was a mistake, and I only made it once.

"I was just a kid!"

"A kid who was deemed borderline schizophrenic and in need of psychiatric treatment."

"*What?!*"

"So, I ask you, Ian," he ploughed on smoothly. "Have you been receiving treatment?"

"I don't need pills," I spat.

"That is not what I asked. I am here to help you, to divert a potential disaster where innocent children could be harmed: your schoolfellows, Ian. Is that what you want?"

I couldn't disagree with the twisted way he said his words. It would look bad, and I was already in the hot seat.

"No sir," I said through clenched teeth.

"I didn't think so, which is why I would like to do a further evaluation in the coming weeks."

I felt like cussing every bad word I knew and a few

from Bankhir I'd learned from Corbin. Further evaluation. Ha! More like a waterboarding interrogation.

Silivus put away my file and folded his hands over a second file he didn't bother to look at.

"It's good to see you again, Ms. Hernfeld. You seem to be improving."

Again? They knew each other?

"Wait a sec," I said. "How do you know Ari?"

Ari's face purpled, and she wasn't breathing. Silivus's lips parted in a greasy grin.

"We've crossed paths before. Arianna here has a bit of a record. Didn't she tell you? No? Well, Ms. Hernfeld has a penchant for explosive and violent behavior. More than once she has put one of her classmates in the hospital."

That was old news.

"That's not fair. It wasn't her fault," I said. "You can't hold it against her if it was an accident."

"So you do know about those unfortunate incidents. Did she also mention that the young girl she attacked was in the hospital for three weeks with severe electric burns?"

"No," I said, reluctantly. Ari's eyes were red and she was gulping back tears. I couldn't let Silivus win. "But I do know it wasn't intentional."

"That may be," he said, unconvinced. "And it may not be, but I think that pairing up two of the school's more . . . *unstable* students is undesirable."

Oh, he was having fun now. My blood boiled in my ears, and I took slow, even breaths to keep my temper in check.

"From today on, Ian will return to his previous schedule in his more challenging classes and Arianna will remain where she is at."

"But you will risk Ian failing his courses," Mr. Bertolio finally spoke up. "It's nearly the end of the semest—"

Silivus held up his hand and silenced him. "It is a risk I am willing to take. You are dismissed."

We left the office. I didn't get far out into the hall before I lost it.

"Stinking, slimy, meddling . . ." I couldn't say *magician*, so I opted for "jerk! Who does he think he is, anyway?"

"The superintendent," Ari said miserably. "He can do whatever he wants."

"It's not right," I growled, but knew, under the anger, she was right. He was a powerful magician and not a person I needed to get on the bad side of. If he was powerful enough to flush me across the galaxy, he was most definitely powerful enough to make my Earth life a living hell.

"Things are going to be different now that he is here," Ari said, stepping away from me and yanking her gloves back on. "He'll be watching."

"That part is obvious," I said. "I didn't know you two knew each other."

"A little too well," Ari said. She held her face in her hands like she was covering up tears. "I gotta go. Bye, Ian."

I couldn't choke out a good-bye. Anger and disappointment left a bitter taste in my mouth. Mad as I was, it didn't last long. I was going to fix this, and I was going to fix it now. I bypassed going back to Calculus and made a running beeline for Coach Corbin's office.

Booking up three flights of stairs did a number on my lungs. I was wheezing and coughing by the time I stumbled through the door. Corbin was reclining in his chair with his feet up on the desk, looking like he didn't have a care in his meatheaded world.

"Morning, lover boy," he smirked and stretched. "You here for courting advice?"

I shook my head, my heart pounding in my ears, gasping for breath.

"It's . . . it's S-Silivus," I puffed. "Silivus is here . . . at—at the school."

For a brief second, I thought I shocked Corbin off his chair. In actuality he had done a perfect back flip, landed on his feet and made a dive for his sword in the equipment locker.

"Where is he?" Corbin bellowed, as he swung the lethal weapon in a whistling arc. "I'll slice him in half before he draws another breath."

"Cool it, Conan," I wheezed. "You can't go dicing up people in broad daylight. You're on Earth, remember? Besides, he's disguised as the new superintendent."

Corbin's face darkened, but he lowered his sword. "I don't care where I am, that sniveling liar will pay."

"Again, still on Earth," I said, finally catching my breath as Corbin calmed down. "What do we do? He took me out of all of Ari's classes. He painted me as a total head case to her."

"That sounds like Silivus. He'll be after me too," Corbin said as he checked out the window and down the hall, looking for the magician in the empty halls. "I doubt he has forgotten that I tried to behead him."

"Come again?"

Corbin shoved me aside and shut his office door. He shut the blinds covering the window and sat on the edge of the desk so we were eye to eye.

"Look, kid, you need to be careful. Silivus wouldn't be

here if he didn't think you had a chance to pull this off. Your father may have blind faith in him, but I don't."

"Could you explain that better?" I said. "Why did you try and behead a magician? Don't get me wrong, I'd love to help you off the guy, but . . ."

"Later. My history with him isn't important. What is important is that you toe the line and stay out of Silivus's way."

"I'm already on his radar."

Corbin winced. "I know. I've always known."

I didn't like the sound of that. Before I could ask him any more questions, he grabbed my shoulder and dragged me to the door.

"Get to class, kid, and keep your nose clean," he said.

"What are you going to do?"

Corbin tucked his sword under his arm and deposited me in the hallway. He didn't look me straight in the eye, which made me suspicious about his intentions. I didn't want to hear about a grisly murder on the five o'clock news and his mug shot flashing on the TV screen.

"I need to think."

10

The Nevada desert in fall wasn't all that spectacular. The few plants that grew here went from half dead to completely dead in a few short weeks at the end of summer's baking hot sun. What little vegetation was left had dried up and dirt clung to everything.

Not that it mattered. The one girl I knew could take me back to Bankhir away from this misery was out of my life for good. Silivus made sure of that, painting me as a type-A head case. I didn't want to go home yet after slogging through an abnormally long day at school. I hadn't seen Ari since that morning when Silivus yanked me out of all her classes. Needless to say, I was irritable. I walked past where I lived on the edge of town and just kept going. Who knew where I'd end up? I didn't care. I kicked viciously at a clod, exploding it into a cloud of dust. Stupid magician.

The dirt cloud didn't settle on the ground. Oddly enough, it started changing color. It grew until it was almost as tall as I was, then rammed into my chest, full force, knocking me flat on my back with a person lying on top of me.

"Ian?

"What the . . . ? Ari?"

Ari, not the dirt, had rammed into me. My chest cushioned the force of her fall. Quickly she got up off me and dusted herself off.

"Sorry about that," she said, helping me to my feet.

"Oh my gosh! I was just sitting in my room freaking out over Churchill, and I knew I had to see you, like right now. I got up to leave and here I am. I've never done that before!"

"Well, for your first try, you've got really good aim," I said.

I slapped the dirt off my jeans, not caring that she had knocked me over with the force of a wrecking ball. She was back!

"So, what did you need to see me for?" I said.

"I, uh, wanted to talk to you," she said, speaking to my knees. "Only if you want to. I'm dangerous and all that, so if you don't want to, I understand."

She was asking my opinion? After she had heard that I was delusional and needed mental help? And she still wanted to talk to me? I couldn't help it. I laughed. "Ever heard of a phone?"

Ari managed a wan smile but didn't say anything for the longest time. When she did bring herself to open her mouth, her chin was quivering. "I never got to say thanks," she said, still talking to my knees. "You had my back in the principal's office and I didn't say anything to defend you. So I guess I should say sorry too."

"Don't worry about it," I said. It wasn't very eloquent, but at least she looked up and tried to meet my eyes.

"You deserved to be defended. Churchill can really get cruel. He pushed hard to have me put in juvenile detention, saying the attacks were intentional. I was lucky the judge was nice."

I didn't know what to say. I hated Silivus and I had only known him for a few minutes after a fifteen-year stretch. However, as far as first impressions went, the magician was

top-grade jerk. I started walking out into the desert again,
and Ari fell into step next to me.

"So, uh, what was that psych evaluation about anyway?"

"I was five," I said. "I had an overactive imagination." It
was a lie I hoped wouldn't come back to bite me in the butt.
I couldn't let Silivus win this one. "If it means anything
at all, the therapist got his degree from an online school
in Kenya." At least that part was true. I didn't place much
faith in shrinks anyway.

"I should have guessed as much," Ari said, shaking her
head. "Churchill is a slimeball. He always twists the truth."

Unfortunately, Silivus was spot on in my case, at least
with the coming-from-another-planet part. Yet, having Ari
come to my defense made me feel an inch taller.

"So what do you want to do about it?"

"How do you mean?"

"Are you going to let Sil—Churchill walk all over you
this time?" I blurted. I didn't usually egg folks into rule-
breaking, but the warrior inside me was waking up. Gentle
waves of Deep Magic wafted over me and made me bold. I
wanted to fight back.

Ari's eyes narrowed as she thought it over. Her answering grin was slow but steady. "Are you kidding? Not this
time," she said. "Not when I've got you, Ian."

Call me an opportunist, but I couldn't take that one
lying down. Besides, my gut was doing flip-flops, cartwheels, and a double back handspring.

"Dang it, Ari. I'm blushing. I don't know what to say,"
I kidded.

Ari punched me lightly in the arm. "It's just that now
that I can release some of the excess magic in me with-

out hurting anyone, it'll be a whole lot easier to stay off Churchill's radar."

"Sure it will. The only problem is that he took me out of all your classes. You don't want me to hang out at your house, and my house is out of the question."

"Who cares? We can still talk between classes and hang out at lunch."

"Please don't say you want to pass notes too," I groaned. "I always hated that."

Ari stopped short and she stared, fixed on the horizon and not seeing it.

"No, what we need is a cheat sheet."

I didn't like where the conversation was headed. "Like the stuff you have written in magic on your hand?"

"Exactly, but a two-way communication. What we need is an interchange or—or a pact."

"We aren't going to spit in our hands and shake on it, are we?" I mumbled.

"No, silly, I'll need to bind you to me," she said, waving me off as she paced back and forth.

"Even better," I said. "Except I don't have handcuffs. Wouldn't that be awkward?"

"Handcuffs? Are you nuts? I didn't mean a literal binding, Ian. Now hush up and let me think."

Ari paced for a while. As she moved, bright arcs of static electricity would fly off her shoulders and crash against the ones emitting from her legs. The air was so charged my hair lifted straight up and crackled.

"What we need is an exchange," she muttered to herself. "Something tangible. I've found that when I own something, I can manipulate it with magic." She turned on me and held out her hand. "I need something of yours."

"Like what?"

"Anything. What do you have that is yours that nobody else owns?"

"Uh . . ." I drew a blank. Everything I had was shared with ten other kids. All my possessions had been pre-owned before I got around to them. "I don't have anything."

"Come on, you've got to have a lucky hat. Or a watch? Favorite trading card?"

I shook my head. "Really, I don't have stuff like that."

"It won't work unless we have something of each other's," she said. "Look, I'll show you." She pulled her hair away from her neck and unclasped a necklace hidden under her collar. "Here. This pendant will work best."

She strung the necklace upward until the pendant slid off and dropped into her hand. It was a half-moon disk of solid silver, and as shiny and smooth as I remembered when I saw it last, fifteen years ago. It was the crescent pendant around her neck when Silivus flushed her into oblivion.

"I've had this ever since I was a baby," she said, her cheeks flaming. "Go ahead and laugh. I know it's lame to hang on to it for all these years."

"Lame?" I scoffed. Not even close. I remembered that necklace. It was the only relic Ari had from Garfel. She had a piece of her home on her. If anything I was jealous. Well, not jealous of the *pendant* per se.

Ari held out the pendant and I took it from her.

"I'll take good care of it," I said.

"It's weird, but I know you will," she said then tapped her foot impatiently. "Now it's your turn. You've got to have something. Anything!"

In actuality, I had zilch. I was a foster kid living on hand-me-downs and secondhand goods. I didn't have anything to give. Well . . . come to think of it, I did have one thing. Though just the thought crossing my mind made my mouth run dry and my heart thump into my throat.

"Uh, well, I do have something. Sort of," I said. Absently I rubbed at the tip of my ears. They felt as if they were going to spontaneously combust.

"Okay, but understand that it has to be all yours."

Yeah, that was the problem. I stepped closer to Ari, about an arm's length apart, and stifled the urge to bolt.

"Just don't slap me," I said. Ari's forehead furrowed, confused.

Here goes nothing. I took her hand, concentrating everything I had on one thing. Bankhir. My people, the Warriors of the Galaxy. We were the protectors of the weak, fighting for those who couldn't fight for themselves, and I was their future king. It was the memory of who I was.

I lifted her hand upward and kissed it: a court-like gesture for a princess.

Ari gasped like I'd shocked her and ripped her hand out of mine. Yep, I was going to get slapped for sure. I braced myself for the blow.

"Where is that place?" she demanded, gripping her hand where I'd kissed her. "What did you give me?"

"A memory," I said, grateful she wasn't going to knock me flat for being too mushy.

"But it was so beautiful. I've never seen any place like it."

"It's my home. It was where I was born," I said. I felt like a fool now that I'd given her something that personal.

"It's the only thing I have that's mine. Sorry. It was stupid to try. I bet it didn't even work."

Ari held out her hand where we could both see it. "Let's find out. Quick, think of something to say, but don't say it."

The first thing that popped into my head was 'Churchill is going down!' A dim bluish light shone in her open palm and the words *Churchill is going down* scrawled across her palm in my handwriting. I grabbed her hand and checked it out.

"Dang," I said, "my penmanship sucks."

"It's not that bad. Now it's my turn to try," Ari said excitedly. She clamped her eyes shut tight like she was thinking up a novel. When she opened them again she lunged for my hand and inspected my palm.

In clear, precise cursive, as if written by a glowing blue ink pen, was scrawled *I can't believe this worked! Woohoo! We can talk anywhere, at any time, and about anything. You're awesome, Ian!*

Once I read the last word, the script disappeared and my hand went back to normal as if nothing weird had happened at all.

"You think in complete sentences with correct grammar and punctuation," I said, making a mental note to at least try to do the same. "Impressive."

Ari, too excited to respond, did a half-jump thing and flung her arms around my neck. The warmth of Deep Magic spun around my shoulders and tamed the heat of the afternoon desert sun with a cool sea breeze. I barely had time to respond when she let go.

"Sorry. Didn't mean to do that," she said, taking a hasty step away from me.

"Don't apologize," I said, snapping back mentally to Earth from Bankhir.

"Well, I've got to go. My mom is going to wonder where I've been if I stay any longer," she said as she started to walk back toward town. "We'll talk later."

And with that, she waved good-bye and disappeared in a cloud of blue smoke and desert dirt.

My jaw was flapping open and my hand was still out, palm up. My mind cranked like crazy. This had to be the weirdest way to communicate: texting by magic through my skin. Yeah.

I headed back home as the first clouds of a storm began to roll in over the mountains and make a stink with thunder and lightning. I snarfed a quick dinner and went to the quiet sanctuary of my closet-sized room, which kept getting smaller. I barely fit with all my books. As I started in on my pile of homework, I dug out Ari's pendant and balanced it on the open pages of my calculus book.

Absentminded, I formed a fist and thought, *I wish my homework could do itself, unless you are volunteering*, just to see if I could get a response. When I opened my hand, Ari had written, *Nice try, genius.*

It was worth a shot, I replied.

My homework is already finished.

"Jealous," I said out loud, then thought, *So, what are you doing?*

Ever hear of hobbies? Ari wrote.

If I roll my eyes, will it translate through magic?

Ha. Ha. Probably not. When I am bored, I like to find things by magic.

Like what?

Well, once I found a raccoon in my neighbor's attic.

You must have been super bored. I could understand boredom.

Pretty much, but what else is there to do in Puckerbush?

Agreed, I replied, then wondered, *What else can you do with magic? You can travel, read minds . . .*

I can only see into your mind if you let me, and you have to think of an object very clearly. I can't force my way into your head.

That's good to know. What else have you tried doing?

There was a long pause, as if she was giving it some thought on her end.

I honestly don't know. I've been suppressing the magic for so long, I don't know what would happen if I tried to really use it. In fact, in the past, I've never been able to control it like I can now. I finally feel like I belong in Puckerbush . . . you know, with actual people.

Her thoughts came through fast and jumbled. When the space on my palm was gone, her words traveled up my arm.

Nice to know this deadbeat town has something good going for it, I replied.

There was a pause, then: *Oops! I probably shouldn't laugh out loud. My parents just gave me the weirdest look. I'd better get going.*

Me too, I sent. *I have a ton of homework to catch up on.*

Sounds fun. And I said that sarcastically, in case you were wondering.

It came through loud and clear.

Good. Hey, Ian?

Yeah?

I'm glad we're friends.

I managed a *Ditto* even though the reply was far from what I was actually thinking.

"If only it were that easy," I said out loud.

11

For the first couple of days after creating the bond with Ari, I was in good with the Princess. Silivus (under disguise as Mr. Churchill, the slime-infested superintendent) spent his time slinking through the halls like a surly snake ready to strike. He kicked the vice principal out of his office and settled in to take over the school. So far, Ari and I had successfully avoided him. The only wrench in the works was Corbin. The dude needed bells on his shoes.

I was stuffing my backpack full of mega-thick books for Honors English, *Great Expectations* being at the top of the "Must Read or Flunk" list, when Ari chimed in from Remedial Algebra class. My hand glowed a faint blue-green, and I had to hold the pack open with my teeth to read it.

Is it cheating if I ask you somewhat leading questions while I take my math test?

I gripped my hand shut for a second and shook my head. *Yep. It's still cheating.*

Boy Scout, she wrote out on my palm in irritated penmanship. In my mind's eye I could imagine her glowering at me and I chuckled.

You got this. I don't know why you are worried about it, I replied. I'd spent half the previous night tutoring her after all. While waiting for her to write back, I zipped up my backpack and shut my locker.

"Hello, lover boy."

I about jumped out of my skin and had to stifle a yell.

Corbin had been standing behind my locker door for who knows how long. I hadn't heard him approach at all.

"Dude!" I gasped. "What is wrong with you? You have seriously got to knock that off!"

"It's called stealth, Nancy. Every warrior worthy of his sword can get around unheard and unseen," he said. "Unlike humans and their incessant stomping around like mountain fledge."

"Fledge?"

"A species of Bankhir Troll."

"Oh." I shouldered my pack and headed toward class. "You know, about that, I keep getting this zinging thing up my neck."

"I take it you get it when Silivus is around? Use it. Warriors get a five-second forewarning before danger strikes. Don't heed it, and you'll lose your head."

"So if I get a five-second warning, how come I don't know when you show up?"

"I'm not the enemy," Corbin said. That made sense. At least some of my warrior skills worked.

Corbin fell into step with me, following me to class. Grudgingly, I had to admit he was pretty light on his feet for how enormous he was.

"Look, I know we have one month and two and a half weeks before the sixteen year deadline," Corbin said.

"Not that you were counting or anything," I said.

"But do you think you could speed things up? Having the magician nearby is making me jumpy," he said.

"I'm going as fast as I . . ." I caught sight of my hand turning a faint blue. I held it off to the side to read it where Corbin couldn't intrude.

My parents are working late. Can you hang out after school?

I couldn't answer right away, but it was a no-brainer. Of course I wanted to hang out.

"You've grown six inches. Being around Deep Magic has got to help narrow the gap between you and the Princess," Corbin said.

"That's great and all, except for my jeans being too short. But I can't rush this," I said.

"What can't be rushed? Doesn't this girl like you?"

"As friends."

My hand glowed again and Ari wrote, *Hello? Ian?*

"What do you mean by 'friends'?" Corbin said. "You spend every spare minute with each other. How is that friends?" I stopped in the now-empty hall and faced off with Corbin.

"I'm doing the best I can. Besides, I'm comfortable with things the way that they are. I can handle being 'friends,'" I said. It was safer that way. There was nothing quite like a flat-out shutdown from a girl to destroy a guy's ego. Although, in my case, it was my ego and two planets.

Corbin peered closely at me. "Do you even like this girl?"

My hand was flashing and I couldn't hide the blue light pulsing from my skin.

What are you talking about? Destroy what?

"Ah crap," I muttered. I needed to learn how to control what went on in my head and what stuff got passed on to Ari. "Just a sec."

I gripped my hand shut and quickly thought, *Hanging out sounds great. See you at lunch.*

"What in the name of the stars?" Corbin demanded and grabbed my hand just as Ari made her response. "She marked you?"

The last of her reply faded under Corbin's nose. I didn't get to read any of it.

"She didn't mark me. It was an exchange."

"You let a Garfelian mark you," Corbin said frankly. "Why on Earth, Bankhir, and Garfel would you do that?"

"We needed a way to communicate," I said. "It's not bad. It's sort of like texting."

"Except with your mind and through your skin!"

"It's not that bad," I repeated, but it was sounding increasingly bad, judging by the look on Corbin's face. His mouth opened to reply, but both of us stopped and froze. My shoulders tensed. Corbin gripped the front of my shirt, his arm out protectively as my Warrior Neck Warning System went off like a fire alarm, buzzing all over the place.

"Really?" a silky voice intruded. Corbin and I turned slowly on our heels to see Silivus, suited, slick, and smiling smugly. How much he had heard, I didn't know, but I was sure it was plenty.

"And what, may I ask, is not so bad that you would risk further punishment by being several minutes late for your next class, Mr. Quicksilver?" He turned to Corbin and acknowledged him, saying, "Morning, Coach. How good to see you . . . alive."

Corbin took an aggressive step forward with a growl. I grabbed his arm to stop him. Last thing we needed was a puddle of magician's blood in the hallway.

"It was nothing," I said. "I was just on my way to Honors English."

Silivus took a step forward and I fought the urge to punch him. The halls of my high school were not the right time or place to exact revenge.

"Ah," he said with a bland smile. "I find you particularly interesting, you and your sharp memory. I bet you have a hard time forgetting things."

He was baiting me. Willing me to strike first. I wasn't falling for it.

"Which means I should probably get to class so I won't forget what I'll be tested on," I said, backing away toward my class.

"Not so fast, Mr. Quicksilver," Silivus smirked. "Hold out your hands."

In a wild panic I sent Ari a message. My thoughts were fast and jumbled. The sentence was short, and I prayed it translated, because I had one shot at it. *Don't respond. Churchill* was all I said. Then I wiped my mind blank. I brought my hands up and flashed my bare palms, front and back. It was plain by the grimace on Silivus's face that he didn't see what he wanted to.

"You may have the teachers in this second-rate institution fooled, but I am not," he said, turning to walk away. "One toe out of line, Quicksilver, and I'll have you kicked out before you can blink," he called over his back. "One toe. That's all it takes."

Silivus threw open the main office door and disappeared inside. It wasn't until the door shut that Corbin and I began breathing again.

"Thank the stars that girl didn't write anything," he said, sighing heavily.

"That was too close," I said. "How did he know what I was doing?"

"Because magic sends off a beacon that can be traced, that's why," Corbin said.

"Like an alarm?"

"More like sonar. How do you think I found you on Earth? Though, until now, your signal was so weak, it was almost as silent as a human. It took me fourteen years to track you down."

That explained a lot. Especially how he showed up anywhere at any time when I was least expecting it. It also explained how Ari found it so easy to magic herself to me without really trying. I'd have to be more careful.

"Right," I said. "I obviously need more help than I thought."

"Name it and I will see it done."

I had never liked Corbin much, but I had to give him credit. When the chips were down, he came through.

"I need to know everything about the magician," I said. Corbin opened his mouth to protest and I added sharply, "With no editing, Corbin. It's time I knew. Especially if we are going to beat Silivus."

"When?"

"Tonight at my house. After dark."

I left Corbin in the hall and slipped into my English class with a halfhearted apology. The lesson had already begun, but I was intent on writing other things. I blocked out the teacher and ran dialogue through my hand.

Coast is clear. Thanks!

You're welcome, Ari quickly responded. *What did Churchill want?*

The usual: my head on a platter.

Slimeball.

That's exactly what I was thinking, I wrote. *Not to change the subject, but what did you want to do after school?*

Ari's handwriting shifted to an excited, untidy scrawl.

It's a surprise! You won't believe what I found out in the desert!!

If a day was doomed to be long, today took the cake. Normally I didn't mind homework, but today my backpack made an audible thud on Ari's front porch. Ari tore off her gloves and tossed them with a grateful huff. Her skin wasn't glowing today, as regular messaging kept her in control.

"Okay, what's the big surprise?" I said as Ari dropped her bag next to mine.

"Well, last night, while I was waiting for you to finish your homework, which took forever by the way," she said in mock annoyance, "I was sending out feelers into the desert. I never pick up on anything because this place is such a drag."

"I've been saying that all along," I said, sitting down on the top porch step next her.

"Yeah, but sometimes the desert can surprise you," she said. "Anyway, so I was putting out feelers, and I found something. Well, a lot of somethings, and they were moving really fast."

"Now you're just winding me up."

"Maybe, maybe not," she said coyly. "Do you want to find out?"

Ari was so excited, she couldn't sit still. How could I say no to that?

"Anything to delay going home is fine by me," I said. Ari bolted off the porch and strode toward the garage. "Where are you going?"

"To get a car."

That got me off the porch and running after her. "Are you kidding? You can't drive."

"Why not?" she said, pulling the garage door open. "I've had a learner's permit for three months."

Ah, the crux of being a foster kid. Driving lessons didn't come cheap, and a license was out of the question.

"You need a licensed driver in the car with you. It's not legal," I said as she ripped open the door of a dusty Jeep Cherokee. "Can't you magic us there?"

"First of all, I can't find things with magic and travel at the same time. I've already tried," she said, getting into the front seat. "And secondly, why are you being so uptight? Live a little."

Live a little? I'd always been the good kid, the one that came home on time, the one that never made a scene. I knew I was a prince. But I also knew what I had to do to get a quest done, and getting into the car and driving out into the desert with Ari appeared to be part of that.

I skirted around to the passenger side and got in. When I turned to Ari, she was grinning triumphantly.

"Don't think for a second that this is going to become a habit," I said. Ari laughed as she kicked the engine to life.

"A little rule-breaking is good for you," she said. She floored the Jeep out of the garage. "It'll put hair on your chest."

Or put me in jail, I grumbled internally. Unfortunately, my thoughts wrote out on Ari's hand. She read it before I could block it.

"Oh stop whining," she said. "This is going to be fun."

She headed straight south, right off the end of the

pavement and out into the wide-open desert. There was literally nothing to see for miles. The closest civilization was Las Vegas, three hundred and eighty miles away. Ari drove with her foot slammed into the floorboards for about an hour. Apparently she knew exactly where she was going because she turned to the left to follow along the mountain range and then parked. She leaned forward and folded her arms on top of the steering wheel to scan the horizon.

"This is it," she whispered.

"Uh, it is?" In every direction there was nothing. Brown dirt mountains, brown dirt valley, and not a tree or house in sight. Even the trailers of Puckerbush had disappeared over the horizon behind us.

"Get out of the car," she said, climbing out. I followed her as she walked into the desert. There was no sound. Not even bugs. I could hear our breathing and nothing else.

"Ari?"

"Shhh! Can't you hear that?"

If I had Corbin's warrior ears, maybe I could have. It sucked that I was ages behind even Ari. I was about to say that I couldn't hear squat when the dirt clods at my feet started vibrating. I could hear something now: it sounded like distant thunder.

"What the . . . ?"

"I know, right?" Ari said excitedly as a cloud of dust rose at the base of the mountain. It grew bigger and bigger, getting louder and louder. It was headed straight at us, forming into legs, necks, and bodies.

"A herd of wild horses?" I said. "Out in the middle of nowhere? How do they survive?"

"I don't know, but isn't it amazing?"

"Amazing and headed right at us," I said as the thundering cloud of wild beasts closed in fast. "And we're going to get run over."

"I didn't think about that part," Ari said. We spun around to run back to the Jeep, but the herd was too fast. The only thing I could do was grab Ari and shield her from the worst of it. I gripped her tight and braced myself for the first hit. It never came. Wild horses passed on the right and left of us, dirt and rocks flew from their hooves, but we were unharmed. They passed on by. When the thunder faded, a new presence breathed hard at my back. It drooled warm spit down my neck too. I turned and came face-to-face with the most enormous horse I had ever seen.

"Whoa!" I jolted back a step in surprise, gripping Ari to my back, using my body as a barrier between her and it.

The wild horse grunted and dipped his head as if he were greeting me. Weird.

The beast was a brilliant white. Instead of a sheen of sweat on his flanks, his coat had a silver, metallic tint to it. His mane was a tangled mess and so was his tail, but he wore it proudly, as if to say "so what." The unnerving part was the way his dark brown eyes watched my every move.

"Do you think he's tame?" Ari said over my shoulder.

Call me crazy, but I could have sworn the horse rolled his eyes. "I doubt it."

"But look at him. He's definitely not a scruffy wild mountain horse. He's got better breeding than an Arabian."

The horse's eyelids lowered into an unmistakable glare. Horses couldn't do that, could they?

"Do you think he'll let me pet him?" Ari asked, and held out her hand around my arm. The horse parted his lips and did one distinctive chomp of his long yellow teeth: an unmistakable warning. Either the horse was off its rocker or I was.

"I don't think that's a good idea," I said.

"I think you're probably right," Ari said, and quickly pulled her hand behind my back.

Then, if I didn't already think I was slightly insane for thinking a horse could express human emotions, it very horseishly shook its mane and sniffed my pockets, looking for treats or whatever else interested horses. When I turned up empty-handed, he started using my chest as a scratching post for his face.

"I think he likes you," Ari said.

"Yeah, but why? I've never seen him before."

The horse lowered his head so we were eye level and cocked it to the side, daring me to look twice at him. Then he lifted his head up so we were nose-to-nose.

I lied. I had seen him before. I'd seen his long face a long, long time ago. I just needed to see him from the right angle to remember it. This creature was at my branding ceremony when I was presented my sword. He was my horse. In an instant it felt as if the other half of my heart started beating again.

My memory tripped on, and I whispered, "I know you. You were there . . ."

The massive horse responded with a knowing smirk. I moved away from Ari and ran my hand down his long nose.

"I don't remember your name, though," I said, which probably meant I'd never heard it. Regardless, the horse stuck out his tongue and lisped a whinny that ended in a thick guttural cough. He looked expectantly at me like it was perfectly clear what he said and that I'd be totally stupid if I couldn't figure it out. I should probably point out that I was not exactly fluent in Horse.

"Uh," I said, confused. "You might want to repeat that."

He tried again, but for the life of me, it sounded like no words I was familiar with.

"All I'm getting is the gacking sound a cat makes hurking up a hairball," I said. The horse huffed out a frustrated sigh.

"What's wrong with him?" Ari said, stepping in for a closer look. "He sounds like he's going to be sick."

"Told you," I muttered to him. The horse grumbled irritably. I turned to Ari and said, "I think we should name him Bob."

"Bob?" Ari said, skeptically.

"Sure. Why not?" I said. "I think it kind of fits." Besides, it was better than the alternative. I wasn't going to call my horse a name that sounded like I was hacking up dust bunnies the size of basketballs.

Ari tilted her head and studied my horse. For the way he was sticking out his tongue and grimacing like the entire idea of naming him Bob was literally going to make him ill, the name fit.

"You know what?" Ari said. "I think you're right. Bob really does fit him."

Bob's eyes flew open wide in surprise and dismay, but it was too late. The name stuck.

"Bob it is then," I said.

"Bob the Horse," Ari snickered. Bob grunted out a cantankerous snort.

"Deal with it," I whispered to him. "It's way better than your real name."

Ari didn't try to touch Bob, but looked him over. "He must be some kind of war horse."

"What makes you say that?"

"Well, look at him. Can you really see him doing farm work or hooked up to pull something? He's big, but he's also athletic."

Bob stood still for his inspection. He proudly curled his neck and flexed his wide chest muscles. I rubbed him lightly on the nose. "Show-off," I muttered.

"How do you know so much about horses?" I said, daring to reach up and scrub my fist between his ears. Bob blew out his breath and let his tongue loll out of his mouth. I guess that meant he enjoyed it.

"My parents went through a phase two years ago. They thought that if I went to a farm for damaged and handicapped kids, it would take away the magic. You know, so that I could become like any other kid. Sometimes it helps handicapped kids cope, but with me, it just made the magic more intense."

She said it so indifferent, but there was nothing casual about it. I wasn't all that impressed with Ari's parents. In fact, a swell of irritation rose in my chest. How could anyone not see how amazing she was?

"But you're normal," I said, because to me, who wasn't human in the first place, she was.

"I'm not normal, Ian."

"Sure you are. You just have a little magic-induced issue. Besides, you can manage it. You haven't lost control in weeks."

Ari gave a short humorless laugh. "You make it sound like I've got warts or something."

"Your parents shouldn't try to take it away," I muttered. "It's who you are."

"Thanks, but seeing as how you are the only person I've met that can stand being around me, it's hard not to see it as a curse."

I could see her point, but I wouldn't want her to be any different. Besides the fact that I could breathe without hacking up a lung when I was around her and that I finally had someone to talk to, I just plain liked her. Even if our worlds weren't depending on it, I would have still liked her.

The wild desert wind blew Ari's jet-black hair into her face, and she brushed it away from her bright green eyes. It was unexplainable, but I felt like putting my arm around her and letting her rest her head on my shoulder. She seemed so vulnerable. She was stuck on a planet where no other magic but hers existed—so beautiful and unique and not knowing why. It couldn't be easy to deal with. I stifled the urge.

When Ari looked up, it was obvious I was staring. Not cool. At least my mouth wasn't hanging open.

"We should get back," she said, checking her watch. "It's a long drive, and I should at least look like I have been trying to do homework or something when my parents get home."

Foiled again. Bob burrowed his head under my arm and shoved me forward after her. Even my horse was playing matchmaker. I pushed his face away and felt instantly guilty about it. Half of my birthright had been found. I rubbed his velvet nose.

"It's good to have you back, Bob," I said as Ari climbed into the Jeep. It roared to life. It was cruel to leave him there out in the dusty desert, but I couldn't bring him home with me. I had nowhere to put him. Reluctantly, I pried myself away from him and got in the Jeep.

I glanced out the back window as Ari floored it back toward town. Bob stood in the middle of the desolate valley and watched me abandon him for the second time.

Some warrior I'd become.

12

A deafening quiet settled over the trailer that night. Everyone had been put to bed, and the TV had been turned off. It was the time between the bugs and heat of summer and the howling wind and snowdrifts of winter, and it sounded like . . . well, silence.

I waited until it was fully dark out, when only the stars gave off light. It was a moonless night. Pulling on my shoes and a jacket, I climbed out my bedroom window. I barely fit now, especially across the shoulders. However, once out, I made my way to a cluster of bushes where all my private conversations seemed to be taking place lately. I still couldn't see in the dark, which irked me. Earlier, I considered taking a flashlight, but the importance of tonight made me want a little privacy.

Standing out in the desert waiting for Corbin to arrive, I clasped my hands behind my back and stared up at the stars. There were billions of them, undimmed by light pollution from cities, which is the one advantage to living in the middle of nowhere. I wished I knew which stars were Bankhir and Garfel.

"You look a lot like your father when you do that," Corbin said, materializing out of the dark with his steel-blue eyes glowing. He stood next to me and looked up. "He would stand out on the castle terrace overlooking the warrior barracks and search the sky."

"What was he looking for?"

"You."

I shouldn't have asked. My chest ached in the worst way, and it had nothing to do with asthma. "Which one is Bankhir?" I said, pointing to the night sky.

"I wish I knew. It might make living on this half-dead planet more bearable."

I nodded dumbly, not trusting myself to say anything. Corbin was quicker to recover.

"What happened to you the day you were sent to Earth? I need to know before I tell you anything about Silivus."

Corbin had helped me reclaim my memories. I found myself reliving them often. Especially the day I was flushed down to Earth. There was so much about it I wanted explained. After a moment of thought, I opted for the undiluted truth.

"I was taken to a dark place with no sunlight. I remember it being cold."

"The place between the planets. It's where all the magicians lived," Corbin said.

"Ari was there with me, and we were laid on an obsidian altar," I said, leaving out the more cruel aspect of how we were treated. "Then Silivus picked Ari up, cursed her to forget who she was, and gave her more power than she could handle."

I took a deep breath, angry that the magician's words still stung like I had been cursed yesterday. I shoved my hands deep into my pockets and gripped Ari's silver pendant. I was looking for comfort, but the coveted piece of Garfel only made the guilt worse.

"I should have done something, Corbin. I could feel that the magician was treacherous, but I just lay there and watched as he dropped her down that big whirlpool toilet. He enjoyed watching us suffer."

"Don't beat yourself up, kid," Corbin said. "You were only three months old."

"But she needed me and I failed her," I said. Corbin reached out and gripped my shoulder.

"What happened next?"

"He picked me up by the arm and drained me of my strength. It hurt. Somehow he tainted the Deep Magic," I said bitterly. "I barely knew the guy, but I wanted to punch him."

"A justifiable reaction," Corbin said. "But you are sure he only took your strength?"

"No. He wanted me to remember what I had lost. And I do remember. He took everything I had. I came to Earth with nothing but a name and a quest."

Corbin took his hand off my shoulder and punched it into the air. "I knew it!" he exclaimed triumphantly. "I knew I hadn't gone mad! And now I can prove it!"

"Your sanity was in question?" I said. "Why am I not surprised?"

Corbin ignored the jab. "Silivus is going to get what's coming to him now."

"Sounds great," I said. "When do we start?"

"We don't," Corbin said. "I was exiled, and I can't go back to prove I was right."

"I thought you said you could help."

"I am helping," Corbin said.

"Maybe you should try a different tactic."

"Look, kid, I was just the son of your father's general. Any say I had with the War Council was a minor one. The whole lot of them put their trust in Silivus, and I was the only one who could see him for the sniveling, power-hungry magician he is."

"And?"

"I went after him. The General was charged with keeping your blade and your horse until you were born, and they were supposed to go with you when you were sent to Earth. It was the only way the King would agree to send you away," Corbin said. His entire attitude changed, almost as if he were back on Bankhir living out the glory of being in the King's army. "A few months after the magician sent you to Earth, I was on night duty along the border of the capital. I picked up the trail of a stallion and heard what sounded like an injured horse. I was following the sound when I caught Silivus slinking around in the dark. He was carrying something long and shiny under his cloak. I have perfect eyesight; I couldn't mistake what I was seeing. So I went in for a closer look. He had your sword. You can't confuse it with other warrior blades because it's the only one, besides the King's, with a Bankhir Emerald on it. I called for him to stop, but he disappeared. Then, I went to the King. I told him I saw Silivus with your sword and heard your horse calling."

Corbin's face fell and he closed his eyes to block out pain.

"At that point, I may have said a few things I shouldn't have. I accused Silivus of . . . well, treason, really. Silivus talked a good line, said it wasn't true and all he wanted was for your quest to succeed. I begged for a search, and when the sword and the horse were sent for, they were not on Silivus or where he lived. Of course, I was the only one who had seen them that night."

"So you were exiled for thievery and not Silivus," I said. Corbin grunted his agreement. "Did Silivus send you here?"

"Sort of. I was supposed to be executed."

"For stealing? That's harsh."

"Not exactly. I had cornered Silivus after my trial and tried to behead him. That's the only way you can kill a magician, by the way. They have no heart to pierce. Regardless, the General got to me before I could succeed."

I put two and two together, and I didn't like it. "Your own father was going to have you executed?"

"Don't be too hard on him," Corbin said. "By law, he did the right thing."

"But you're still alive, so he must have backed out, right?" Please say yes.

"The King was the one that pardoned me." Corbin looked down at me and his eyes glowed clearly in the dark. "Your father has always been kind to me and took pity on the General's favorite son. He had Silivus send me away."

The magician again! Silivus had his fingers in everyone's business. He was good at messing up their lives.

"So you were sent here."

"Yes."

"And you came looking for me for what? To regain your honor?"

"In a sense," he said, simply. "If I helped you with your quest, I might be able to regain the King's good graces."

I knew the truth, but I still felt sour. "Nice to know I'm everybody's favorite pawn."

"You don't get it," Corbin said. "I will show you."

He gripped the back of my neck with his giant hand that glowed silver, pinching his meaty fingers into the base of my skull. My eyes blinked on like spotlights and pushed aside the night darkness. It was the weirdest thing I'd ever experienced.

"This is Bankhir," Corbin said. We stood on the beach at the edge of an enormous stone city. The sand was real. The ocean was real. But it smelled and felt like the Nevada desert at night. For a mirage, it was pretty detailed. "It is a planet roughly the same size as Earth. Your father rules the whole of it. He is a good king, sired by many generations of noble kings. We have one purpose in our galaxy: war."

"Why?" I asked, confused. "Why war?"

"We are the protectors. When weaker planets are attacked, we are the ones to fight for them. It is what we do, and we do it well. We do not farm or cultivate because our reward for protection is sustenance."

"Where does Garfel fit in this war machine?"

Corbin turned my head to look out over the ocean. We had an unobstructed view of the sky where an enormous planet, nearly the exact size of Bankhir, was rising over the horizon.

"Garfel is the only planet in our galaxy that produces Deep Magic. It is the fuel that feeds our bodies and makes us strong. Without it, we would never have victory. Without it, we would be the ones in need of protection. Look."

My feet pulled out of the sand, up into the clouds, and out into wide-open space. There were planets everywhere, rotating and orbiting. However, only Bankhir and Garfel seemed to give off light, a pulsing bluish-green of Garfel and bright silver of Bankhir flashing in the abyss. They were two bright lights in the darkness of space.

"You may think our wars are petty, but what would

happen to the people on these planets if we weren't there to protect and fight for them? What would happen if Bankhir and Garfel were destroyed and everything that is good in our universe was destroyed with it? Can you not see why your quest is so important?"

I could see it, and I understood it. A fire of pride ignited in my chest. I could not fail. I would not. Corbin released my neck and I plunged back into the cold desert night.

"I get it, Corbin, but why Earth? Why couldn't we have tried to fall for each other on our own planets?"

"For many reasons. All of them, unfortunately, were Silivus's ideas. Earth is the farthest planet away from Bankhir and Garfel. It has never needed our intervention. The people of Earth fight their own wars and have been left alone by other species for centuries. They don't need us, which means that in a galaxy where Bankhirians are pretty much involved in everyone's business, Earth was the prime planet to have you two grow up."

"And be forgotten."

Corbin huffed out a short laugh. "On Earth, you are nothing more than a scrawny kid living in the middle of the desert. At home, there isn't a Bankhirian who doesn't know your name."

"Even better," I grumbled.

"Frankly, I wouldn't trade places with you," Corbin said. I rubbed wearily at my face and tried to keep all the information straight in my head.

"What does Silivus stand to gain in all this? Why would he curse me and Ari if Bankhir and Garfel are so important?" I said.

"Silivus has always had a plan. The spell he cast over

our planets, sending you so far away, the sixteen-year deadline . . . all his ideas. I'm not going to lie; he fooled us all. At the time, especially when both kings were left with so few options, his offer of help seemed exactly what we needed," Corbin said.

"Nobody noticed the rat in the room? Even at three months old I knew Silivus was evil."

"The face he showed to us was not the one you experienced. We had no reason to doubt him. The magicians had always been good. They were a gift to us from the stars; for eons they have been helping us, creating good things out of the magic our planets generate."

"And nobody suspected maybe one of the magicians might get a little greedy?" I said. "You were born with magic, Corbin. I wasn't. Now that I'm around it a lot, it's addicting. I can see Silivus wanting the Deep Magic all to himself."

"As can I," Corbin said. "And yet, here we are."

"Yes, we are," I glowered.

"I know that look," Corbin said. "Your father looks the same way when he's cooking up an idea. I'd advise you to stop."

"Why?"

"Because it'll come to no good. The magician is too good at what he does. He is too slick. If there was a way to rid myself of Silivus forever, I would have thought of it by now."

"Then what do you suggest?"

"The best way to defeat Silivus is to complete your quest," Corbin said.

"But that won't get rid of him for good."

Corbin sighed. "I am afraid not, but it may buy us the time we need to regroup and recover. There may be a chance yet to get rid of him."

The weight of my world lay heavily on my shoulders. "One month and two weeks," I said. "That's all I have left."

"Are you stating defeat?"

"Never," I said.

Corbin cracked a rare smile. "Good man," he said. "Now you are thinking like a true warrior."

"Will that get me out of gym class next semester?" It was a long shot, but I had to try.

"Ha! You wish."

"Can't blame me for trying," I said.

"If I can get even a little meat on your bones, I'd be happy," Corbin said darkly. Who knew my scrawniness irked him so bad?

"Well, if it helps your mood, Ari found my horse," I said. "He was out in the desert about fifty miles south of here."

Corbin's eyes got wide. "Running wild?"

"Wild, with his own herd. They about ran right over the top of us."

"Theovan is strong. I hoped he would escape Silivus and try to find you."

"What did you call him?" I said.

"Theovan. Theovan Hugrok," Corbin said. "That was what he was named at birth."

"So that's what he was trying to tell me," I mused. "No wonder it sounded like he was going to be sick. Ari and I named him Bob."

Corbin shook his head. "I knew Theovan. Bob probably works better as a name for him anyway."

Good thing too, because his real name was a gagging mouthful.

"Well," I said, turning toward my foster home. "As long as I put out enough magical sonar, maybe I'll find my sword too. Night, Corbin."

As I headed back to my window, a dome of faint light was rising in the eastern sky. I wasn't going to be sleeping off tonight's conversation. Dragging my feet wearily across the desert, I heard Corbin bid me farewell.

"Good night," he said quietly. "Your Highness."

I spun around, not sure if my ears were playing tricks on me. In the dark I could see nothing but a shadow of Corbin's mass disappear into the night.

13

Midmorning sunlight poured in through my window. I scrunched my eyes shut to block it out. After staying out late last night, I didn't want to get up yet. Not that I could sleep if I wanted to. The rest of the foster kids were up stomping around like elephants. The TV blared early-morning cartoons. I felt wrenched out of shape, like a big slab of taffy getting worked over in a candy puller. Even my bones felt stretched.

I kept my eyes shut and tried to tune out the noise, but someone was messing with my head. Literally. It was as if wide lips were clamping down on my tangled hair and pulling it out of my scalp like blades of grass.

"Gerroff," I muttered, swatting at it, only to have whatever it was blow hot, smelly breath impatiently on top of my head. It reeked like . . . horse.

I sprang upright, nearly braining myself on a shelf above my head.

"Bob?" I said, rubbing at a goose egg forming on my forehead. "What are you doing here?"

Bob huffed, irritated, like he felt it was about time I got out of bed. His thick neck filled the entire window.

Despite the jolt of adrenaline I got by being woken by my horse, I still felt like a train wreck functioning on no sleep.

"Ughh," I groaned, and scrubbed at my face to circulate some blood flow. "Remind me to never try and make plans to save the world in the middle of the night. School on no sleep is going to bite."

Bob nodded knowingly. He strained forward to yank my shirt off the hook on the wall and passed it over to me.

"Uh, thanks," I said. This whole horse-acting-like-a-human thing was a little weird. I was in the middle of getting my shirt over my head when I was shoved against the wall.

"Hey! Knock it off!" I said, forcing my shirt down over my ears. But it wasn't Bob I had yelled at. "Ari! Sorry about that, I thought you were Bob."

Bob shoved Ari off his face and she grabbed my arm to steady her balance. Between me, Bob's big head, and Ari in my room, it was for a tight fit for the three of us.

"Never mind that," Ari said. "You completely missed first period and Coach Corbin keeps tailing me asking where you are. Haven't you gotten any of my messages?"

I looked down at my hand, where the words *If you don't answer in the next five minutes, I'm coming after you!* were fading into my skin.

"Apparently not," I said. "I had a late night and slept in a bit.'

"A bit? If Churchill gets wind that you skipped class, he'll fry you. Now hurry and get dressed," she said.

We stood there nearly nose-to-nose with me bent double hanging onto a pair of jeans. "I will. I wouldn't mind some privacy though."

"Right. Sorry," Ari said, and turned around to face Bob, who, with a longsuffering sigh, allowed her to scratch his nose "So, uh, this is your room?"

"It's more like a closet," I said. I pulled on my jeans,

but there was a problem: they didn't fit. "And it keeps shrinking."

Ari turned around and eyed me critically. "No, more like you grew. What happened? It looks like you shot up ten inches in one night."

How could I do that? I had been talking to Corbin most of the night, and I didn't notice anything different then. I stood up straight to my full height and my head slammed into the ceiling. Instead of seeing Ari eye-to-eye, I was now looking down at the top of her head. I had to be well over six foot.

"I don't think this is going to work anymore," I said.

"I agree. You look ridiculous."

"I was referring to my room," I said. "What are you talking about?"

"Your clothes. They're a good six inches too short."

She was right. My T-shirt showed my gut and a few ribs, and my jeans fell just below my knees.

"Don't go anywhere," Ari said. "I'll be right back."

I had to brace my hands against the ceiling to not get knocked around by the rush of bluish Deep Magic as Ari disappeared. Bob looked me over once she was gone and sniggered.

"Oh shut up," I muttered. "You look pretty stupid with your head shoved through a window. If you get stuck, I am not helping you out."

Bob stuck his tongue out at me. Good grief. If I was going to take him anywhere out in public, he was going to have to learn to act more like a horse.

Ari wasn't long. When the wisp of bluish smoke began to form, I was ready for her. But, ready or not, she still slammed into my chest with the force of an auto collision.

This time I caught her with one arm so she wouldn't fall back on Bob's head. I couldn't tell if it was the jolt of Deep Magic that warmed my insides better than scalding hot chocolate or if it was just that Ari was pressed up against my chest. Whichever it was, it made me delay letting her go.

"Okay, I raided my dad's closet," she said, being the first to pull away. "He's about six foot two." She looked up at me, with my head bent to the side and crammed into the ceiling. "It looks as if you are at least that and then some, but this should work better than what you've got." She handed me a few shirts and jeans and turned around again.

I stared at the back of her head for a few seconds. Her long glossy black hair fell over her shoulders around a soft pink sweater. I decided right then that I liked it when she wore pink.

"Thanks," I said, quickly re-dressing.

"Anytime," she said. "No worries. So did you go out and bring back Bob last night? Is that why you were up so late?"

"Uh, no. Bob found me on his own," I said. "When I woke up, he was slobbering drool on my face."

Bob's head popped up over Ari's shoulder. If the horse could talk, it was plain on his face that he would have said "I don't drool, buddy."

"That's odd," Ari said as she ran her hand down his nose. "I've never heard of a horse doing that."

No other horse could locate his owner via magical sonar either, but I wasn't about to tell her that.

"I've never heard of a horse getting his head stuck in a trailer window, and yet here he is," I said instead.

146

Ari scratched Bob behind the ears, making him lean his big head into her while he enjoyed it. He lolled his tongue out of his mouth. He panted like a dog, dripping spit all over my pillow by the time I was ready to go.

"Okay," I said, grabbing my backpack. "If we hurry, we should make it in time for third period."

"Shouldn't we get Bob out first?"

"Nah, he got his head in, he can get it out," I said. Bob nodded curtly in reply.

"Then how am I going to get out the window?" Ari said. "Your foster parents aren't going to be happy when a girl walks out of your room with you."

"I honestly don't think they'll notice," I said and grabbed her hand. "Come on!"

I couldn't have been more right if I had handed Janet and Phil acting scripts. Phil was sacked out in his recliner, scratching at his potbelly with a fat roll of duct tape. Janet puffed away at a cigarette in the kitchen while rinsing breakfast dishes.

"Good morning," I said as I made a beeline for the front door with Ari. "I'm off to school."

Neither Janet nor Phil made a move to acknowledge us. I could have done handstands and cartwheels and they wouldn't have blinked.

"That was easy. Are they always that oblivious?" Ari said.

"As a rule? Yes. It used to bother me, but recently, I find their lack of interest comes in handy," I said. I cracked my neck and worked the kinks out of my back. If I grew any more, I'd consider sleeping outside. With Bob around, that might not be a bad idea. Then again . . .

Bob got his head out of the trailer, but he was still stuck. Foster kids mulled around his muscular legs, pulled his tail, and ran under his belly like he was a playground jungle gym. He had a toddler hanging off his face, and he was going cross-eyed trying to keep watch on all of them. Even Carrie, the girl I'd rescued from being flushed by the Evil Twins, was in on the action as she hugged Bob around the neck.

"At least he's a good sport," Ari said, a little nervous. "For being wild."

Bob caught sight of us. His ears perked up and he gave a pleading whine for assistance. The toddler slipped off the end of his nose, and he began plucking kids off his legs with his teeth and plopping them down in the dirt out of the way. The second he got one kid off, another one would reattach. It was kind of entertaining.

"Hey!" Janet hollered from the kitchen window. "You kids gerroff t'school!"

There was a general chorus of complaint until Janet threatened to belt their backsides off if they didn't clear out of there. Bob looked comically relieved.

We skirted around the trailers and headed for school. Bob caught up with us, thoroughly enjoying himself, doing a slow, flashy-looking high-step trot behind me.

Ari kept watching me like I'd just sprouted tentacles or something.

"What? Why are you looking at me funny?"

"Am I?" Ari said and shook herself out of a half trance. "Sorry, I was probably staring, but have you seen yourself lately?"

"Why?"

"Well, for one, you are freakishly tall. I could have sworn yesterday you and I were the same height."

I looked down. My feet *were* farther away than I was used to. The cool part was that my hands and feet didn't look too big for my body anymore, like I had finally grown into them. Sweet!

"Also you have a lumberjack five o'clock shadow thing going on. Scruff is not in, so you might want to shave."

I had a beard? No way! I ran my hand across my chin. My fingers scraped across rough stubble.

"Lastly, and this is the part that kind of freaks me out, you look way too much like Coach Corbin. Not kidding. You could be brothers. The only difference is that he is twice as wide as you are. It's weird."

It wasn't weird to me, but the comparison was unnerving. If Ari noticed, I wondered if anyone else would make the connection.

"Uh, I guess I had a growth spurt," I said. It wasn't exactly a lie. I just omitted parts of the truth. It didn't take great intelligence to see that every time Ari put out a ton of magic, I grew. It was no wonder I was too big for my room. Ari was pumping out enough Deep Magic to supply a small army.

"Seriously?" Ari said skeptically. "That's one heck of a spurt. You aren't taking steroids, are you?"

"What? I would never . . . ," I exclaimed as Ari laughed.

"I'm only joking," she said. "Don't get your boxers in a wad."

"Don't even kid. I would never do something like that."

"Right, I forgot. You have your perfect Boy Scout image to uphold."

"You know, it's not that bad of an image. I like staying out of trouble."

"I didn't say anything about getting into trouble," Ari said, innocently. "I'm talking about basic living."

"That's rich," I scoffed. "Coming from a girl who has stayed locked up in her house for years and is scared to touch people."

"True, but that hasn't kept me from experimenting with my magic when my parents aren't home."

"That's devious," I said. "Are you always like this?"

"Look, you have to admit if you had a limitless supply of magic, you would want to try it out."

"Probably," I said, fairly.

"Even if that means that every once and a while I hide their stuff using magic when they really annoy me," Ari mumbled around a grin she was trying to hide.

"I take it this happens a lot?"

"More frequently than I care to admit. But I'm never mean, and I always return their stuff before they get too frustrated."

"Wow," I said, blandly. "You are really a rebel."

Ari sighed. "It's not like I'm all that easy to live with."

"Hanging with you is far better than living with the Barfuses. I'd say your parents are lucky. Though, I can't wait to leave Puckerbush."

"Where would you go?"

The safe answer would have been "anywhere but here." But that's not what came out of my mouth.

"Bank . . . kok," I fumbled to avoid blurting out "Bankhir." Lies were not my specialty.

"Thailand. Really?"

"It was the first thing that popped into my head," I shrugged. "So I guess that means my subconscious likes spicy food."

Ari laughed. "I think your subconscious is mental."

"It's not like I am going anywhere," I said. "The foster system in Puckerbush, Nevada, isn't exactly a foreign exchange program, and Phil and Janet are more interested in the slot machines than world travel."

Ari glanced up at me with a kind smile. "Maybe your parents will come back for you and things will be different. You never told me what happened to them."

How would I explain that one? *My dad, the King, was duped by a messed-up, power-hungry magician who exiled me down to Earth to fulfill an impossible quest*? That wouldn't work.

"They, uh . . ." *Think fast, doofus!* "It's kind of top secret," I said lamely. "In their line of work, it's difficult to raise a kid." If I thought I was only mildly craptastic at lying before, then I was definitely stinking it up now.

"Your parents were spies?"

"Not exactly. More like very important military personnel." At least that part wasn't a lie. I could tell Ari wasn't buying it so, like a fool, I kept talking. "But they'll come back for me. That is, if they survive whatever they are doing right now."

Dude, shut up! I clamped my mouth closed before I could brand myself as an idiot any further.

"Well, at least you aren't very bitter about it," Ari said.

Nope. I didn't have time for it. Besides, I had a job to do. It was my duty to complete my quest. Everything else was just details.

"What about you?" I said. "It's not like you'll want to stay in Puckerbush forever."

"Actually, Puckerbush is the only place that feels like home to me," Ari said.

"You have got to be kidding." She wasn't laughing, so I couldn't tell if she was serious or not.

"Nope. I have left on vacation, but none of the places we went to felt quite like it does here. I don't think I'll ever move too far," she said, and the weird part was that she sounded excited. "To me, it feels safer. Someday, I'll find a place of my own and put a little distance between me and my parents' rules. Though I swear if it ever gets out that I am using more magic than ever before, my next residence will be in a cage."

"It's that bad?"

Ari nodded. "I think I scare my parents. When I was little, it wasn't so bad. It would take a year or two for the magic to build up inside of me. Even then I couldn't do much besides shoot off bluish light and static electricity. But every year it gets stronger and harder to control."

"So they keep you holed up and out of the way," I said.

Ari looked up at me. Her darkened facewas too sad for someone as amazing as she was. "In a sense, yes. I think my parents wish they could fix me. They haven't stooped so low as to have me tested or put in an asylum, but they keep treating me like I am a ticking time bomb, ready to explode."

"Don't they realize that you can't help it?" I said. "You are different, not dangerous."

"I don't think they'll ever see it that way because, to everyone else but you, I am dangerous."

I was getting irritated with her parents. Whom I'd never met, by the way. But they were turning out to be monsters in my mind.

"You know what, Ian?" Ari said, wrapping her arms around my waist out of the blue. "I think you are the only person who can see the real me. You have no idea what that means to me."

Okay, I'll admit it: my insides went bonkers. It wasn't exactly a manly warrior thing to do, but I put my arm around her shoulders and pulled her a little closer. A very small—and mushy—part of me was ready to confess to her that I was falling for her. Good thing I hesitated.

"You're like a really cool protective big brother," she said, pulling away.

And . . . boom. I was back in the Friend Zone. We walked up to the school grounds and headed to the front doors. I felt beaten, but Ari skipped along like she didn't have a care in the world.

"Do you have any big plans after school?" Ari asked as I opened the door for her.

"Nothing besides homework."

"Good, because I'm thinking we should take another drive out in the desert."

Call me crazy, but after getting cut off at the knees, I wasn't exactly feeling like breaking the law.

"I could magic you out there, but I wouldn't know exactly where to put you and you might hit something," she offered.

"That sounds tempting," I kidded.

"Oh, come on, please?" she begged. "It's just a little drive. I've been working a bit of magic to see if I can grab objects and bring them to me. I know I can push things away, but I'm trying the reverse."

"So, I'm going to be your test rat?" I said, scratching at the base of my neck that was vibrating oddly. I half registered that it was a warning.

Ari's cheeks colored a faint pink. Her mouth opened, but what I heard next wasn't her voice.

"Well . . . ," Silivus said, equal parts triumphant and silky slimeball. "My two favorite students decided to come to school today."

I think my heart stopped. The halls were empty. Third period had started without us. We turned slowly to face Silivus, who was beyond smug.

"Detention," he said. "Separate detentions for both of you."

"For what?" I said before I could stop myself. Ari gripped my arm, and the influx of magic-induced endorphins certainly didn't help me keep my cool.

"Tread carefully, Mr. Quicksilver, you are already on dangerous ground. But if it must be spelled out for you: detention for leaving the grounds during school hours without permission. And, I might add, an extra detention for you, Mr. Quicksilver, for bringing an animal onto school property."

Ah, heck. I knew what that meant. Bob stood in the hall behind me, swishing his tail irritably as he glared at the magician. He must have followed us in while we were talking. As if having him in the school wasn't enough, he cocked his tail and dropped a steaming pile of manure on the linoleum floor.

"The authorities have been summoned. That animal

will be taken into custody and another day will be added to your sentence," Silivus said, turning on his heel and strutting off down the hall. "Enjoy purgatory," he sang.

14

Detention was the last thing on my mind. I could do purgatory. Heck, I'd been in foster system hell for fifteen years and counting. But put Bob in custody? Over my dead body! I had to get Bob out of the school fast.

I shucked off my backpack and handed it to Ari.

"Can you hang on to this for a second?"

"Sure," she said, confused.

I rolled up the sleeves of my shirt, my brain cranking hard on what to do about Bob. I had no holding pen or rope to tie him to a tree. I didn't even know the basics of what a horse needed. Bob stood patiently for me to make my first move.

"Okay," I said, pacing. "We've got to get him out of here before the sheriff shows up."

"And put him where?" Ari said. "You can't exactly take him home."

"The yard isn't fenced," I said. "I know, what about your place? You have a fence."

"It only goes around three sides and it's a dinky four-foot-high picket fence. Bob could walk right through it if he wanted to."

Crud. My hands were shaking. I could hear sirens. The sheriff, who probably never used the sirens on his patrol car before, was really pulling out the stops for something as trivial as animal control.

"We're running out of time here, Ari," I said, pulling

Bob's face around to head for the door. He wouldn't budge. "Help me! What do I do?"

"I wish we had a rope," Ari said. She chucked my pack and hers into the corner and joined me. Bob would let me lead his head anywhere, but his body stayed stock-still.

"Why isn't he moving?" I grunted as Ari and I leaned into his chest. We might as well have pushed against a stone statue for all the good it did. It was if he had dug his hooves into the linoleum and was going to stay there forever.

"What if you walked outside and had him follow you?"

It was worth a shot. I walked past Bob, down the hall toward the doors. Bob's eyes followed me until I pushed against the lever. It must have been the critical move because his ears pricked up and he lifted a front hoof.

"Come on, Bob," I coaxed. "All you've got to do is go outside."

Curse my big fat mouth. Bob swung back around to face forward and stomped his hoof so hard into the floor the linoleum cracked. He was not going to move. Sirens blared, practically making the bricks vibrate in the mortar. The sheriff must have gone over the speed limit, actually rushing for the first time in his life. I ran back to Bob and slapped him on his wide backside.

"Move it, Bob!" I shouted. I might have well have slapped the wall. Yet, even though I was annoyed with his bullheadedness, my gut wrenched with guilt that I had resulted to hitting him. "Please?"

"Come on, Bob. You have to go," Ari pled desperately as she pushed against his face. He would not move. "What is wrong with him? He spent all night finding you; you'd think he'd be a little smarter than this."

"He is smart. Too smart," I said. No matter where I went, Bob was going to find me and stick to me like wart glue. I rubbed my hand up the flat front of his face and gripped his tangled forelock in my fist. It was time to have a straight talk with him, even if I did look loony talking to a horse like he was human.

"Look, Bob, if you don't get out of here, they'll haul you off," I said. Bob replied with a short grunt and glared. Obviously that was a no. Angry, I stepped back and pointed a stern finger at him. "Get out of here, you big fleabag! If you don't I'll . . ."

I couldn't think of a decent threat, at least none that I would actually follow through with. Let's face it, this was Bob—and he was mine. Deep down, I didn't want him to go.

"Well, that's not something you see every day," the sheriff said from behind me. I spun on my heel to see him with the scrawny volunteer deputy, Bert from the gas station, and Andy, a self-professed cowboy. Frankly, I'd never seen Andy do anything besides sit in front of the gas pump and spit tobacco out from under his grungy ten-gallon Stetson.

Bob took it all in. The corner of his mouth lifted into an unmistakable smirk. Horses weren't supposed to smirk. I stepped in front of his smug face before anyone could notice that he wasn't normal.

"Ah, it's about time you got here, Sheriff," Silivus said coming out from the main office. "Haul this animal off school property."

"Wait!" I said, eyeing the rope and chain they'd brought and the mean-looking bat Andy was leaning on. "I'll walk him out of here. There is no need for any hauling off. I'll take him home."

"Not when you are facing double detention, Ian," Silivus said silkily. "Go to class and let the professionals do what they came to do. Leave and you face suspension."

"Now, that's a tad harsh, Mr. Churchill," the sheriff said.

"Which is why I am the superintendent and you are not," said Silivus. The sheriff shook his head, but he didn't argue.

"Step aside and let us get on with it," he said.

"At least let me walk him out," I said. My blood pressure spiked as Bert made a loose noose with the chain.

"We'll be fine," the sheriff said. "This doesn't have to be a rodeo."

I could have sworn Bob chuckled deep in his barrel and I cringed. It wasn't mirth. It was a challenge. Bob was going to dish out a rodeo whether they wanted it or not. I didn't move, standing there between the slapped-together animal control team and Bob. Then I said possibly the stupidest thing I could come up with under Silivus's pale nose.

"I'm not going to let you haul him off."

"Ah, move aside, kid," Andy said around a lip full of chew. "I don't got time for this."

Andy was a born slacker. He only broke a sweat when he absolutely had to, so really, I could care less what he said. It was Bert that shoved past the sheriff.

"I'll make short work of this," he said, elbowing me aside. In an instant he had the chain up over Bob's head. I didn't have a second to react, but it wouldn't have mattered. Bob didn't move a muscle. He let on that he was as sweet and docile as a spring afternoon. Bob turned his face slowly and deliberately to me and winked. Winked! Horses don't do that. This wasn't going to end well.

Bob sprang into action, rearing up on his hind legs and jerking the chain upward. Bert didn't lose his grip on it. Naturally, Bob swung his neck around, grabbed the chain in his mouth, and ripped it out of Bert's hands. Then he flung it in a deadly arc toward the deputy and sheriff, who were only saved from being gutted because the chain was too short.

"Bob! No!" Ari screamed. Bob didn't pay her any attention. He kicked out at a row of lockers, mangling them beyond recognition and spilling the contents out onto the floor. If it weren't for the completely controlled, calm look on his face, I'd say he'd gone off his rocker, but no. Bob was having the time of his life.

"Rope him in!" the deputy hollered. He and the sheriff plunged forward. Bob danced away, overestimating the width of the hall and crashing into the drinking fountain. The fountain wasn't made to handle the force of a horse's backside. It crashed to the floor, spewing a geyser of water into the mess. Bob's ears flattened as he jerked around to face off with his new attacker. Water poured out into the floor and Bob kicked at it, widening the pipe hole and making more water come out.

"Watch the rear!" Andy called out as he stayed a safe distance away and shouldered his bat. The deputy ran to Bob's side and tried to rope him around the neck again. Bob was distracted by the waterfall he'd created, but he still was able to jerk free of the rope. He'd had enough of making a mess and started charging animal control. He would dash toward whoever was closest, throw his head around, and bay like a wild beast.

He was having too much fun. Irritated, I lunged for him, catching the end of the rope that was wet and whipping around. Bob turned to stomp on me, stopping short when he realized who was on the other end. He spared me a short grunt of apology.

"Knock it off, Bob!" I demanded. I gave him credit; he would have obeyed if Bert hadn't grabbed the rope out of my hands.

"I got him!" he yelled triumphantly, then bellowed in dismay when Bob jerked him off his feet. Bob dragged Bert through a puddle of sodden homework and soaked books.

"Keep him busy, Bert!" the deputy said. He snagged Bob's hind foot in a makeshift lasso and pulled. With Bob's back leg wrenched high and out of use, the warhorse was stopped short. He backed up to kick, but the sheriff caught his front hoof in the rope and yanked. In the time it took to blink, Bob went from having a little fun to being pissed off.

He reared, bucked, kicked, and threw himself on the ground, anything to get rid of the ropes. And yet, the ropes crippled him. I ran forward in the middle of the fight and grabbed a handful of hair between his ears. Frenzied, he whipped around and bit my arm. Not as hard as he could have if it were someone else, but enough to make pain shoot down into my hand. He left bloodied imprints of his teeth in my skin. I didn't let go.

"Enough, Bob," I ordered. Bob dropped his head, submissive. He was pulled in four different directions, hooves out and trembling. I hated myself. My stomach was sick with guilt. A trickle of blood ran down my arm, and when he got a whiff of it, his eyes teared up. His remorse made me feel worse.

"Don't . . ." I barely got out a word when Bob threw his head back and wailed. I don't know how he did it, because it wasn't like anything I'd heard from a horse before. It was too human, like mourners scream-crying at the top of their lungs.

"Ah, hell," Andy grumbled. He popped the bat off his shoulder and sauntered across the hall. "I'm gonna put an end to this. Say nighty-night, horsey."

"No!" Ari screamed over Bob's crying. I released my grip on Bob's mane and shoved his head out of the way at the same time Andy swung the bat around. The bat skimmed the top of Bob's ears and slammed right into the side of my head.

Bam! Lights flashed in front of my eyes and everything went wonky. I fell to the floor. I didn't feel it, but I did register the shift in visual angle. Bob spun around and headbutted Andy so hard the half-baked cowboy fell like a mighty oak. He crashed, out cold, on the linoleum. Bob prodded him with his hoof to make sure he was going to stay down, then huffed, satisfied. It was only then that he would allow Bert and the sheriff to haul him off. The entire scene swam dizzyingly.

My vision dimmed and the pain in the side of my head was excruciating. The last glimpse I got was of Silivus, who stood off to the side of the mess, unruffled, neatly pressed, and looking entirely too satisfied with himself. Where was the bat when I needed it?

"Ian? Ian? Can you hear me?" Ari said as she pushed at my shoulder.

Nope.

Everything went black.

For being knocked out, snoozing it off wasn't so bad. As long as I didn't move. My head thumped and my left ear throbbed. I wondered if Andy was still using my head for batting practice the way the blood pounded through my skull. Forcing my eyes to open, I stifled a groan. Vision hurt.

In the fog, someone was pacing the room. I deduced we were still in school because it was the only place I knew of that had a medical cot in the copier room. An ancient printer was spitting out worksheets in the corner. After rubbing my eyes, things got clearer. The person pacing looked familiar. I couldn't mistake the blue sheen to Ari's jet-black hair.

"So nice of you to stick around," I said. Ari spun around and nearly magicked herself to the cot. "I didn't drool or anything gross, did I?"

"I wouldn't know. Miss Reeder wouldn't let me in here until school got out," Ari said, imploding my mental image of her fretting over my lifeless body.

"Good to know I was dumped here and left to rot alone," I said. I tried to sit up. The head rush and explosion of pain did more damage than Ari stomping on my ego. "Ow."

"Don't get up." Ari helped me back down and I kept my eyes shut until the swirling in the room stopped. "The nurse said you should be fine in a day or two. The bat didn't even break the skin. It was weird. I saw how hard Andy hit you and your head should have been bashed in. It's like your skull is ten times thicker than most."

If my head didn't feel like it was threatening to split open from the inside out, I would have laughed. "Wow, thanks," I grumbled. "Nice to know you think I'm thick-headed."

"I didn't mean it like that," Ari said. "I'm just glad you're okay. You got off better than the rest of them."

Recalling the all-out rodeo with Bob was difficult. Getting a bat smashed into my head messed with my perfect memory. Images flashed and shorted out again. Thinking about it hurt. Pressing my palms into my face didn't help much, but I wanted to physically make the images stop. Maybe, just maybe, having a blank mind would halt the pain.

"It's okay," Ari said, softly patting my arm. "You can cry if you want."

She thought I was going to what? I jerked my hands from my face and swatted her hand away.

"I'm not crying," I snapped. "I just got beaned in the head by the village idiot."

"Okay, so you're mad," Ari said. "Do you want to talk about it?"

"No, I don't want to talk about it."

"So, you'd rather yell at me?"

"I'd really like for my head to stop pounding," I said, waspish from the shooting pains.

"I can't fix that, but I want you to promise not to bite me. You need someone to clean up your lip," Ari said, very patiently, considering that I just chomped her head off.

"My lip? I thought I got whacked in the head."

"You did, for the most part," Ari said, pulling up a folding chair. She grabbed alcohol and cotton swabs from the shelf beside the cot. For the most part? After getting hit in the head with a bat, what else could have happened?

Ari reached out to work on my face. She was fully covered, head to toe with thicker-than-normal compression sleeves. I don't know why it bothered me so much, but my tolerance level was paper-thin. I grabbed her wrist before she made contact with my face.

"Take the gloves off."

"A 'please' would be nice."

I took a deep breath to steady my head and try and sound less like a jerk. "Please."

Without a word, Ari peeled off the gloves with an electric crackling snap and stuffed them in her back pocket. There was no low blue-green glow to her skin. Today, she was nearly pulsing like a lighthouse beacon, making the florescent light in the workroom look dim in comparison.

"I put out more magic when I'm worked up," Ari said, pressing the cotton ball into my split skin. "Why does my wearing gloves bother you so much?"

"It doesn't," I said automatically, wishing my vision would stop sloshing back and forth. In the swell of it, I heard Ari huff out an exasperated sigh.

"Enough already! You are such a pill when you don't feel good."

"You take a bat to the head and tell me what it's like afterward. Trust me, you wouldn't be in a fantastic mood."

"I'd at least try to be nice to the person helping me out," she said. I honestly had nothing to reply with. No comeback at all. If the circumstances were reversed, she would be nice.

"Sorry," I grumbled, more angry at myself than at her.

"Better," she said. "Now hold still."

I obeyed, but to ensure that I was immobile, she lightly pressed her fingers into my forehead on the uninjured side and concentrated on cleaning off my bottom lip. Deep

Magic poured over my scalp in a slow flow like warm liquid fudge. Relief flowed with it. I sucked in the stuff, grateful for the release as the pain just went away. Gone, like the bat incident never happened. The blinding Ari-light went out and her skin was normal again. My nerves settled.

This was nice. My asthma had cleared up a while back, and I reveled in feeling healthy once more. Before Ari, that was a rare feeling.

"Sorry," I said. This time, I actually sounded like I meant it.

"I already forgot what I got mad at you for," Ari said, flicking the bloodied cotton ball in the garbage and getting a fresh one. She moved my head to the side and began wiping again.

With my head clear, I sifted through the sequence of events that got me out cold on a medical cot. I remembered everything up to Bob getting mad, the bite, and my run-in with the bat. After that, there was nothing.

"Ari?" I said. "What happened?"

"Which part?"

"Everything after I got knocked out."

"I—uh, I'm not sure. There was a lot of chaos getting Bob out the door. He nearly killed Andy and you fell into what was left of the busted drinking fountain."

"So that's how I got the bloody lip."

"Yeah."

"Anything else?"

"Well, Miss Reeder and I got you into the sick room, and they hauled off Bob."

"Where did they take him?"

"I don't know."

I shot upright, scattering cotton balls all over the floor.

"You're telling me that they just left with him? Gone. Just like that and nobody said anything?"

"It's not like Bob was acting innocent . . ."

"Don't say it! He doesn't deserve it," I said bolting to my feet. My head sloshed, but not near as bad as before it got jumpstarted by magic.

"Of course he doesn't, but what is it about this horse that has got you in such a twist? You barely met him like yesterday."

"It's not like that."

"Okay then, explain it to me," Ari said, getting to her feet. She stood patiently and watched while I took my turn at pacing.

How could I explain it? I couldn't put into words what it felt like to get back something that had been torn away from me for years. Bob was half of what made me who I was: a Bankhir Warrior.

I took a deep breath and ran my hand over my thoroughly tangled hair. I could talk, but where would I start? I didn't think I could stomach lying to her anymore.

"I don't really like animals," I said, then stopped and shook my head. "Let me try that again: I've never particularly liked or disliked any one specific species. Never mind, that sounded even worse."

"No, I understand. You are indifferent. Nothing is wrong with that," Ari said. "Go on."

Hoo boy. Here goes.

"I've never really had anything of my own." I shrugged. "But when we were out there with that herd of wild horses and Bob just stopped, it was like he wanted me to touch him. Even though he was wild. Does that make any sense at all?"

Ari didn't laugh. I'll give her credit for that. "It makes sense," she said. "He picked you."

"Yeah," I said, relieved she wasn't going to poke fun of me. "He wanted me to own him, and the weird thing is, I already feel like he's . . ."

I paused long and hard. He was what? He was mine even before I was born? Because he was. As if that didn't sound lame enough.

"He's a part of you."

Oh brother. I rolled my eyes. "Sap fest. I was thinking more like I feel like he's already mine."

"In other words, he's a part of you."

"You aren't going to let that die are you?"

"That horse left his herd, traveled over fifty miles in the dead of night to find you, and, even though you've known him for barely twenty-four hours, I bet you feel like you've known him all your life. Am I right?"

She was dead on. Bob was half of my birthright. He made me feel like a whole person for the first time in my life. He made me feel like a warrior—not just wish for it, but actually feel it. "Yeah, but when you put it like that, my Dude Levels drop like ten points."

"Your Dude Levels?" Ari snort-laughed. "You don't know where your horse is or what is going to happen to him, and you are worried about how manly you are? Give me a break."

"Fine," I said. "You want the mush? Here it is: I am freaking out. They hauled off Bob to heaven knows where. What if he's hurt? What if they kill him? Wild horses around here are treated like rats. It's not like they are on a protected reservation or anything."

Ari's mouth pressed into a thin line and she stood still, thinking, for a full minute. "You're right," she said. "We don't know where he is."

She turned, walked straight to the copyroom door, and opened it.

"Wait a sec. Where are you going?"

"I'm going to go find him."

15

It was embarrassing to admit I could only stand and gape at her. The second I found out Bob was gone and nobody knew where he was, I was planning on going after him, alone. I hadn't thought to drag Ari along.

But there she was, standing half out of the doorway ready to chase Bob down. I have to admit, it did something funny to my gut. Normally, I'd get the swooping roller coaster sensation jumping around between my spine and navel. This time I was busting with something new, and if I had to put a word to it, it would be *loyalty*. Apparently I had a soft spot for it, bad. Like full-on goo. And I didn't do mushy.

In one stride I was at the door, lifting Ari off her feet into a spine-crunching hug.

"You're welcome," Ari said when I finally let her go. "Now, let's get out of here."

Ari and I booked it out of the school and ran to her house, where we picked up her Jeep. Clouds had rolled in. The beginnings of a hard desert rain began splattering fat drops on the windshield.

"Where do you think we should check first?" Ari wondered. "The sheriff's office?"

I didn't feel like talking to the man who was in charge of hauling Bob off, but I didn't have another suggestion. Ari turned into the police station parking lot, which was a tin shack with *POLICE* stenciled on the metal. The sheriff was on duty. He kicked back in an old wooden armchair with his feet up on his desk and a cup of coffee balanced on his gut.

"Afternoon, kids," he said, scratching at his mustache. "You'd better not be lookin' to get into trouble. You're lucky I didn't arrest you earlier."

"No sir," Ari said, sweetly innocent. It was time to schmooze. "We were just wondering where you took the wild stallion?"

"Mr. Churchill said you might drop by asking about that," he said. "He said I should tell you to clear off. He also said he'd take on the horse. Not that I mind much. That horse was flat out of his mind."

The sheriff shook his head, his eyes open and staring blankly. A thin trickle of tainted magic curled out of his mouth and dissipated into nothingness.

"Don't know why I just said that," he mused. "I didn't think it was any of Mr. Churchill's business. That horse isn't school property."

"Why would Mr. Churchill want Bob?" Ari said to me. I put my hands up like I didn't know, but I did. Silivus had taken him before. I'd place bets that he wanted him back just to spite me.

"Beats me," the sheriff said around a smelly coffee burp. "But I know we about dragged that devil of a stallion out to Doc Saunders up at the veterinary clinic. It's the only place in Puckerbush that could handle a horse like that."

If I were dumber, I'd think that this was a rare moment of humanity, but this was Silivus. The most humane he got was a deep shot of euthanasia. I grabbed Ari by the arm and about jerked her out the door.

"Thanks, Sheriff!" she called over her shoulder before the door slammed shut. We were off toward the other end of town where Dr. Marvin Saunders held a small practice in the front half of his ranch house. He had plenty of room on his land to house sick animals.

"Can't you drive any faster?" I said. I was antsy to get going, but I had a rotten feeling that I was going to be too late.

"I only have a learner's permit, remember? I'm going as fast as I dare."

It didn't help that the deluge of rain made going seem slower. When Dr. Saunders's Mountain Home Veterinary Clinic came into view, I didn't wait for Ari to park. As soon as the Jeep rolled to a stop, I was out running for the front door. I bolted up the steps and skidded to a muddy wet stop on the welcome mat.

"Doctor Saunders?" I called through the screen door. I pounded on the wood siding. If there were a doorbell, I would have laid into it, too. Ari joined me and added to the racket.

When the wiry old man finally heard us, he limped to the door with a friendly smile. "Well, hello there," he said, and slowly opened the screen. I was stuck in a geriatric nightmare where everything moved at half speed. "What can I do for you this afternoon?"

"We're looking for a horse that came in today," I said, dispensing with politeness. "A wild horse brought in by the sheriff."

"Oh, I remember something like that this morning," Dr. Saunders said, taking his sweet old time. "A big white stallion. Healthy beast he was, and he had a temper on him."

"That's the one," Ari said, excited. "Where is he?"

"He's not here. I was given an order to put him down."

All the air left my lungs in one big rush. Ari gripped my wrist hard like she was trying to separate my hand from my arm.

"When did you do it?" Ari said.

"I didn't. I told them I don't put down healthy animals. It's just not right. That horse had a whole lot more living to do."

"You . . . didn't?" I could hardly believe my ears.

"Them?" Ari said. "Who was it that wanted to put him down?"

"It was a *him*, really. The new superintendent up at the school was the one. I told him to clear off my land. That's when he said he'd take that horse down south over the border to Mexico. Wanted to take him off to a slaughterhouse if I wouldn't do it," Dr. Saunders shook his head. "It's a pity they didn't leave the beast here. A horse like that doesn't deserve to be slaughtered."

Relief turned to dread in an instant. My ears started ringing, blotting out the rain pounding on the porch roof.

"He's going to kill my horse?" I said.

"I'm afraid so," the doctor said. "I did my best to stop him. Offered him good money for the stallion too."

"When? When did he . . . ?" I couldn't finish.

"About two hours ago. Bought off the cattleman with a hundred bucks to haul the horse off."

"Ari," I said. For the first time in my life, I sounded helpless. "Please tell me you can track him down." She could search with magic. It was my last hope.

"I can't."

"Why not?"

"I, uh," Ari paused, looking nervously at Dr. Saunders, calculating how much was safe to say in front of him. She lowered her voice to a barely audible whisper. "It takes time to locate . . . things . . . and I only get a general shape. If there is more than one semitruck on the freeway, I wouldn't know which one he'd be in."

"He's going to kill my horse," I said, not wanting to believe what just came out my mouth. I'd heard about the cattleman, and he wasn't someone you'd want to meet in a dark alley. That was a low blow and it hurt. Physically hurt.

Silivus. He was like a revolving door of evil. Magician or not, it was time to settle the score.

"Give me the keys," I growled at Ari. She held them out of the way.

"Auto suicide is not the answer," she said. "We still have time to find Bob before it's too late."

"I'm not so sure, missy," Dr. Saunders said. "The cattle trucks rolled out for Mexico at three, and it's almost half past four already. I hate to admit it, my dear, but that horse is long gone."

The old vet's words lashed out like a barbed whip. I couldn't take it any longer. Silivus screwed with my life one time too many and I officially had enough.

I wanted revenge.

"Ari," I said. "Keys."

She handed them over without a word.

I ran to the Jeep, got in, and yanked the gears into drive. Blinded by anger, I floored it to the school. I wasn't sure what I'd do if Silivus wasn't there, but it was a place to start. Besides, trashing his office seemed like an additional perk to ripping off his head and dropkicking it across the galaxy.

The school parking lot was half empty. It was nearing the end of the semester, which meant that most of the staff was still there entering in grades.

When I threw open the main office door, I was soaked through and muddy up to the knees. Miss Reeder didn't look too pleased to see me drip gunk on the carpet.

"I need to see Mr. Churchill," I said.

"He's out. But you can wait in his office until he gets back in," she said. "He only stepped out for a minute or two."

I walked straight into his office, shut the door, and stood there. Common sense was slowly returning. What was I going to say to him? *You rotten scumbag, I'd like to rip your head off for cursing me and killing my horse?* If Silivus had any cunning in him at all, he'd use that to lock me up forever in the loony bin.

Running my hands over my hair, I sent a river of excess water down my neck. No, I couldn't lose it. I had to think smart.

I was lost in thought for a few minutes, trying to find a way to pin Silivus down without backlash, when I heard a rattling sound in Silivus's otherwise-silent office. I stopped pacing to make sure I was hearing what I thought I'd heard. The next time I heard it, it was more of a shuffling rattle. Whatever it was was on the move.

Silivus's office was obnoxiously messy with files and stacks of paper strewn over his desk and in the corners. The noise came from under a deep pile between two tall metal filing cabinets. The rattling thing made the papers shake and slip down the pile.

Digging under piles of stacked and stapled paper is harder than it looks. The rattling increased to an all-out violent vibration. I was knee-deep in files when I came to a long wooden box wedged between the baseboards and the file cabinets. The contents were fighting to get out, but when I put my hand on the lid, the rattling stopped.

What on Earth . . . ?

I put my shoulder to one of the cabinets and pushed. It budged a few inches. That was enough. I had just enough space to pry the lid open and have a look inside.

"Hello, magical sonar," I said under my breath. Thank the stars for Ari and her neverending supply of Deep Magic. It made me a beacon for Corbin, Bob, and Silivus, but it also made me a beacon for my sword. Light from the window glinted off the high-gloss silver blade. From the angle I was viewing it, I couldn't see it from end to end, but the hilt was unmistakable, with a fat emerald embedded in the gold handle. It was a blade fit for a king.

The lid opened just far enough for the tip of my finger to brush the gem-studded hilt and nothing farther. I wanted to get it out. Free it. I felt as if a section of my soul was trapped in the box with it, and my fingers ached to grip the hilt for the first time.

Ring! Ring! Miss Reeder's phone blared, and the noise through the door jolted me back to reality. I couldn't take my sword and walk it out the front door under the receptionist's nose. Parading a massive weapon around would raise panic. It would also alert Silivus, heaping more trouble on me. Reluctantly, I closed up the box and put it back behind the cabinet. It was a wrench to walk away from the last missing piece of my birthright, but I'd have to come back for it another day. Half sick with a renewed sense of loss, I pushed the cabinet back into place. I was picking up files spread over the floor when the main office door opened with a deafening bang.

"Miss Reeder, where are my messages? How can I efficiently rehabilitate this school if you insist on being incompetent at your job?" Silivus barked at her. I pushed the last of the files to the top of the pile. My Warrior Alarm System vibrated like mad, but the danged files wouldn't stay in place and kept slipping back to the floor. I gave it a few more tries before I heard Miss Reeder say tartly, "Your messages, *sir*, are by your phone, and you have a student waiting for you in your office."

Crud. I was holding a stack of manila file folders when the knob began to turn. I tossed them on top of the pile, vaulted over his desk, and fell into a chair just in time for the door to open and Silivus to walk in. I prayed the pile would hold, though it looked as if it would topple to the side at any given second.

"Mr. Quicksilver," Silivus greeted me coolly. I am sure I was the last person he wanted to see after school hours.

I got up and brushed off my jeans like I'd been waiting for a while. I gave him a tight, ice-cold smirk of a smile.

"Sil—Mr. Churchill," I said. I purposefully slipped his name, letting him know that I was far from forgetting that I knew exactly who he was.

"You wanted to speak to me?"

"I did. I want to know why you took my horse."

Silivus slid behind his desk and regarded me, completely devoid of emotion. "That animal is not yours," he said silkily. "It is a pest of the desert and was taken to slaughter this afternoon."

He was so cool, so in control, just waiting for me to

make the first strike so he could mow me down. I fought the urge. I desperately wanted to accuse him of killing a noble animal of the Royal Stables belonging to the King of Bankhir. I wanted to, but I didn't. The door to his office was still open and Miss Reeder would hear what would have sounded like the ranting of a delusional maniac.

"That was all I needed to know," I managed to get out in forced politeness. I held out my hand. "Thank you."

He took my right hand to shake, the hand that Ari concentrated her magic on to send me messages. It was undoubtedly stronger than my left. We shook. Then I started to squeeze.

His knuckles cracked and his bones bowed under the pressure. The pain of it was evident on his face. I leaned forward so we were eye-to-eye.

"I appreciate your honesty," I said through gritted teeth. "I'll never forget it."

I let him go just as he buckled under the pain, gasping as he cradled his squashed hand against his chest. I knew I had to get out of there before he could retaliate. Leaving the office, I forced myself to walk. However, once I was clear of the door, I ran full tilt for the exit. I was nearly home free, just around the next corner, when I collided, face first, into Ari.

"Thank goodness I found you," she said, and ran with me to the door. "Come on, we've got to get out of here."

"Why? What's going on?"

"It's Coach Corbin."

16

Ari wouldn't say another word until we made it back to the Mountain Home Veterinary Clinic. The rain had eased up to a drizzle and mud was caked on everything. Ari led the way into the house without bothering to knock. Down the hall and past the waiting room, we entered into the back surgery where an enormous man was laid out on a wide silver gurney, dripping blood onto the floor.

"Corbin! What happened?" I ran to his side as he lifted his head with a groan.

"Hey, kid," he said. Blood trickled out his mouth. "This is just small stuff. Paper cuts compared to what I'm used to."

"These are pretty deep paper cuts," Dr. Saunders said as he prepped a tray of needles, sutures, and cotton swabs. "I'm surprised you weren't killed."

"Ah, it was just a few hundred head of cattle," Corbin said weakly, waving a banged-up hand.

"Corbin went after Bob," Ari said, pale and staring, like she couldn't stand not to look at the gore. "Miss Reeder told him all about Bob nearly killing Andy during lunch and he decided to go after him."

"Wha—?"

"That's right," Dr. Saunders said. "Nearly took my head off when I told him about it. Though I don't know how he knew where to look. That dunderheaded sheriff was about ready to do whatever Mr. Churchill wanted."

"Sonar," Corbin coughed weakly. I shot him a warning glance, and he clamped his bloodied lips shut. Nobody knew about magical sonar except us.

"Whatever it was," Ari said, "Corbin found Bob before they got too far out of town. He made the cattle truck stop, but at the same time the rig unhooked from the hitch when it went off the side of the highway. All the cattle and Bob were dumped out the back. Right over the top of him."

"But he got your horse back, son," Dr. Saunders said, threading a needle. "I don't know whether to give him a medal or call him a fool, but the man's got guts, that's what."

I looked down at Corbin, not sure what to say. His steel-blue eyes were barely glowing, as if they were threatening to go out. He glared back at me, unblinking and challenging, and I knew he'd do it all over again. No questions asked. My chest filled nearly to breaking point with pride. He was my kin.

"Definitely a fool," I said.

Corbin coughed out a laugh. He touched a bloody finger to his forehead and saluted me. "You're welcome."

"It's time you kids run along now," Dr. Saunders said. "I should get started cleaning him up."

"Don't you think we should take him to a hospital?" Ari said.

"Nah, I was a medic in the Korean War. I remember the important stuff," Dr. Saunders shrugged his old bony shoulders. White hair poked out from under his surgery cap. "I think it's time you two waited outside."

"I can't leave him," I said. "Not now." Not after everything he'd done for me. It just felt wrong. Dr. Saunders only shook his head slowly.

"I'm in good hands, kid," Corbin grunted. "Go on out and I'll be cleaned up before you know it."

Corbin managed a painful half smile before resigning himself over to Dr. Saunders. I couldn't bear to leave him. Soft, warm fingers slipped down and around the palm of my hand. The gentle pressure helped as Ari led me out of surgery. She took me through to the back half of the house where the kitchen connected to a covered porch. The rain had stopped and Bob was prancing around in mud puddles under a scraggly elm, catching fat drops of water that fell from the leaves with his tongue. For the damaging ordeal he'd been through today, he didn't show any signs of letting it get in the way of a little fun.

Ari leaned up against the porch railing, still holding hands with me. I wasn't stupid enough to call attention to it, but weirdly enough, a low flow of calming magic flowed up my arm. It kind of dulled the worry. It didn't make it go away or anything, but it did quiet it. It was as if Ari had a magical remedy for everything.

Ari's hair hung limply around her face. Thick mud smeared across her chin. She was still beautiful to me. I ran my thumb over the back of her hand and wished that I could tell her everything. Where she came from, who she was, and who I was, too. She didn't deserve to be lied to anymore. But the afternoon was too perfect, with the sun turning the parting clouds a flaming red and Ari standing close to me. Besides, the timing was hardly prime with Corbin laid out in surgery. I could wait another day.

"I hope this was all worth it," she said. "Almost trading a life for a wild horse."

"It's worth it," I said. Corbin would have thought so

too. "Look at him. No wonder Dr. Saunders couldn't put him down."

At the sound of my voice, Bob's ears pricked up. He stopped monkeying around and trotted over to us. He shoved his muzzle under my hand, willing me to pet him. He was covered in muck and mud and he smelled like cow. Hardly any of his metallic silvery-white coat was visible. Ari scratched him behind the ears.

"Are you going to break him in?" she said. Bob stopped enjoying her ministrations and yanked his head out from under her hand. I had a feeling being broken in was not on his agenda.

"No. I'm not sure what I'm going to do with him. I suppose he could stay wild," I said. Bob scrunched up his nose like he didn't like that idea either. "On second thought, I wonder if he'd let me ride him."

Ari's hand gripped mine tighter even though Bob was nodding vigorously. "Don't do it," she said. "We already have one person in surgery, we don't need two."

"What's this? Coming from the girl who calls me a Boy Scout and says I don't live enough?" I teased. "It's not like I am attempting to BASE jump off a cliff. It's just a little ride. Besides, you've been around horses before. You can give me pointers."

Ari reluctantly let go of my hand. "Okay, but don't come crying to me if you get bucked off."

"I swear. I'll suck it up."

Ari led me over the to Bob's side and put her hand on his neck to keep him steady. It wasn't necessary; Bob stood quieter than a statue.

"Okay, step in close so he knows you are there and grab a handful of his mane."

I did as she asked. "Like this?'

"Perfect. Now swing your leg up and over his back."

In the movies, they make that part look easy. It's not if you've never done it before. I swung halfway over his wide table-like back and had to scramble the rest of the way.

"That was good," Ari said, but she spoke too soon. Bob swung around and jumped into a gallop. He got about ten feet away from the house before I bounced off his haunches and landed on my back in the mud.

I started to laugh. I was sure I looked like a first-class idiot.

Ari ran over and fell to her knees at my side. "Ian! Are you okay?"

"Do I look okay?" I chuckled. "I think I did something wrong."

I sat up in time to see Bob come to a stop. He looked over his shoulder to see where I'd gone. Ari tugged on my arm and helped me out of the squelching mud.

"You didn't hold on with your legs," she said, suppressing a grin. "They were flapping all over the place. It was hilarious."

"Thanks," I said, flinging some mud at her.

Ari held her hands up to shield the worst of it and laughed with me. "Let's try it again, but this time leave your legs long and tight around his barrel. It's easier to stay on, especially if you put your heels down."

"Excellent tip, Miss Hernfeld," I joked as Bob trotted back to us. I tried again. Bob waited until I had both hands wadded up in his mane before taking off.

This time it was better. The horse walked a few steps, then turned his head toward the open desert and kicked in gear to a full run. Once I understood his rhythm, I found

I liked riding. We made our own wind, which whistled in my ears as mud splashed up in every direction under Bob's pounding hooves. I never wanted it to end.

Bob made a wide loop out in the valley and galloped back toward the clinic. He ran toward Ari, who was waving me in, then slowed to a slow high-stepping trot, like he was on parade for millions of spectators instead of just one girl. He really threw himself into it as he circled her once and then stopped.

"You did better this time," Ari said.

"Yeah, amazing what can happen when you are given vital information," I said. "You want to take a ride?"

"I don't think Bob likes me very much. I don't think he'd let me get on his back."

"He likes you," I said. Bob swung his head around and eyed me skeptically. "His head is full of desert dirt if he doesn't. Come on, swing up behind me."

"Actually, I should get home."

"Please, Ari," I pled. I held out my hand while Ari considered Bob, who was studiously ignoring her. Finally, she relented, and I swung her up behind me.

"So," I said. "The trick is to hang on with your legs."

I was kidding. Ari pulled herself up on Bob's back and wrapped her arms around my waist. A zing of adrenaline coursed through my veins, far better than any jolt of Deep Magic. Bob took the extra weight as a sign to ease into a canter, thoroughly enjoying himself as he stretched out his neck and rolled with the gait. I didn't feel like saying much. For the first time in years, I felt content, like I was always meant to be there with Ari and Bob, riding through the desert. I didn't want it to end, but Bob had a better feel for the passage of time than I did. Sooner than I wanted, we were at the clinic and sliding off his back.

Bob allowed Ari to thank him by giving him a scratch under the chin, but he soon left in search of a feed bin.

"I'll see you tomorrow, Ian," Ari said, tramping off through the mud to her Jeep. She waved once and then was gone up the drive and into town.

"That's quite the girl you have there, young man," Dr. Saunders said. He came up behind me, wiping blood off his hands with a towel.

"We're just friends," I said.

"Have you told her that?"

No, it was what she kept telling me. It was maddening. "What makes you say that?" I said.

"I don't need my old man glasses to see the way you look at her," he said.

Great, now I had sappy eyes.

"You'd better snap her up while you've got the chance," Dr. Saunders said as he walked toward the barn. "Girls like that don't stick around forever. Oh, the coach is starting to come around."

"Thanks," I said, heading back into the house.

Corbin was up, gingerly pulling a shirt over his head. "I think I'm getting old, kid," he said as he tried to get off the gurney. I gave him an arm up and he took it gratefully.

"You can't be," I said. "How old are you anyway?"

"I'll be one hundred and fifty-two in the spring."

I shook my head in disbelief. Longevity: another bonus of not being human. "You don't look it."

"I'm feeling it," he muttered. I helped him limp toward the door as he leaned heavily on my shoulder. "I shouldn't be aging for another seventy-five years, but I've been away from home too long. My body doesn't like Earth's lack of magic."

I took Corbin out to the porch and sat him down on a high-backed rocking chair. He looked out into the muddy valley and grimaced. "That punk magician really knew what he was doing, sending me here."

"I thought you said not to curse the magician," I said. I sat across from him on the porch railing.

"It doesn't matter much now," Corbin shrugged. "I've gone and done it again. Went against orders and against Silivus. There is no way I will get back into Bankhir at this rate. No, I will die a slow, drawn-out, weakling human death, and Silivus will laugh himself all the way back to the stars."

"You make it sound so agreeable," I said wryly. "It's not over yet. We have six weeks left."

"Are you saying there is still hope?"

"I am saying there is a possibility that this will all blow over without much chaos," I said, falling far short of telling him that even the veterinary could see I had it bad for Ari. A slow smile spread over Corbin's face, and he took a deep breath that ended in a painful round of coughing.

"Ah, stars," he grunted, clutching his ribs. "I hate cows. Stupid animals used me like a springboard to jump off. If it weren't for Bob, I would have gotten my head smashed in."

"What did he do?" I said. "Fight his way in and pull you out by the scruff of your neck?"

"Just about. A good warrior never leaves a comrade behind. Warhorses are no different. He lived up to his name today," Corbin said.

"As Theovan or Bob?" I said.

"Theovan Hugrok," Corbin said. "His name comes from an ancient Bankhirian dialect. It means *Courageous Hero*."

For a name that horrible, I had hoped it had a cool translation. It was odd, but I could believe Bob lived up to it. Not that I was going to stop calling him Bob, but it was nice to know his real name had a good meaning. Bob acted very little like a horse, with his human reactions. I wondered what else he could do. "I think it's time I told Ari everything," I blurted.

"Go right ahead," Corbin said. "Heaven knows you've been stalling for long enough as it is. It's about time you got that girl squared away."

"I didn't mean *that*, exactly. I want to tell her who she is and who I am."

Corbin held up his hands, shaking his head vigorously. "Not a chance, kid. We have not come this far to chuck horse droppings into the fan. You tell that girl she's not human and from another planet, and she'll boot you to the curb."

"She has earned the right to know," I said. "Besides, she is throwing off enough magic to fortify an army. She gets stronger every day. What makes you think she couldn't believe she comes from a planet where controlling magic is common and completely normal?"

"Because she doesn't remember a stitch of it, kid. Put yourself in her shoes. Would you take news like that well?"

"I would learn to deal with it," I said, stubbornly.

"Listen to yourself," Corbin said. "Even you can't deny it would be a hard pill to swallow."

"But she'll have to find out eventually," I said. "Which would be worse? Telling her now and letting her adjust to the news or later when we turn sixteen and are carted off back to our home planets to be presented as king and queen?"

"Nice to see that you are finally warming up the marriage idea," Corbin said, slickly changing the subject.

I rubbed at my face and hair with a frustrated groan. Why did he have to keep bringing that up? It made it everything worse. "I'm not warming up to anything," I grumbled. "And pressuring me into it won't make it better. I'll turn tail and run if you don't knock it off."

"No, you won't," he said. "If you think I'm bad, just wait until you are back under your father's thumb. Besides, you like this girl, don't you?"

Yeah, something like that.

Dr. Saunders came up from the barn trailing a half-empty oat bucket behind him. Bob followed, trying to get his nose into it. "That is one queer horse you've got, son," he said. "I could have sworn he laughed at me when I slipped and fell on my backside just now."

"He probably did," I said. "He was never taught good manners."

"Well, manners or no, he's welcome here anytime."

Bob leisurely left teasing the doctor out of his oats and came to me, using my back as a scratching post for his face. I wanted to stay and ride him again, but the sun was dipping low over the mountains.

"Do you mind if I leave him here for a few days?" I said. "Just until I find him a permanent place."

"Sure. We all worked hard to keep him alive. I can

keep a close eye on him for you. He can stay as long as he likes, free of charge," Dr. Saunders said. "Muck out his stall and keep him clean, and I can do the rest."

"Thank you," I said, getting up off the banister. "I'd better get going."

Dr. Saunders and I shook hands. I almost left, but then I was struck with an idea. I turned back and stood beside Corbin's rocking chair.

"You know I can never repay you for getting Bob back," I said.

"I was doing my duty."

"Regardless," I said, cutting him off. "I will pay you back in kind. If it is the last thing I do, I will get you home."

Corbin froze for a full minute, not blinking. Then, slowly and painfully he stood up. We were nearly the same height now. He was broader and thicker and three inches taller than me, but there was no need for me to strain to look up at him any longer.

"You're willing to swear on it?" he said, holding out his hand. I extended my arm to shake on it, but Corbin grasped me by the wrist, forcing me to do the same. It must have been one of those binding Bankhirian Warrior things.

"I swear on my horse and my sword I will see you home," I said, thinking of the only two things I owned I could swear on. I must have said the oath right because the crusty old warrior's face broke into a grin.

"Thank you," he said, but if I read his eyes right, he silently added "Your Highness" just as he had the other night.

17

The end of the week passed. I sat out two of the dullest hours on record in detention on Friday. Actually, 'dull' wasn't the right word. The truth of it was that I was entirely on edge. I wanted my sword back in the worst way. By the end of detention on Friday afternoon, I was on the verge of an anxiety attack. I had a plan. I had worked and reworked it over and over in my head until it was foolproof. Well . . . except for one glaring problem. I needed help.

I went straight from school to the vet clinic. The first person I could think of who would understand what I needed was Corbin. I pushed through the front door and strode down the hall to a room in the back of the house where Corbin was staying.

"Corbin, I need your help stealing my swo—" I said, barging through the bedroom door. I stopped short when Dr. Saunders turned with a handful of bloodied bandages.

"And good afternoon to you too, young man," he said blandly.

"Hello, Doc," I said, plastering an innocent smile on my face. "How's the patient?" I held the door open for him as he walked past.

"The coach is fine. Wipe that smirk off your face. There's no need to fake it for me," he said. "You have guilty written all over you."

"Thanks for the tip," I said, shutting the door after him.

"You really need to work on your deception skills,"

Corbin said from a bed in the corner. He was still bandaged up pretty good, but he looked a lot better.

"You'd think honesty would be a desirable trait." I kicked a chair over to the side of his bed and sat down. Or at least tried to. I couldn't sit still for long.

"So what are you stealing?"

"My sword," I said, too excited to keep silent about it any longer. "I found it, Corbin. I finally found it!"

"When do we go after it?" Corbin sat up, much too quick. Even I could hear sections of him rip. He gasped in pain and sunk back down to the pillow. His face went from eager to despondent in less than a second. "When do *you* plan to get it back?" he said through gritted teeth.

"I wanted to go tonight," I said. In the pit of my stomach, I knew he wasn't able to come with me. "But it looks like I'll be going alone."

"Sorry about that, kid," he said. "You don't think you could wait a few more days, could you?"

I could try, but I'd go stark raving mad. My impatience must have registered on my face.

Corbin nodded knowingly. "Don't wait on me, kid. That sword is much too important." He shifted uncomfortably on the sheets and rubbed at his ribs. "What I wouldn't give for a healthy helping of Deep Magic right now. I wouldn't have to lie here like I'm dying and wait for my body to mend. Where is a Garfelian Healer when you need one, eh?"

I didn't reply, mainly because I was struck with a brilliant idea. I turned toward the window and clenched my hand into a fist. My thoughts came out in a barely legible jumble.

Ari, we need to hang out. As in, right now. I kept it vague on purpose and waited.

It felt like forever. "Come on, Ari," I said out loud, and started pacing.

"You're not taking the girl, are you?" Corbin asked.

Again, I didn't reply. My hand lit up. I could barely stand watching the slow scrawl of perfect cursive write out on my palm.

Can't . . . talk right . . . now, Ari wrote. *Parents.*

Crud. That meant I couldn't reply. When I needed her the most, her stinking parents got in the way. I'd have to rework the plan and go in alone to steal my sword.

"Gotta run, Corbin," I said abruptly as I headed for the door.

"Hey! What happened to visiting the wounded?" Corbin said.

"Oh, right," I said. I paced over to the chair and sat down, my knee bouncing impulsively. "Sorry about that. So, how are you?"

"Fine," Corbin said, watching me closely as I fidgeted. "Thanks for asking. Now what's the plan? How are you going to get your sword back?"

"I'm going to . . ." I blew out my cheeks. Without backup, I had nothing. With unveiled anticipation, Corbin waited for me to fill him in. Then my hand flared brightly. Across my palm read: *My dad . . . has me running . . . laps. Won't have time . . . to hang out until . . . tonight. Save me!*

It wasn't a flat-out yes, but it was all the confirmation I needed. *I will. I promise,* I replied as the letters on my hand faded.

When I looked up again, I was grinning even though

Corbin was glaring at my dimly glowing hand like it was the author of all things evil.

"I'm going after it tonight," I said.

"I still can't believe you let her mark you," Corbin grumbled.

"Do you want me to tell you the plan or not?" I said. I wasn't in the mood to argue. Luckily for him, he let it drop. I leaned forward to tell him everything.

I was in my room, crammed in like an accordion, working out the final details Corbin had added, when the rest of the trailer finally fell silent. That was my cue.

I grabbed some rope, a hook borrowed from Dr. Saunders's barn, a thick blanket, and a ball of baling twine. Going out my window was out of the question. My shoulders were too wide. So I crept out the front door. I don't know why I bothered with stealth; it wasn't as if I'd be missed.

It wasn't long before I was out on the road, using the light of the full moon to guide my way. I considered whistling for Bob, but for this mission, all I wanted was Ari. That is, if she agreed to come with me.

All the windows at Ari's house were pitch-black and the porch light had been turned off for the night. I skirted along the fence line to the back left corner of the house. Scanning the side of the house, I looked for the corner window over the garage. I had climbed out of it once before and I'd not forgotten where it was. I picked up a handful of rocks, thinking it was juvenile to be chucking pebbles at a girl's window, but I kept it up until a light switched on in her room. The window slid open and Ari leaned out.

"Hey, Ari!" I called in a hoarse whisper. "You said you needed saving?"

"Ian? What are you doing?"

"Breaking the law," I said bluntly. "Want to come with me?" I crossed my fingers and prayed she'd say yes.

There was a long pause before she said, "It's the middle of the night."

"So?" What better time was there to break into the school and steal a sword?

"Uh, okay. Let me get dressed and I'll be right out."

Sweet! Elated, I waited patiently under the eaves of the garage. There was hasty shuffling, then she turned off her light and climbed out the window. She made it down the garage roof fine until the edge, where she stopped with her sneakers hanging over the drainpipe.

"I think I should have tried going out the front door," she said. "Or magicked myself down. I should have thought of that first."

"No, you're doing great," I said and reached up to grab her ankle. There were definite benefits to being freakishly tall. "Jump down into my arms."

"You swear you'll catch me?"

"I'm not going to cross my heart because that's just lame," I said. "But I give you my word, I won't let you fall."

Ari scooted to the edge of the roof and let her legs dangle over the side. She was too high to grab her by the waist. I shouldered the rope and held out my arms so she could grab them. It took her a second to work up the courage to do it, but she finally slipped off the drainpipe. I caught her.

"See, that wasn't so bad," I said and put her on her feet.

"Yeah, but the trick will be getting back in," she said, pulling up her elbow-length gloves. I was half hoping she'd leave them behind. On second thought, considering what we were about to do, she probably had the right idea.

"Details. Worry about it later," I said, and grabbed her by the hand. I led her through the shadows, around the fence, and out into the street.

"So, what sort of law-breaking are we doing?" Ari said as we headed toward the school.

"Breaking in and thieving mostly," I said casually. I left it at that. For breaking the rules, I was surprisingly calm. It couldn't be stealing if I already owned what I was stealing, right?

"What's gotten into you?"

"Nothing, why?"

"Ever since you went after Mr. Churchill, you have been acting totally different," Ari said.

"Like how?"

"Well, you're way more confident, for one, and for being a total Boy Scout, you don't seem to mind breaking the rules now."

I stopped and turned toward her. "Do you want me to take you back home? I won't force you to come with me, 'cause it sounds like you're backing out."

"I am not backing out, I'm just noticing you've changed a little."

"Is that good or bad?"

"Undecided. Now tell me what we are stealing."

I debated how much of the truth I dared tell her. I could sugarcoat it. After talking to Corbin, I was gun-shy about telling her everything.

"You know how weapons of any kind are banned in school?" I said.

"Yeah, it's been like that for ages."

"Well, when I was at the school waiting for Churchill, I was in his office. Let's just say he is hiding a weapon that would get him into big trouble if it was found."

Ari mouth hung open. "He is?"

"He is," I said. "Which makes it the perfect thing to steal to get him back for trying to kill off Bob."

"He can't say anything because he shouldn't have something like that in school."

"And he can't report it, either. Which is why I am going to break into the school and steal it."

Ari laughed. "You've totally lost it."

"Thanks."

"No, this is great. Whatever you need me to do, count me in," Ari said as we started off to the school.

Ah, there was that loyalty again. It was like a crooning musician singing a love song to my soul. It made me want to do mushy things like hugging or holding hands. Or, better yet, kissing her. Though planning a serious bout of rule-breaking wasn't exactly romantic.

"So, what was your parents' deal this weekend?" I said to pass the time as we walked. "For a while there I thought maybe you'd run out of magic."

"Yeah, sorry about not writing too many messages. My dad read in some magazine about how consistent exercise helps teens deal with pent-up emotions," Ari said. She kicked viciously at a rock on the side of the road. "It's one of his stupider ideas, though I think the time when he enrolled me in a survival school was worse."

"That actually sounds interesting," I said.

"It would have been if the instructor wasn't so big about drinking your own pee when you've run out of water and are battling dehydration." Ari shuddered in disgust.

"Gross."

"Exactly. The class was more for crackheads who needed to get clean, so thankfully, that didn't last long."

"I'd say. What did he have you do today?"

"Run a couple miles. He says he wants me to work up to twenty miles and he'll help me qualify for the big Las Vegas Marathon in spring."

"Sounds like he and Corbin would be best buddies," I said, caustically. "I think Corbin gets a kick out of torture via exercise."

Ari sighed. "Really, I think it's just another barely veiled attempt to get me so tired I can't use magic. The fact is, I really hate running, so qualifying for a marathon isn't high on my list of things to do."

"But hanging out with me where we could get into big trouble is?"

"Heck yes. Way better."

I was torn between genuine satisfaction and disappointment that her idea of fun was so skewed.

"We need to work on your priorities," I said. "Not that I like running any more than you do, but I'm just saying."

"Don't get preachy on me, Boy Scout," Ari said. We skirted around to the back of the school. "You're the one who invited me on this adventure."

We stopped in the pitch-black alley below Corbin's office. I looked up, hoping he'd left his window open.

"How are we getting in?" Ari said, zipping her jacket up further to keep out the cold.

"Through that window on the third floor," I said pointing to it. "Corbin always leaves it open."

"That's way up there. Are we going to climb?"

"That's what I brought a rope for," I said, pulling it off my shoulder. The look of skepticism on Ari's face was apparent even in the dark.

"How about I make this easier," she said, taking the rope from me. "What is the layout of Corbin's office?"

I faced her and quoted from memory, "If you are the window, his desk is on the right side of the room. A big metal equipment cabinet is in the corner on your left."

"That's easy enough," she said, walking closer to the school wall. "Don't wait up."

In a dim flash of bluish-green light she was gone. A second later I could hear a crash and swearing coming from Corbin's window. Ari leaned out and tossed down the rope.

"You forgot to mention the chair," she said.

"Sorry! Are you okay?"

"I'm fine, except for my shins," she said. "Hurry and climb up. Being in Coach Corbin's office alone creeps me out."

I grabbed the end of the rope and started a pretty decent upward climb like a mountaineer. A month ago, I wouldn't have made it two inches. But as I braced my feet against the bricks and hauled myself up, I had to admit, hanging with Ari had definite benefits. I traded in my asthma for a bit of muscle. I couldn't complain.

"So," Ari said companionably as I cleared the second floor. "How's it going?"

"Great," I grunted. Sweat trickled down the back of my neck. "I love rope burns."

"You know, I probably could have magicked you up."

"How do you propose to do that?"

"I'm not sure. I've never tried it before, so I don't know what it would do to you."

"I'll pass."

"I'm just saying, it might make this operation run a little faster."

"And teasing me with it isn't helpful either," I said. I reached the base of the third floor windowsill and stopped to take a breather. My arms were on fire. My shoulders protested.

"Give me your hand and I'll pull you up," Ari said.

I looked up to where Ari was leaning far over the side of the sill and holding out her bare glowing hand. I outweighed her by a lot, and if I put too much of my weight on her, I'd yank her out the window.

"Trust me," she said, sensing my hesitation.

Here went nothing. I reached up. The instant our fingers touched, I was propelled upward and through the window in a spiral of bluish mist. Deep Magic zinged around the inside of my body like a steel ball in a pinball machine. Aching muscles repaired and the only thing left of my climbing ordeal was a layer of sweat that dried to my back.

"Thanks," I said, and a puff of blue green smoke blew out my mouth. "You know, I think you are getting stronger."

"I didn't yank you up, silly." She put back on her gloves, blocking out the dim glow that lit the room.

"No, not you. Your magic." I shook my head, trying to calm the nerve zapping I was getting.

"Did it hurt?"

"Nope. More like a straight shot of caffeine into my

blood stream," I said. I pulled in the rope and wound it up.

"I don't know if that should make me feel proud or worried," she said.

"Go for proud," I said. "It's easier to deal with. Come on."

I took Ari by the hand, unlocked Corbin's office door, and slowly looked out. The last time I had broken into the school, I hadn't bothered to be careful. Yet, with Silivus in as the superintendent, I couldn't be sure the school was empty. The coast was clear. I led the way out into the hall and down the stairs, checking around each corner just in case.

At the main office door, I grabbed the handle and turned, expecting it to push open. It didn't budge. I should have known that Silivus tightened security.

"What's the problem?" Ari said from behind me.

"It's locked."

"Uh, I don't think I've ever unlocked anything using magic before. I could magic my way in. That is, if I can slip in right behind the door. I don't want to crash into anything again," she said, rubbing absently at her shin.

Call me dense, but I wanted to try my own way in first. Excess Deep Magic coursed down my arm and into my hand, leftovers from Ari pulling me through Corbin's window. If the stuff were a drug, I'd be high on it. I twisted the handle until the locking mechanism broke. It was easier than opening a jar of pickles.

"No need," I said, and opened the door. I walked into the main office but was stopped when Ari pulled me back to the door, inspecting it.

"What did you do?"

"I broke the lock," I said.

"With your bare hands?"

"Basically, yeah," I said.

Ari stared at me.

"Stay here and keep watch. I'll be right back."

I had a hunch that Silivus's office was going to be locked up with a deadbolt or more. He was too particular, and his office housed an object too great of value not to. But if I remembered correctly, the door to his office was wood. I pressed my fingers into the paneling and felt for the weakest point.

"You aren't going to break the door down, are you?" Ari said.

"That is the general idea."

"I think it would be a good idea to stop breaking things."

"Do you have a better idea?"

A muted poof behind me blew my hair into my eyes. I spun around just in time to see Ari disappear. The door clicked and a deadbolt slid back. Ari opened the door with a smug grin.

"Well," she said and slipped past me. "That was easy."

I think my mouth flapped open into shocked dork–mode. Nonchalant, Ari took her station at the main door and cracked it open to check the hall.

"Have I told you lately how seriously awesome I think you are?" I said, impressed.

Ari grinned. "Hurry up."

Silivus's office was in the same state of chaos as it was the last time I was in it. The piles were messier, but as I stood at his desk, the rattling behind the file cabinets was unmistakable. In no time at all, I shoved everything aside and lifted the long, heavy wooden box out. Carefully, I laid it on the desk. Despite the Deep Magic running races through my veins, my heart was pounding double time. This was it.

The lid swung back easily. There in the dark, with the moonlight glinting off the blade, was my sword. It was more beautiful than I remembered. I lifted it out of the box by the hilt and held it with the blade pointing to the ceiling. It was perfectly balanced in my hand, as if it were forged as an extension of my arm. I ran my thumb across the edge. It was still sharp and sliced easily through the first layer of skin. On the handle where the blade met the hilt was written *Danthis* in bold script. My sword had a name? Sweet!

I gripped the hilt tighter, reveling in the feel of the metal melding into my hand as if it were built especially for me. I wondered how the swordsmith knew what size my hands would be and why it felt more comfortable to hold in my right hand than in my left. It was amazing, as if I wasn't lost anymore. No longer a stray alien on a magicless planet. No, I was home. I was billions of miles away from Bankhir, but I was finally home.

I wanted to stand and stare at Danthis. The weapon was terrifyingly beautiful, perfect in every way. I was so wrapped up in looking it over; I almost missed seeing that my hand was glowing.

Hurry! I think someone is coming! flashed across my palm.

Time to go.

I laid out the thick blanket I had brought with me and

rolled Danthis in it. The broadsword was too long to be completely hidden. I did the best I could to cover all of it and then strapped it to my back. In a rush, I put Silivus's office back to the way it was, which wasn't hard. Replacing a mess back to a mess was a piece of cake. Soon, I was done and ready to walk out the door, which was when I was struck with an idea.

I wanted Silivus to know I took Danthis. I wanted him to feel the same frustration I felt for years. I wanted him enraged and not being able to do anything about it. Just thinking about it gave me a sense of savage glee. I grabbed a pen off his desk and a sticky note and wrote: "I took what is mine."

I stuck it to his planner and then got out of there, shutting the door silently behind me.

"What took so long?" Ari whispered nervously. "Someone just entered the school!"

Crud. We froze when footsteps echoed down the hall. There was a low buzz at the base of my neck. It was a warning that no one dangerous was in the hall. Still, I'd rather not get caught.

"Can you get us out of here?" I whispered.

"I've never done a double travel before. What if I drop you or leave half of you behind?"

"Then I'll just have to hold on tight."

Yeah, I know. It was a cheesy line. Under the circumstances, I didn't have time to think of something better. The footsteps were getting closer and the light of a flashlight shone under the door. My heart jumped into my throat.

Ari ripped off her gloves and shoved them into the back pocket of her jeans. Then she wrapped her arms around my chest and gripped my jacket in her glowing fists. I did the same around her shoulders.

"Don't let go!"

18

Okay, so not letting go while traveling by magic is apparently one of those mandatory things. Ari shot us out into the atmosphere, blasting me with an overdose of Deep Magic. Staying conscious was proving tricky. That much magic pulsing through my body made my vision swim and dark spots of color flash in front of my eyes. I held on for as long as I could, but when my grip on Ari slipped, I couldn't recover.

I felt myself slide out of Ari's arms and fall toward the desert. I bounced a few times and rolled. My half-conscious state made me flop around like a ragdoll while my sword slapped against my back. Somewhere above me I heard Ari scream.

When I finally came to a stop, I rolled to my back, staring up into the frosty night sky, unblinking at the haze of stars. The air had been knocked out of my lungs and I struggled to recover. Other than hitting hard ground from who knows how high, I was feeling top-notch. Deep Magic rocked!

Ari appeared out of thin air at my side and grabbed me by the shoulders. "Ian? Are you okay? Can you hear me?"

Sure, I could hear her. Nothing worked yet and my lungs were screaming for air, but I could hear her loud and clear.

"Oh gosh, what if I killed you," she moaned. She leaned over me, listening at my mouth for breathing. "Not breathing. Okay, CPR. I know how to do this."

Say what? She was going to give me the kiss of life? This night couldn't get better than that. Though she needed to step on it; my lungs were killing me and the rest of my body was joining in on the complaint.

Ari pried my mouth open and pinched off my nose. It was weird being awake for all this as she bent, pressed her mouth over mine, and blew. It wasn't just air that Ari blew into me. I could feel the pleasant tingle of magic pour down my throat and spread outward like wildfire. My chest unstuck itself, thank goodness. I sprang upright. I didn't need to cough or recover. No, I was flying high. I jumped to my feet and did a victory fist pump into the air.

"Yes! Whoo baby! That felt good," I said as Deep Magic exploded out my nerve endings like a volcano blast.

"You were faking it?" Ari said, half angry as she got to her feet.

"Absolutely not," I exclaimed. "CPR was exactly what I needed. Thank you."

I grabbed her by the arms and did the stupidest thing a guy can do under the circumstances. I kissed her. Sort of. I made it a millimeter shy of hitting home on her lips when she recoiled.

Ari's reaction was immediate. She pushed me away and slapped me across the face. Her fingers stung sharply against my skin. Her hands lit up with electricity, adding an extra zap to her slap.

"Don't ever do that again!" she shouted. Good thing we were far out into the desert. Her voice echoed for miles. "I thought I'd killed you!"

"Uh, sorry?" I said rubbing the side of my face. I was sure there were distinct fingerprints embedded in my skin.

"Sorry won't cut it. I was so scared that we were going to get caught! I used way too much magic," she said. "Then you went limp and I could have sworn I felt your heart stop!"

"Well, I'm definitely not dead," I said. "With that much magic I only blacked out."

I should have kept my mouth shut.

"WHAT? Why didn't you tell me?"

"I didn't think it was that big of a deal."

"It. Is. A. Big. Deal. To. Me!!" she said, pounding her fist into my chest with each word she yelled.

"Whoa, hey," I said, and grabbed her wrist. "Calm down. I'm okay, so everything worked out just fine."

"It's not fine. I dropped you at least twenty feet," she said. This time her voice had lowered a few decibels.

"No worries," I said, fighting the urge to grin. "I bounced."

"It's not funny."

"Too bad we couldn't get it on film."

Ari's arms dropped to her sides. She stared at me blankly like I was completely out of my mind. "You are *such* a guy," she said at last.

"That's a good thing," I said, turning toward the lights of town. "But we should get back before it gets too late."

"We're walking this time," she said, stalking past me, irritably shoving her hands into her gloves. "No more traveling by magic."

"I wouldn't write it off completely," I said, catching up to her. "I kind of like it."

"You like passing out and falling to your death?"

No, I liked the feeling of irrational power coursing

through my veins, like a mega dump of endorphins. "I haven't died yet," I said. "And the adrenaline rush is, well, fantastic."

"That explains a lot."

"It does?"

"Yeah, my magic burns brain cells."

"Hardly," I said. I adjusted my sword so it fit more comfortably between my shoulder blades. "It's more like a heightened sense of awareness, jumpstarted by a boatload of irrational behavior. Oh, and I can't leave out the complete lack of self-control."

"That would explain a lot," Ari said. I kept silent. Common sense was returning as magic began seeping out of my body, allowing my head to clear.

We walked in silence for a long time. It was getting harder for me to separate the desire to be with Ari from the desire to leech magic off of her. Don't get me wrong; I had my moments. I could count a handful of times where magic had nothing to do with the acrobatics raging in my gut when she was around. I seemed to take any opportunity to hold hands with her. And that almost kiss?

Hmmm.

At the time, I had too much Deep Magic pumping through me to make sense of that one.

"Ian?"

"Hmm?"

"Why did you try to kiss me?"

Why did I? I didn't know, so I opted for logistics over soul-baring.

"I'm not sure," I said. "One thing I do know is that while your magic harms most humans, I'm probably the only guy out there that likes being zapped by you."

"You said you absorbed it, but what does that have to do with . . ." She couldn't finish. I must have embarrassed her too badly.

"It has everything to do with it," I said. "Your magic feels euphoric to me. I can control it when it's in small amounts. But when you go whole hog on me like that, I end up doing something I wouldn't . . . normally do."

Even as I said it, I knew it was a lie. Maybe I had to say it out loud for me to come to grips with the truth. It was less to do with magic and more to do with the fact that her magic took what I wanted and made me bold enough to get it.

"Oh," she said. Her voice came out flat.

I wasn't sure how to respond to that, so I let it drop. We turned on her street and kept to the shadows to get around to the back of her house. I stood under the garage eaves and looked up at her window.

"Are you going to magic yourself up or would you like me to give you a boost?"

Ari rubbed wearily at her face. "I'm too tired to concentrate on it," she said. "Can you give me a leg up?"

"Sure." I interlocked my fingers and created a step for her. Ari put her foot in my hands and gripped my shoulders to keep her balance.

Most of the magic had run its course and I was feeling more like myself. It was the perfect timing. I hoped.

"Ari?"

"Yeah?"

What was I going to say? I was bent far enough to be eye-to-eye with her, but it was hard to judge her expression in the dark. *Here goes nothing.*

"I just wanted to say, uh, that it's not all about your

magic. That's just an added bonus." That didn't come out right. I tried again. "I think I want to like you . . ."

I was going to end the sentence with a very lame 'more than just friends.' And the 'like you' part was so far from the truth, my ears burned white-hot and began to itch. I didn't get the chance to finish anyway, so I guess it wouldn't have mattered if I sounded like an idiot or not.

"Don't, Ian," she said. She wasn't harsh about it, either. "After tonight—after hurting you like I did—I think it's best that we stay friends."

Shot down. Not even cut off at the knees. We were talking full-on buckshot to the vital organs.

I nodded.

"I'm sorry."

I gave her credit: she sounded like she meant it.

"No really, I get it," I said, getting a better grip on her foot. Ari gave a little hop and I boosted her up to the roof. I wanted to get out of there. My ears were ringing; they were burning badly. I rubbed at them to make the burn stop. "Hey, Ari, if you ever change your mind . . ."

"You'll be the first person to know," she said, pulling her legs up over the drainpipe. I waited for her to scramble up the roof. The window slid shut and I headed out.

Okay, I wasn't bleeding out any internal organs just yet. It was only a smidgen of hope, but at least Ari had left me with a maybe instead of a flat-out no.

I could work with maybe.

19

Monday morning I left early and swung by the vet clinic to give Bob a carrot and check on Corbin, who had decided to stay with Dr. Saunders over the weekend. Corbin was fully dressed and looking a bit more alive than when I saw him last. He said he felt well enough to teach. It wasn't cool, but I walked with him to school and took the opportunity to fill him in on what he'd missed over the weekend.

"So, you finally got Danthis back," he said, impressed.

"Thanks to good old-fashioned magical sonar," I said.

"I bet that'll get Silivus's pants in a twist. Filthy rotten liar," he glowered. "You really left him that nasty note?"

"Dead center on his desk," I said proudly.

Corbin chuckled. "Kid, you've got more guts than your father, and that's saying something."

"I wish," I said, my head still buzzing with Ari's refusal. "I tried to come clean with Ari last night."

"You didn't tell her about Garfel did you? I'm telling you, it's too soon."

"Uh, not that part," I said getting hot under the collar. "The other part."

"And?"

"It didn't end so great," I said, truthful this time. "It freaked her out that she had knocked me out and dropped me, so . . ."

"She shot you down," Corbin said, blunt as ever.

"Pretty much."

Corbin swore. "Well, I suppose you've got to start out somewhere."

"That's comforting."

"What can I say? I've never seen a kid work so hard to win a girl over before. I got my three wives to marry me without half your headache."

"Three wives? I can't even handle one girl!"

"Yeah, well, I didn't marry them all at once. And I wasn't in the time crunch you are."

"There is divorce on Bankhir?" I said, curious.

"I was widowed, numbskull," Corbin said.

"Good to know," I mumbled.

"Although, I wouldn't be too hard on her," Corbin said. He scratched at his chin, deep in thought. "She could have killed you."

"How is that possible? I thought we needed Deep Magic to live."

"We do, in regulated amounts, but even the best things for the body can be dangerous in an overdose," Corbin mused. "You were lucky she is young. In ten years, if she tried a stunt like that, it'd be like putting electric paddles on your heart and jump-starting it with a million volts."

"Oh," I said. "Well, I guess that rules out traveling by magic."

"Not really. She just needs to learn control. Warriors have traveled by magic countless times. We cross the bridges the Garfelians make to get to the outer planets and never have much trouble. She'll get the hang of it. More to the point, it was probably the bond between you two that caused the problem."

Not this again. "I'm not going to break it, Corbin. There's no point in harping on it."

"Watch your tone, kid," Corbin said. "I was going to point out that when you are that in-tune with a Garfelian, they can sense where you are a mile off. No warrior would consciously do it because it ruins the element of surprise in battle. It's my guess that she could feel your heart stop and panicked."

That made more sense.

"Well, I already blew it with her, so now what?"

"Steer clear of magic for a while. She'll come around."

"You think so?"

"No. But it's all I got," Corbin shrugged. "Bankhirian women are a whole different ballgame. They either like you or want to run you through with a knife, which eliminates guesswork. No Warrior has ever tried to woo a Garfelian."

Great. Now what was I supposed to do?

Corbin limped up the front steps to the school just as the first bell rang. He stomped off toward the gym. I headed to my locker, where Ari was waiting for me. You'd think that after our late-night break-in mixed with my almost confession of feelings, things would have been weird between us. For Ari, it was a regular Monday.

"So, how long do you think it'll take for Mr. Churchill to explode?" she said. "I bet twenty bucks he blows before the tardy bell."

I turned to tell her she was on, but over her shoulder I caught sight of Silivus. He'd finished his morning tour of the school and was entering the main office.

"I'll raise you to fifty and say he'll start a riot in about one minute."

"You're on!" she said, shaking her watch out from her jacket sleeve. I slammed my locker shut and leaned against it, waiting for the show to start.

"Thirty seconds," Ari announced.

"You're timing this?"

"With fifty dollars on the line? Of course I am."

"How much time do I have left?"

"Rounding the horn at forty-five seconds."

Come on, Silivus. Don't disappoint.

"Five left!"

At about one second to go, I figured I'd have to borrow some cash off Corbin when what sounded like a bomb going off reverberated in the halls. An aggravated howl emitted from the main office.

"Pay up," I snickered. I was usually a peacemaking guy, but I had to admit: it felt good to exact a little revenge. Ari dug a wallet out of her bag and slapped two twenties and a ten in my hand.

"I don't care that I lost," she said, biting down on a satisfied grin. "That was worth every cent. Do you think he'll figure out who did it?"

"I am sure he will."

"What makes you so confident?"

"I left him a note saying I did it."

Ari gripped my arm. Her eyes got wide as she listened to garbled shouting coming from the office. "I think it's time you went back to being a Boy Scout, Ian. Mr. Churchill is going to burn you."

He already screwed up my life enough as it was. What more could he do?

"I say, let him," I said. The front office door crashed

open. "But I think you should get to class. I didn't put in the note that you helped, yet I wouldn't put it past Churchill to assume that I had you along."

"I said I was all in, Ian," Ari said, stubbornly staying by my side. Silivus burst out of the office, trailing papers behind him. "If you get in trouble, I get in trouble."

Hoo boy. It was bad timing, but when she talked all loyal like that, I was reduced to putty. I probably had the biggest love-smacked look on my face. I grabbed her wrist and took her gloved hand off my arm.

"Not this time. Go," I said, pushing her gently in the direction of her first class. "I can handle this."

"Ian!" Ari complained, but there wasn't time to argue. Silivus was closing in fast, beyond furious. His face was a spotty puce color and his black eyes were rimmed with red. I half expected him to hit me.

"YOU!" he bellowed into my face, just inches away from the tip of my nose. I'd like to note that I towered over him. It felt more empowering than if I was still a shrimp.

"Yes, Mr. Churchill?" I said, perfectly calm.

"Get into my office, now," he hissed.

"Yes, sir."

For being in trouble, I was incredibly cool. Normally, I kept my nose clean and stayed out of regular kid problems. But when it came to taking my sword back from someone who had no right to take it in the first place, I had no fear.

I swung my backpack over my shoulder and dug my hands into my pockets. People stared as I walked by, wondering who that kid was who would be the first student knocked off by the superintendent. Silivus pushed me into his office, past a pale-faced Miss Reeder, who was frozen in shock. His office looked like a tornado hit it. I kicked past toppled piles of papers and took a seat across from Silivus's desk.

"Stay here, Mr. Quicksilver, and when I get back, you will confess to everything," Silivus said, waspishly.

In your dreams, old man.

Silivus's office was a disaster. The two metal filing cabinets were thrown on the floor with the drawers hanging out. Files and papers were scattered everywhere—except, I noted with satisfaction, for a hole dug through to the floor where the empty sword box lay.

I waited for a long time, listening to Silivus bark orders at Miss Reeder to phone in the sheriff and hurry up about it. Judging by the clock tipped over on his desk, first period had about ten minutes left. At last, Silivus was back with the sheriff in tow.

The sheriff looked confused. "I'm telling you, Mr. Churchill, I can't arrest the boy for stealing when you won't tell me what he stole," the sheriff drawled.

"That is not important," Silivus snarled. "This child is unstable and dangerous. I order you to arrest him directly."

"Well, now, hold on to yer hat, sir. I think we should get to the bottom of this first before any cuffs are involved. Now if you would just sit down for a moment, I want to ask a few questions."

It took all I had to keep a straight face. A weak, magicless human was ordering the most powerful magician in the galaxy to chill out and sit down. And I had a front row seat.

"Question him then, you half-wit!"

The sheriff took a deep, patient breath and turned to

me. "Now son, Mr. Churchill here believes you took something out of his office."

"Stole," Silivus corrected. The sheriff chose to ignore it.

"Tell me straight, son. Did you take anything from this
office?"

"Like what? Paper?" I said, just to see Silivus's face turn
redder.

"See, he admitted it!"

The sheriff sighed deeply, shutting his eyes to muster up
some patience. Maybe it was too early on a Monday to be
interrogating a teenager. Maybe he needed a few more cups
of coffee in him. "Sir, I'm going to ask you to keep a lid on
it, or I might insist that you leave," he said to Silivus.

Classic. I sat quietly, watching as Silivus's head threatened to explode.

The sheriff turned back to me. "Son, these are serious
allegations against you, so I am asking you to be honest,"
he said. The more he spoke, the more I liked him for it.
"Did you or didn't you take something that was not yours
from this office?"

Awesome. I didn't even have to lie my way out of this.
I looked Silivus straight in the eyes and said, "No. I didn't
take anything that wasn't mine."

"There you have it, sir," the sheriff said, putting his
hands up. "He didn't do it."

"How would you know?" Silivus shrieked.

"I saw a special program on the TV all about how to
spot a lie. This young man isn't lying. That, and I've been in
law enforcement for twenty-five years. I can spot a criminal
in my sleep."

Ka-boom. Silivus lost it.

"Get out!" he said, pointing a shaking finger at the door. "I will deal with this on my own."

The sheriff ducked his head in farewell and left. Silivus slammed the door shut. Kicking files out of the way, he paced behind his desk, struggling to keep his temper in check. It took a while, but he finally sat down and glowered at me. His solid black irises bored into me angrily.

"There is no sense in beating about the bush," Silivus said. "You know what you did."

"Maybe," I said. "Maybe not. But I didn't steal anything."

"Liar," Silivus spat.

"Say what you want," I shrugged. "I don't take things that don't belong to me. Search my room. Heck, search my whole house if you want. You won't find anything."

"I will tear apart this town piece by piece."

"If that'll make you feel better," I said. "What are you looking for, anyway?"

I figured I could play dumb for a few more minutes. Silivus snatched up the note I'd left off his desk and held it up.

"*I took what is mine,*" he said, quoting it from memory. "Left on my desk where I wouldn't miss it. You are a long way from Daddy, Ian. Do you really want to go head-to-head with me?"

So, he was finally going to drop the charade. It was about time.

"I'd go head-to-head with you any day," I said, not breaking eye contact. "Bring it on, old man."

Silivus chose his words carefully. I let him take his time.

"Being cocky won't get you far with me. You royals are

all the same. The same arrogance; the same sense of entitle-ment. I have ways of knowing your secrets," he said, lifting his hand above his head and snapping his fingers. A perfect blue-green replica of me entered the room, pulsing like a beacon. I watched my image unearth my sword, read the message on my hand from Ari, and strap the weapon to my back. Silivus snapped again and my magical replica disap-peared. If his intention was to shock some fear into me, it wasn't working.

"Was that supposed to surprise me?" I said. "I wanted you to know I was here. However, if we are coming clean with each other, you should know that Bob didn't make it to the slaughterhouse in Mexico. Corbin got to him first."

"Corbin," Silivus sneered. "You put so much trust in a man who is the laughingstock of his kingdom. He was cast out for treason and can never go back. You do realize you are only his meal ticket to get back into the King's good graces? He's using you."

"Gladly. In fact, I am willing to help anyone who wants to get rid of you."

Silivus leapt to his feet and pounded his fists into his desk. "You would not exist without me!"

"And for that, I owe you nothing. You burdened me with an impossible quest. You took from me my sword, my horse, and my strength, and then you sent me here to suffer a weak human life," I said evenly. "You may think you've won, but I will not fail. No matter what you take away from me."

"Ha! Spoken like a true bullheaded Warrior who doesn't have the brains to see past his small pointless existence, to know that the age of the Warriors is at an end. Your mighty race will dwindle while the age of the magicians begins. I have made sure of it. It's taken years of patience and careful planning, but I have drained the magic from your people. While you wander around on this dead rock, chasing after a girl who doesn't care for you, I will take everything good away from your people. You *will* fail. And I will rule them all!"

"Is that what you're after? Good to know," I said. "Great villain monologue, by the way. Top score for evil."

I was cool on the surface, but internally my blood was boiling. Never before in my life did I want to win so badly. It raged inside of me like fire. I had all the tools to fight: my sword, my horse, and Ari.

"Listen closely, little prince," Silivus hissed as he leaned forward. "Abandon your quest, or I will make you suffer in ways you never thought possible."

"Dream on," I said. "You'll have to kill me first."

Silivus's mood switched. He smiled greasily. "Killing you would be too easy. Much, much too easy," he said, sitting back into his chair and interlacing his fingers. "I'd rather see you suffer. It would be easier to return you to the King alone. I want you to stand before him and tell him how you failed, miserably, and watch your faces when you all realize that your doom is sealed."

Honestly, I didn't like the sound of that. I wasn't sure how he was going to pull it off, but I didn't want to find out. "Well, it sounds like you are going to be busy. I should to get back to class," I said. On cue, the bell ending first period rang. I spoke lighter than I felt. I wanted out of there.

"By all means," Silivus said, motioning to the door. "In

fact, I believe the lovely Princess of Garfel is waiting for you just outside the door. You should go to her before she worries."

I froze half out of my seat. This was too easy. My Warrior Alarm Radar was going haywire, the vibration at the base of my neck buzzing out of control. Silivus stood and walked me out of the office, staying a foot or two behind me as we left. Ari was across the hall talking to another girl, nervously gnawing on her bottom lip.

Silivus stood behind me, too close for comfort. I could feel waves of hatred crash down on my back.

"Know this, warrior prince," he whispered. "For every second she suffers, it was because of you."

And then I entered a nightmare.

Silivus slowly raised his hand and snapped his fingers. The sound echoed in my ears as Ari's hand came up as if she was attached to marionette strings. To everyone else it looked as if she was going to pull her long glossy black hair out of her face and tuck it behind her ear. I could see an arc of electricity form on her palm and mix with a bolt of sickly-looking blue-green magic. It was tainted and too dark to be from Ari. Silivus had tainted it. However, the electricity and the polluted Deep Magic building up on her skin was a killer combination, even for me. But it wasn't for me. It was for the girl Ari stood next to.

Ari's hands stiffened. Any second now she would lose control, and judging by the expression on her face, she knew it was coming.

"Enjoy hell," Silivus whispered. He snapped his fingers once and Ari's body went rigid. It was that horrible second before an explosion when you know what is going to happen next and can't do anything about it. Ari gasped and her eyes flew wide open. Her hands lifted and her skin went supernova-bright.

I ran forward, ready to take the blow for the human girl who was the unfortunate object of Silivus's cruelty. All I needed was to place my body between them and stop the flow of energy.

"Ari! No!" I could hear myself yell it, but my gut reaction was to jump. I grabbed the girl, bowling into her as Ari blasted me full force in the chest. The pain of thousands of volts of electricity and Deep Magic pounding into my skin made me scream like a wounded animal. Burned flesh and hair invaded my sinuses. Deep Magic heightened my nerve endings, making the torture excruciating. I wanted to die. I wanted to peel off my skin and bleed myself dry. My eardrums popped and my teeth vibrated in my skull. I just couldn't take it.

"Ari," I garbled around blood that clogged my throat. "Please!"

What felt like an eternity of pain finally came to an end. I tried to breathe, taking short gasps so not to make it worse. My vision swam and tears coursed down the sides of my face to mingle with the blood that trickled out of my ears. The hall exploded in chaos. Amid the sea of faces, Corbin struggled to get to me. He pushed through the crowd and knelt down to lift my head, making it easier for me to breathe.

"Hang in there, kid."

Ari stood off to the side, white as ash and staring in horror. I held my hand out to her, or at least I thought I did. I was more distracted with the blood coating my fingers. She didn't move for the longest time, scared stiff. Then she turned and bolted out of the school at a dead run.

I held on for about two seconds longer. Just enough time to see Silivus give me a courtly bow. He slipped behind the crowd and disappeared into thin air.

Then I blacked out.

20

U_{gh.}

I hated life. Literally every breath made my chest ache. I tried moving. Yeah. Bad idea. Nothing worked right, and my muscles screamed in protest right along with my splintered bones.

"He lives!" Corbin said with forced bravado at my side.

"Where am I?"

"At Doc Saunders's place."

"I hope I got some human doctoring before the vet took over," I said, finding that speaking didn't hurt as bad as moving.

"Nope. Marvin volunteered to take you in. They'd ask too many questions at a hospital. Annoying ones, like why your bones are thick and dense and your anatomy is all wrong. Marvin stepped in and intervened before the ambulance had a chance to cart you off," Corbin said.

"That's not exactly comforting news," I grunted.

"He saved your hide," he said. "Give him some credit. For a human, he is surprisingly likable. We've been taking turns waiting for you to wake up."

"Excellent," I said. "Nothing like knowing two grown men have been watching me snore. That's not disturbing at all."

Dr. Marvin Saunders came into view and chuckled. "At least you haven't lost your sense of humor, son. It could be a whole lot worse."

I wasn't sure how my being laid out unconscious could be good. Last I knew, Silivus had disappeared, and Ari . . .

I sprang upright.

"Where's Ari?" I demanded.

"She already went home," Marvin said. "Thought it was right nice of her to drop by."

I looked to Corbin, who was avoiding making eye contact with me.

"She didn't say much. Her parents were with her," he said. "Said she'd be back later to pick something up."

"Like what?"

"Not sure," Corbin said. "She didn't say."

Marvin put his hand on my shoulder and pushed me back down to the pillow. Everything hurt with even the slightest movement. I didn't care. My mind was on things other than the pain.

"Easy there, son," Doc said. "You don't want to start bleeding again. You Warriors are a tough bunch. You don't know when to stay down and give your body a rest. Never seen a man take a beating like you did and live."

I tried to obey. Lying down seemed to be an arduous task. However, I looked to Corbin, who didn't seem to notice that the old doctor had mentioned anything a little off.

"Is he in on this?" I said.

"He figured out about half of it, and I filled him in on the rest," Corbin said. "He took it pretty good. Only passed out once."

"I said I was a little dizzy," Marvin said. "That's a whole different ball of wax."

"How'd you figure it out?"

"X-ray. Your bone structure is thicker and you got more ribs than a human. That, and did you know you have a bone plate protecting your heart? Completely blocks the organ from view. It's fascinating!" Marvin said. "I wish I could take a few samples. Maybe test to see what's in your genetic makeup."

"Are you sure it's safe to be here?" I asked Corbin, who was shaking his head with a long-suffering grimace. "I feel like a frog on a dissection table."

"Shut it down, Doc," Corbin said. "Go tend to your animal patients."

"Oh all right." Marvin grumped out of the room, muttering under his breath about being ordered around by aliens.

"Are you sure telling him about us was a good idea?" I said when the door shut.

"It seemed to be at the time, though I didn't tell him everything. Just the need-to-know stuff."

I rubbed at my face, realizing I was bushed. I didn't feel up to sleeping it off. With my hand up near my face, I noticed that the tips of my fingers were blackened. Which made me wonder.

"So, how bad is it?"

"Bad," Corbin said, frankly. "I'm not going to sugar-coat it, kid. If you hadn't jumped in when you did, Arianna would have killed that girl. About killed you too if she had held on much longer."

"I'll recover, right?"

Corbin paused. He was struggling with absolute truth. "For the most part. You will have some scarring. Even in the height of war I have never seen a Garfelian use magic on a Warrior like she did on you. Reaching into your chest and ripping out your heart would have been merciful in comparison."

"I thought you said she wasn't strong enough yet."

"It's hard to gauge. I wouldn't have believed it if I hadn't seen it. No Garfelian kid her age is that powerful."

I swallowed back a deep well of bitterness. "It was Silivus."

"Come again?"

"It was Silivus that made her do it," I said. "I was in his office that morning and he threatened me. He said that if I didn't give up my quest, he would make me suffer. I wouldn't back down. I couldn't. Then he took me out to the hall where Ari was waiting and . . ."

I couldn't finish. Words clogged in my throat and I couldn't cough them out.

"Take it easy, Your Highness," Corbin said. "What's done is done. Don't beat yourself up over it."

I flinched. I was so accustomed to Corbin calling me "kid" or taunting me with "Nancy" that hearing my official title from him made me angry.

"I'm no prince, Corbin," I said. "If I had any royal blood in me at all, I would have told Ari who she was ages ago. If anything, I am a coward."

Corbin pulled a chair over from the corner and sat down at the side of the bed. Silently, he straightened the blanket covering my legs and changed out the cooling ointments in rags on my chest. He was kinder than a trained nurse. As if I didn't feel bad enough, I now felt guilty I had ever considered him a jerk.

"You are no coward," Corbin said at last. "You are your father's son. No child of his would be anything less."

"How can you compare?" I said, acidly. "I barely know the man."

"His blood runs in your veins, made apparent when you willingly embarked upon a quest predestined to fail. You fought for your horse and your sword. You took on the most powerful magician in our galaxy, alone," he said. "I've never met a Warrior so fearless. Especially when you fight for the one you love."

"Hold up," I said, balking at the implication. "I wouldn't go that far."

"You wouldn't?" Corbin said. His eyebrow cocked skeptically.

Corbin waited patiently, studying my face. He was right. Less than a minute after regaining consciousness I wanted one person: Ari. Though she nearly killed me, I couldn't stand to be away from her. My body was in pain, but my heart ached because she wasn't there. I was a love-soaked sap.

"Ah, crud," I muttered, finally giving in.

"Told you so," Corbin said.

"No need to gloat."

"Too late."

I reached up and rubbed at my ears. They were patched up with gauze, which didn't help the burning sensation.

"You should rest, Sire," Corbin said as he got up.

"Hey, Corbin?"

"Yes, Your Highness?"

"Thanks."

He made a short bow in reply and left the room. I almost preferred him calling me Nancy. I settled back on the pillow and stared at the ceiling, where posters of dog treat ads, Marine stickers, and warnings against feline diseases were plastered over the drywall. Apparently, I wasn't the first patient to recover in this bed.

I clenched my hand into a loose fist. I didn't care what I sent to Ari, I just wanted to hear from her. I'd sleep easier knowing she was okay.

Hello? Ari? Are you still there?

I waited for what felt like an age. The patch of sun shining through the window shifted from the floor to the wall before I tried again.

Ari, please talk to me. Are you getting these messages at all? Ari?

I barely finished the thought when my blackened hand lit up with a weak, flickering bluish light. My heart leapt into my throat. The words were faint and scrawled in a broken, shaky hand.

C n't talk n w. Be ov r lat r.

The blue-green message began to fade, and I hung on to it for as long as I could. The weak influx of magic took away the sting that seemed to linger in my arms, back, and chest. It was blessed relief that helped me relax just enough to sleep.

When I woke, it was dark, and a lamp on the table next to me was on. I heard voices talking outside the door in a heated argument. I sat up; this time, movement was less painful. The scorch marks on my hands were gone and someone had come in and changed out my bandages. I looked better than the last time I was awake.

There was a knock on the door, so timid I almost missed it.

"I'm up," I said.

It took a while for whoever it was to figure out if they were coming in or staying out. Finally, Ari peered cautiously around the door, like she was afraid I was going to chuck something at her.

"Ari! Hey, come on in," I said. It was good to see her. Better than any healing ointment I had slathered on me. "I was hoping you'd be here."

"Hi, Ian," she said. She slipped through the door and stood next to it, ready to bolt. "I, uh, really shouldn't be here, so I'll make it quick."

"What are you talking about?" I said. "Come sit down; I can't see you over there in the dark."

"I, uh, I shouldn't."

"Okay, now you're being weird. I need someone other than Corbin to talk to. He's driving me nuts."

Ari didn't laugh, which wasn't a good sign. She stood miserably in the corner for a long while before she walked slowly into the light where I could see her better.

Her glossy black hair was dull and hung limp. She looked like she hadn't slept in days. Deep circles were under her eyes as dark as bruises. And, speaking of her eyes, the emerald green that was so unusual and bright was now a flat hazel.

"Whoa, you don't look so good," I said. "What happened to you?"

"I probably look far better than you do, Ian," she said. She sat down on the edge of the chair, as far as she could get away from me. "I really messed you up."

"It's not that big of a deal," I said. "I'll heal."

Ari flinched so hard it looked as if I had slapped her.

"Don't. It's not okay what I did to you."

"It was an accident."

Ari shook her head. "It's over, Ian. I'm done with magic."

"It wasn't your fault. What happened was an accident, and that girl is fine. I'll tell them . . ."

"It doesn't matter. Mr. Churchill put me in a program. I'll stay in Puckerbush, but once a week I am hooked up to a machine that sucks the magic out of me."

"No!"

"It's better this way. If I get rid of it, I won't hurt people anymore."

"NO!"

A tear leaked out her eye and trickled down her cheek. "I've had enough. I came to get my pendant back and . . . and . . ."

I didn't want to know why she was really there. I didn't want to hear it, but the entire house had fallen silent. There was no way to escape it.

"I don't want to be friends with you anymore."

Ouch. I may have had bone plating over my heart, but I just got sucker-punched in the vital organ. "You'll change your mind. This'll blow over," I stammered.

Ari didn't reply and she couldn't look at me. That was when I noticed that her gloves were gone, along with her compression suit under her clothes. Her olive skin was just that, olive and normal like a human. Her hands shook until they glowed a faint, weakened blue-green as she reached out to me. Searching. Her pendant rattled against my chest. The little silver crescent was a traitor. She snatched back the covers and dug it out of the pocket on my shirt.

Like an automaton, I grabbed her hand, not willing to let go of the only piece of her I had.

"Please, don't do this," I said.

"You know what? I think you'll be just fine without me," Ari said. Another tear streaked down her cheek. "You were only after my magic anyway."

I released her in an instant, as if she had zapped me all over again. I couldn't believe she had just said that. I didn't want to.

Ari fled. The door banged against the wall long after she'd run through it. I heard the windows rattle as she burst out the front door. I was shocked into silence.

Corbin came into the room. His normally tan face was white as a sheet as he stared out into the hall where Ari had disappeared. "Go after her," he said.

"No."

"Get off your lazy, half-healed backside and go after her, now!" he demanded.

"It's over, Corbin."

"It is not over. You get out there and save her from that maniac. You can't let Silivus do this to her."

"It's what she wants."

"It's what Silivus wants. He'll suck her dry and then feed her all kinds of lies. Lies that will destroy you both."

I lay back on the pillow. I couldn't decide if the physical pain was enough to cover the level of suffering I felt. Ari had cut me deep. I was willing to bleed out if that was what she wanted.

"You've got to keep trying. Tell her," Corbin said. "Tell her you love her! Heck, tell her whatever you want. And then don't stop until she believes you."

"No," I said to the ceiling.

"Then we are all lost," Corbin said. "We will die. Your mother, your father, and the entire kingdom will die! Doesn't that mean anything to you?"

I rolled to my side and tried to block him out. Soft footsteps came down the hall and paused at the door. There was a full minute of deafening silence.

"Let the boy be, Corbin," Marvin said softly. "He'll come around in due time."

"That's the problem," Corbin sighed, utterly defeated. "We don't have time."

I wanted to explode. There it was again. Pressure. I wanted to blame him. I wanted Corbin to know it was his fault that he'd pushed me onto Ari. I wanted to blame Silivus for cursing us. I wanted to blame my father for being too stubborn to stop fighting. I wanted to shout at him that he'd put his faith in the wrong kid.

But it would be pointless. I had failed, and the only person I could honestly be mad at was myself.

21

In a few days I was up. I couldn't take another day staring at animal posters on the ceiling. I was getting up, ready or not. At midday, when I knew Corbin would be gone, I swung my legs over the side of the bed and forced myself upright. It took work. My legs were sore, and my spine cracked in ten different places as I shuffled to the door.

The house was silent. Usually there was an animal wandering through the hall, mewing or barking. It was too quiet. Today must have been a slow day at the clinic. Hot, dusty air blew in from an open window in the kitchen. I limped past a bowl of fruit and a note on the counter saying I should help myself. I wasn't hungry. I aimed for the ancient landline phone mounted on the wall that had at least ten feet of tangled cord.

I looked up the Hernfelds' number and dialed it on the backlit number pad. It rang twice before I hung up. It was a stupid thing to do since the invention of caller ID. I had no clue what I was going to say.

Actually, I knew what I wanted to say. I wanted to tell Ari that she ripped my heart out by leaving. I was angry that she threw our friendship in my face like it was nothing. And I'd tell her I didn't care, but it'd be a big fat lie.

I did care. Curse my photographic memory. Her last visit was crystal clear in my head. I knew it hurt her way more than it did me when she broke the bond and took her pendant back. The pain on her face was burned on the back of my brain; I couldn't get rid of it.

This time when I dialed, I let the phone ring until the answering machine kicked on.

"Hi! You've reached the Hernfelds'," Ari's bright voice chimed. "Leave your message after the beep!"

Beep!

Now what? I liked answering machines about as much as a root canal at the dentist. I took a deep breath and figured, what the heck, it's not like I was forcing her to talk to me. "Hey, Ari," I mumbled. "This is Ian. Not like you didn't already know that, but I wanted to talk . . . to . . . you." I rolled my eyes at the receiver. My phone skills stank. "Anyway, I'm still at the vet clinic if you can come by and . . ." See me? Hardly. She didn't want me to look at her the last time she dropped in. "Talk. Geez, this is lame. Really, so if you can call or whatever, just do it. Okay? Bye."

I slammed the phone down. I felt like my ears were on fire and ripped the gauze off to give them some air. They were practically burning off the side of my head. I was already pretty irritated, but it seemed like everything itched under the bandages. I hadn't worn a shirt since Ari left and I limped into the bathroom to do some damage control.

Sticky medical tape clung to the undamaged portions of skin on my chest. It prickled my hair; all I wanted to do was rip it off. Marvin's bathroom was straight out of another era, with orange countertops and an avocado-green toilet. A wide mirror took up three quarters of the wall. I stood in front of it and attacked the biggest bandage under my left arm. It stretched from my armpit to the bottom of my ribs, itching and chafing in the worst way.

I grabbed the edge and pulled it slowly away. I was too

sore to do a fast rip. It was a good thing I didn't. As the gauze fell away, my exposed flesh goose-pimpled from the rush of fresh air, making the knotted masses of skin retract into ugly clumps. I swore under my breath. Corbin warned me it was bad, but until I saw it with my own eyes, I had no clue.

I stood in front of the bathroom mirror for over an hour slowly uncovering one wound after another. My left side had the most damage. Starting on my back just above my hip, a streak of split and half-healed scars spread around the front of my chest and up over my right shoulder. Smaller gashes branched out from it, but none nearly as deep.

I didn't know what to make of it. It looked as if the magic had ripped through me from the inside out. And yet, it wasn't the sight of the tangled mess of skin that infuriated me. It was when I noticed that I had dropped from a towering six foot five to six foot zero. I was still big, but the noticeable drop aggravated me more than my itching, purpled wounds. Call it what you like, but it was as if I had lost Ari all over again.

I swore again, louder this time.

"Watch your language, son," Marvin said at the door.

"Sorry, Marvin," I said. The old man didn't deserve my disrespect.

"Don't think I don't understand," he said handing me a warm damp towel. "I've had a few war wounds myself, and there is always an adjustment."

"Honestly, I could care less about the scarring," I said. I gingerly rubbed off the last of the sticky tape residue. "I've looked worse."

"If you're worried what Arianna will think . . ."

I didn't let him finish. "She wouldn't," I said. "She's not like that."

"I didn't say she was shallow, son, but you are tough to look at," Marvin said evenly. "I'm giving her full marks for compassion."

"I don't want her to feel sorry for me either."

Marvin stared at me with his wrinkled lips pressed into a thin line.

"Communicate with me, boy," he said. "Two aliens show up in the same town, drop into my clinic, both in need of severe medical care. I have given you all I've got. No questions asked."

He deserved better. I sighed and gave up. "Again," I said, "sorry. I'm not used to confiding in humans. The last time I did, it didn't work out well."

"Well, I am no Phil and Janet Barfus," Marvin said, then added under his breath, "Miserable excuse for human beings, they are. I have a good mind to call them in to child services and report child neglect. The least they can do is clean that rat-trap trailer of theirs."

That got a wry laugh out of me. "All right," I said. "You got me. I'll talk."

Marvin leaned against the doorjamb. "Who is Arianna?"

"She's the Princess of Garfel."

"That other planet Corbin was telling me about?"

"Yes."

"Any more of you out there I should know about?"

"Well, Mr. Churchill is definitely not human," I said. I scooped my bloodied bandages into the garbage can and sat on the countertop.

"The superintendent up at the school? I wondered," Marvin said, then shuddered. "His eyes . . ."

"Are abnormal and weird me out too," I said. "He's dangerous, so stay out of his way."

"He did this to you? Mr. Churchill?"

"No," I said. Rubbing cautiously at a patch of irritated skin, I considered how much to tell. "Not directly, at least. It'd be easier if he had. No, this was from Ari."

"Did she catch you smarming up to another girl?" Marvin asked, glaring in an accusatory way. If I hadn't been recovering from my guts being torn from the inside out, I might have laughed.

"Definitely not," I said.

"No, I would think not," he said. "You don't seem the type."

I slid off the counter and clapped my hand on his bony shoulder on the way out the door.

"Don't think too much on it, Marvin," I said, unwilling to betray Ari's secret, even to the kind old man. "The truth is more than you could handle. Heck, it's more than I can handle."

Without the irritation of the bandages hindering me, I felt freer. I headed out to the backyard to see if Bob needed company. I still smarted with every motion and I was limping through the door when Marvin spoke again.

"She still cares for you, son."

I didn't look back. "What makes you say that?"

"Call it a hunch."

Hunches wouldn't save me, Corbin, Ari, and our people. I pushed through the screen door and whistled for Bob. He trotted around the barn with his ears pricked up and hay dangling out of his mouth. For a horse, he was way too excited to see me. I couldn't ride yet, but Bob danced out of the way, keeping his wide table-like back as far from me as he could.

"I'm not going to ride you," I said. Bob stopped his sideways dance and wiped my jeans with hay snot instead. "Thanks," I muttered. "The least you can do is be entertaining. I've been staring at dog posters for a week."

Bob's mouth popped open in exaggerated dismay and the rest of the hay dropped to the dirt. First, he shoved me gently out into the yard and stomped the hard ground with his hoof where exactly he wanted me to stand. Then he went into an elaborate show of all his paces, turning in crisp figure eights. When that was done he started hopping on three legs, with his back leg out and his tongue hanging out.

I tired hard not to laugh. It would hurt too much. From behind me I heard a stifled gasp. I swung around, eager to see who else was watching. Marvin didn't have close neighbors and the yard was empty. Or so I thought. Bob ran out into the yard, whinnying in greeting.

In the baking sun I could barely see it, but a faint cloud of bluish-green poofed out from behind a shed. I ran to the front of the house and vaulted over the log fencing, not feeling a thing. I couldn't. Not when my gut was jumping all over the place and my heart was thumping into my throat.

"Ari!" I called out, but by the time I got to the shed, there was nothing. She was already long gone. Disappointment shot through me, along with a jolt of pain.

"Aaugh!" I clutched at my side, where the deepest

wound had opened up again and splattered my arm with fresh blood. I fell to my knees and my vision swam.

Bob ran back to the house and bayed for Marvin, who ran out the front door. Half conscious, I felt him put his arm around me and lift me to my feet.

"It'll be back to bed for you, son," he grunted as we struggled up the front porch steps. I didn't argue. My body felt as if it was threatening to tear in half. I looked back over my shoulder and was certain I saw a section of Ari's black hair blow out from behind the only tree in Marvin's yard.

I wanted to go back and check to see if my eyes were playing tricks on me. Bob pushed on my back to help Marvin get me through the door. With my head spinning and my stomach churning, I lay back down on the bed.

I would have sworn on a stack of Bankhir Warrior blades that I had seen Ari. I tried to get up. Marvin pushed me back down easily, thanks to the pain shooting through my chest. It was nearly unbearable.

"Know when you're beat," Marvin said testily. "And lie still."

"I'm not beaten," I said, trying to roll to my elbow to get up.

"Keep this up and I'll call in Corbin to sit on you," he warned.

"So let him sit on me!"

Marvin struggled to get me down. It took a full minute. When he finally pinned me, he was puffing with his arm braced against my shoulders.

"What is with you people?" Marvin said, wiping away a bead of sweat that ran down the side of his face. "It's like you have no off switch."

"I don't need one," I spat. "She was out there. I saw her."

"Not Arianna again. Son, nobody has seen her for days."

"She was there. I'd swear on it."

"I wouldn't. The front yard was empty." Marvin eased up off my chest when I finally gave up.

She was there. I knew it. I couldn't mistake the lingering Deep Magic behind the shed. Why wouldn't she stick around and talk? Or stay to see Bob? "She was there."

Marvin had his hand on my shoulder, at a loss for words. I tried not to look at him. Though, when I did, his forehead was furrowed and his eyes communicated one thing: pity. I was sure the old man thought I'd lost it.

Marvin rolled me over on my right side so he could work on me. Blood trickled over my skin as it seeped out the new gash I had made in the half-healed wound.

Ari's silence was deafening. She meant it when she said she didn't want me around anymore, but the near miss in seeing her again was torture. If she cared at all, she sure was making it as miserable as possible for me.

Some hunch.

22

Being an alien from another planet had its perks. It took me a week and a half to heal. I didn't have visitors. Phil and Janet certainly didn't notice I was gone. Marvin said nothing about me going back to live at the foster home. He just took me on, no questions asked. I was even surprised to find clothes in my closet and new shoes under my bed.

I couldn't ride Bob, who kept licking me like a dog, which I couldn't figure out. Maybe he thought horse spit would speed up my healing process.

The night I got my sword back, I hid it. Now I wished I hadn't stolen it in the first place. I had paid a high price to get Danthis back from Silivus. I wasn't sure I could stomach looking at it yet. Corbin had turned despondent and quiet. Every time we did talk, we argued. Marvin acted as mediator to us, his surly houseguests.

It was three weeks until I turned sixteen. I felt like I knew the date of the apocalypse and was waiting for death. It was that bad.

As Monday dawned, I got ready for school. I was back in my old clothes. No longer six foot, my shirt hung off my bony frame and my asthma had come back with a vengeance. It stung me every second I thought about how much I had needed magic. It showed, physically, every day as I shrunk away.

I shouldered my backpack and, for a brief second on the porch, wondered if I'd run into Ari at school. That thought alone propelled me from the bottom step where Bob was waiting to send me off with a playful push of his long nose. It was an icy morning, with the desert wind pushing frosted dirt around the desolate landscape. The cold bit into my lungs and made me cough. For the first time in weeks, I had to use my inhaler.

School was dead normal. I didn't have to worry about being questioned about the incident with Ari; kids talked about Thanksgiving and assignments as if nothing unusual had happened. I went back to being unseen. Invisible again, I searched the faces in the hall, but the only person I wanted to see wasn't there.

"It's almost as if she never existed," I said out loud to myself.

"She doesn't," Corbin said from behind me. I hadn't heard him walk up, which was no surprise. My senses were too dulled without magic. "At least, not anymore. Silivus wiped their memories in return for Ari giving up her magic. Nobody will remember a thing."

I stared down the hall of the high school. It may have been a trick of the lighting, but the linoleum looked dingier, the brick walls grayer, and the lights dimmer. It was a dreary existence where day in and day out I would come here to purgatory until my number was up.

"But she's still here," I said stubbornly.

"Technically yes, but even she herself is beginning to fade."

"What do you mean?"

"Her magic, those radioactive-like waves of Deep Magic I was telling you about? It's almost gone," Corbin said. For a second, I could have sworn the man had a hint of a tear in his lamp-like eyes. He shook himself out of his thoughts and pressed his hand on my shoulder. "I got a message from Bankhir this morning. Come to my office during lunch. There is someone who wants to talk to you."

"Who?"

"Someone I'd rather not meet right now," he said cryptically. "I'm sorry, kid, but you are on your own with this one. I'll see you after school to take you home."

And at that, he walked off and left me in the middle of the hall to get slammed into by a tall girl not looking where she was going. Yeah. Being half the size of everyone at school sucked.

Lunch seemed a long way off. I couldn't think of anyone on Earth who would want to talk to me who Corbin would wish to avoid. Personally, I half hoped it would be Silivus. This time, instead of taunting him, I would go straight to punching him in the face.

The lunch bell rang, but Corbin was nowhere to be seen. Even as I trudged from the first floor to the third, I didn't see him. I made it to his office where, through the smoked glass, I could see the broad outline of his shoulders. For a second, I thought he was messing with me.

"Thanks for getting my heart rate up, Corbin," I said as I opened the door and tossed my bag into the corner. "I should have figured . . ."

The man I thought was Corbin turned around, and air left my lungs in record time. In one glance I knew why Corbin didn't want to face off with my visitor. It was like looking at a mirror image of myself. Well, a much larger, six-foot-six-inch version of myself. We had the same blond tangled mop of hair, same blue eyes, and same smirk. The biggest difference was that he had to be five times my size. He was dressed in battle leather and had a whopper of a sword strapped to his belt.

"Is that the way the people on this planet greet family?" he said.

"Uh, no," I fumbled, and tried to force my body to bow. "Hello . . . Father."

The King of Bankhir bellowed out a laugh. "That's not much better. A bow? From my own son? What have they been teaching you on this rock?"

"Nothing useful," I blurted before I could stop and think about it first.

"Now, that's more like it," he said. My dad shifted his sword so he could sit on the edge of Corbin's desk. Calling him 'Dad,' even in my head, sounded weird. The man had an air of regal control and lethal bearing. 'Dad' didn't fit. I wondered how he could be so calmly collected. My insides were jumping all over the place, bouncing between irrational happiness and dread. The King looked me over with his forehead furrowed.

"You are a lot smaller than I pictured you. Are you not eating well?"

"I eat plenty, sir." I said. "I'm undersized because I have been living on the only inhabitable planet farthest from magic. Makes it a little difficult to grow around here."

"But you are in the presence of a Garfelian. Doesn't that help?"

Not when her magic was being sucked out of her like a leech. Thinking about Ari hurt. It was time to change the subject.

"Uh, what are you doing here?"

"Technically, I shouldn't be here at all. I have a few minutes before what little surplus of Deep Magic we have is used up, but I had to see you. Silivus brought word that you failed your quest and I don't believe it. I can't."

"Why? What happened?"

"Silivus drained us. He siphoned nearly all the Deep Magic from Bankhir and Garfel. At first we thought he would help us. He was supposed to save us from destruction by putting a spell over our world to halt the decay. It worked, for a while, until we began to see that the spell was a cleverly cloaked barrier to separate us from Garfel. He cut off our supply of magic. Now, we are dying."

"No," I said, feeling weak, like I'd lost the last shred of hope that kept me going on this dead rock of a planet. "You can't just die. You're the Warriors of Bankhir."

"Now we are only the *people* of Bankhir," he said, shaking his head. "We can't even fight to save ourselves."

"Why not? Why not get rid of Silivus and end this now?"

"He is far too powerful. We tried. Years ago, when he first showed his true colors. But the more we spent our strength fighting him, the faster the magic would drain."

"So you just let him walk all over you?"

"Never," the King growled, looking every inch a fearsome warrior. "But I know when to yield, especially when my kingdom is at stake. Without Deep Magic, we would be weakened. Silivus would send in mercenaries to slaughter us by the thousands to beat us down and humble us. At least this way, when you've completed your quest, you will have a kingdom to come home to and warriors to fight for you."

I flinched a little when he said *when* instead of *if.* The guilt I felt was palpable.

"But the quest," my father said. Hope flared like fire in his eyes. "The quest will break the barrier. We will be strong once more. Tell me, son, are you ready to be presented to the King and Queen of Garfel to ask for the Princess's hand in marriage?"

He was worse than Corbin. And that marriage thing? Who in their right mind would marry off their kid at almost sixteen?

"Hold up," I said. "It's a little early to be talking marriage, but Ari is nearby and we are . . ."

We were nothing. She broke the bond and shut me out, but I couldn't tell him that. I couldn't bring myself to watch his face.

My father motioned for me to continue and said, "And you are what, exactly?"

"We are . . . friends," I said, half choking on the lie.

"Friends?"

"Or were friends. I'm working on it. I still have time," I said.

"So, you were given almost sixteen years to fall in love and you failed? Friendship will not save us."

"I haven't failed yet," I said, but I was spouting more lies. I had wasted too much time over Ari jabbing me in the heart with a dull knife and I had no plan in place to fix it. Granted, I'd left her a series of phone messages—some nearing stalker quality. I doubted she had received any of them. She never replied, and she never showed up at the clinic again. Not since I'd seen her last, disappearing from behind Marvin's shed.

"You may have not failed yet, but my councilors are pressing for action," the King said, getting up off the desk and towering over me. "With Silivus's spell in place, we will not last much longer. It is the wish of the War Lords to devise a plan to leave Bankhir."

"Wait, you want to leave Bankhir? You can't! Not yet."

"The only other option is to let Silivus overrun us. Is that what you want?"

"Are you out of your mind?" I said.

"You have not been a part of our world in almost two decades, child. You don't understand the importance of what is at stake."

"I understand plenty."

"Then understand this," he said, enunciating with a snap of his teeth. "Sixteen years ago we were in the middle of one of the worst wars in the history of Bankhir. I suffered a great loss that day. I'd lost as many of my Warriors as we had killed Garfelians. My people were diminished, and when I stood in the midst of the massacre, I felt the ground beneath me tremble. The very core of Bankhir was failing. It was then that Silivus came to me with a warning: Garfel was unstable as well, and if we kept fighting, both our worlds would be destroyed."

I wanted to interrupt and quip that the entire war with Garfel was caused by Silivus in the first place, but the look on my father's face made me bite my tongue.

"It probably was the only thing I got right," he said grudgingly. "I wanted to give you a chance to rule. So, I went to the King of Garfel. I nearly got myself killed, but we agreed ancient magic could save us."

"Corbin said it was unstable."

"Correct. It is unstable, unpredictable, and powerful enough to obliterate the entire galaxy. And yet, if wielded by a Magic Keeper and a Warrior together, it would create a power more useful than either of us could produce alone."

"It sounds like a long shot," I said.

"No, it was the chance of hope we needed. Silivus hated the idea from the beginning . . ."

"Which should have been a big red flag right there."

The King growled irritably. "I am well aware of Silivus's treachery, son."

"Sorry."

"Silivus wanted you and the Princess to leave home. It was agreed that we were too steeped in our own prejudiced history to not raise you unjaded and impartial. I didn't want to let you go, but as our worlds shook, it was clear we were running out of time. Silivus cast a spell to stop the decay, one that would hold until your sixteenth birthday. At the end of that time, we agreed if your quest failed, Silivus would be given control of our worlds—and the magic they produce—to give us stability.

"Had I had known then his design was to drain us of all our magic, I would have never given you up. Our mistake cost us more dearly than I can express. I lost the faith of my people, the strength of my kingdom, and my only son. If I had known then what I know now, I would have found a way to save ourselves without Silivus."

Slowly, I nodded. I understood. "But now you're stuck."

"Yes, stuck. Even though the word seems a little weak to describe what we suffer. I am bound under a spell that can only be broken by a son I haven't seen or heard from in fifteen years and a princess I have never met," he said. "The union of magic is what is required. Which means only the bond of love between a child of Bankhir and a child of Garfel can break the barrier and stabilize our planets."

Wow. Now *that* was pressure.

"You've lost faith in me," I said, frankly. I wanted to know.

The King held my gaze for a long time, considering what to say. "I've lost everything," he said. "Faith is all I have left."

It sounded like he barely had that.

"Then give me the three weeks I have left. I can complete my quest . . ."

"I am not sure I can grant you one week," my father said, shaking his head. "The War Lords are in agreement against you, son."

"But you are the King!"

"I may be the King, but even I can be overruled by unanimous vote of the council. Do not judge them too harshly. We have been cut off from the galaxy for a decade and a half, and we are dying. My men are desperate. Silivus is tightening his hold on Bankhir as we speak. This may be our only opportunity to escape."

"You can't give up yet," I said. "I can save you, Father!"

"How?"

My father could really nail a guy down with a single syllable. I had nothing. I searched for an answer as I turned away from him and paced the office, running my hands worriedly though my tangled hair. I was a prince of Bankhir! I should know what to do!

A light went on. I was a prince. I didn't look like it, but I was a Warrior too, and with that came specific responsibilities. I had an idea.

"Because, Father, I am a Warrior. Arianna is a Magic Keeper, and without us, the galaxy will fail. Silivus is too greedy with our magic, which means that no matter where you go, he'll be there to suck it away again." I said. "There will be no escape."

"And what of your quest?"

About that . . . I didn't have a plan in place, but I wasn't about to tell him that. "I will not fail," I said. I didn't have much beyond that to give.

My father scratched at his chin, his stern eyes never leaving my face. "You care for the Princess," he said, matter-of-fact.

"Yeah," I said, hoping beyond hope that I sounded more confident that I felt. "Something like that."

He studied me for a minute longer, then said, "Then we will hold." He put his hand up before I could say anything. "But only if by the end of the week you send word to me that the princess has agreed to a courtship."

So was that like a date? By Friday? I fought back the urge to panic as abject terror rose in my throat. There was no sugarcoating it, calling it "hanging out" or "talking on the phone." I'd have to tell Ari what I was . . . better yet, what *she* was. I'd have to tell her why we needed to be together and then have her deal with it . . . in four days.

"You don't think you could tack on a few extra days, could you?"

"Honestly, asking the War Lords to wait even a partial week will cause an uprising. I'm giving you all the time I can spare, assuming the council agrees."

"Sure," I said, my voice spiking up an octave. I coughed and tried again. "Yeah, bring it on. I can do that."

"Good. I will wait for your message," he said as he

walked to the window and peered out into the dreary overcast sky. His solid bulk flickered as if his image was shorting out, which was odd. The magic he had used made him look so real, so tangible.

"Wait! How will I send you a message? I don't even know where Bankhir is!"

The King of Bankhir turned and tapped his chest over his heart. "Magic leaves a mark, son. Hold on to the Garfelian Princess and think of me, and I will know you have not failed. The magic from the message will sustain us until the spell is broken. You will give us hope again."

He flickered again and began to fade. "My time is up. I must go," he said. "Will you do me a favor?"

"Anything."

"Tell Corbin I'm sorry."

He turned back to the window and leaned out. It looked as if he might jump out and plummet to the pavement. However, even as I rushed forward to stop him from doing anything drastic, he put his leg over the windowsill and disappeared.

My heart fell the three floors to the pavement below. Holy blunted blade! I was in the thick of it now, and I didn't know which way I was going to turn first. I'd ignored Ari for two weeks, putting her out of my mind every time a thought of her popped into my head. She wasn't going to be all that excited to see me if I just reappeared on her doorstep. Speaking of doorsteps, her parents weren't going to let me in the front door to talk to her. Me, the kid she almost killed, showing up out of the blue? That wasn't going to happen.

I needed help. Big time.

"I need Corbin," I said to his empty office.

Snatching up my backpack, I bolted out the door. My lungs were screaming in protest, but I ran. I ran down to the office, where Miss Reeder told me Corbin had checked out for the rest of the day and called in a sub.

Then I ran toward home 00like my life and the lives of my people depended on it.

23

Corbin!" I shouted as I vaulted up the front steps of the clinic. "Corbin!"

I made it down the hall by the time I got an answer.

"Corbin is gone," Marvin said, poking his head out a waiting room door with a mange-ridden cat in his hands. "He took your horse out for a ride about twenty minutes ago."

"Did he say when he'd be back?"

"No. In fact, he didn't say much of anything."

I tossed my bag and about howled. "Geez, Marvin, just when I need the guy, he disappears!"

"Maybe I can help?" Marvin said, bewildered.

"Can you win over a girl and get her to go out with you in four days or less?"

"Is this about the Princess?"

"How much do you know about that?"

"Only what I hear through the walls," Marvin said.

Needing Corbin got upgraded to wanting to do him physical harm. The man did not know how to keep his voice down.

"Which would entail . . . ?"

"A whole lot about your people dying if you don't get it together with Arianna. Am I right?"

"That's the shortened version," I said. "And the newest development is that I've got to 'get it together' with Ari by Friday."

"I don't know much about alien courtship, but that seems rushed."

"Just a little! What am I going to do?"

"Son, the last time I went out with a young lady was forty-five years ago. You'll need Corbin for this one."

"Fair enough," I said. "Did you see what direction he went in?"

"Out the back and straight west."

"Thanks, Marvin!"

I headed for the back porch when Marvin called after me.

"Are we in danger?"

"We?"

"Folks here on Earth."

"Trust me," I said, half out the door. "Humans have nothing to worry about."

The door slammed shut. As I turned to head out into the desert, I came face-to-face with the last person I wanted to see: Silivus.

"Humans," he sneered. "Such base creatures."

"Well this is just my lucky day for visitors from outer space," I said. "What do you want, Silivus?"

"Really," he said, "I am tempted to kill them off just for the fun of it. They'd hardly notice in their hurried race to run circles around pointless desires. I'd even make it quick. One snap and *poof*: it'd be like life on Earth had never happened."

Silivus was clearly enjoying himself. He wore a long black cloak over his dark suit. The fabric seemed to absorb light, as if he were an evil black hole sucking away life. Looking at him made my stomach churn.

"You're sick," I spat.

"No, I'm impatient. I see you got Daddy to spend what little magic he had left to check up on you. I'd say it was an admirable act, but really it only made me stronger. The more they use, the more they lose." Silivus smirked. "And for what? So you could lie to him and assure him that you are going to win the Princess's heart? I'd laugh if it wasn't so pathetic."

"I didn't lie. You gave me sixteen years and I have three weeks left to complete my quest. Fair is fair."

"I don't play fair. Never have," he said. "How do you think your dear old dad got into this predicament? Because I lied. Which was as easy as telling him what he wanted to hear. Though I find it fascinating that you still try to defeat me. Makes me want to do something special, just to torture you."

"I can hardly wait," I growled. "Now shove off. Don't you have some secret cave you can disappear into?"

"Caves aren't my style."

"Whatever."

"Really, you should get to know me better than you do. It would make destroying you more pleasurable."

"You know what?" I said, teetering on losing it. "I don't have time for this."

"No? Well, if that be the case, and seeing as you are in a rush, I have a proposition for you."

"Another one? Didn't you do enough damage with the first threat?"

Silivus smiled. The jerk was really enjoying himself.

"The Princess is almost spent. Siphoning her magic has been—" He paused and licked his lips. "Gratifying."

Yep, that did it. He had officially pushed me over the edge. I swung out to deck him good and hard, but my fist punched through thin air. Silivus's image shimmered as he laughed.

"You thought I'd come to you in person? You poor, naïve child."

"What do you want from me?" I shouted.

"I want you to die."

"I thought you said you would rather make me suffer."

"You have been. Look at yourself. You've wasted away to less than human. Your race is dying, and there is nothing you can do about it." Silivus was almost gleeful.

"And what about your proposition? You want me to walk away from my quest?"

"That is an option, but no. I want you to die."

"Why?"

"Because you've irked me, Ian Quicksilver, and I don't like to be irked. I want your world and you keep getting in the way."

"Too bad. You can't have Bankhir. Or Garfel, for that matter," I said. As I watched him glare at me, I could feel waves of tainted Deep Magic waft off of him. He took all that was good about magic and warped it. The feel of it washed over me like an oil slick. My energy sapped, and I felt weak right down to the bone. As much as I wanted to deck the guy, it was a good thing he wasn't there in person to blast me with full-strength evil.

"Look at me, Quicksilver."

I didn't want to, but I could feel his dark magic creep up my arms, into my face, and force my eyes to focus on him. The magician was powerful beyond my worst nightmare. His black eyes seemed to absorb my soul.

"Your quest is over. Your father, the King, has nothing left. No magic, no strength, and no kingdom. You have nothing left to fight for."

"Nothing?" He leeched good sense right out of me. I couldn't think.

"Nothing," he whispered. "Die, Quicksilver. Die and put an end to your father's suffering."

Yeah. I could die.

My brain shorted out. I didn't want to die! I blinked and blotted out Silivus's image for a brief second. I wanted to fight. Fight for my father, for Corbin, and . . . fight for Ari.

In an instant, the air cleared and the creepy oil-slick magic Silivus emanated washed away. My head cleared and suddenly I knew why he was here.

"Yeah. I could die," I said. "Because you know that my death would break my father. And with a broken king, you could rule without a bloody battle. The planets can't exist alone, one without the other. You . . ." I pointed a finger at him and stood straighter, feeling more like the prince I was born to be. "You stole the magic. You were the one who started the war between Bankhir and Garfel. You were going to let them destroy each other until . . ."

My brain sped into hyperdrive as I recalled what my father had said: *after the battle, the ground beneath him trembled.* The dawn of realization made me laugh out loud even though there was nothing remotely funny about it.

"Until you realized that Bankhir and Garfel can't survive without the Warriors or the Magic Keepers. You were forced to save our planets or risk losing your lifetime supply of Deep Magic," I said, triumphant.

"Took you long enough," Silivus sneered. "And to think that Warriors are supposed to be smart."

"And the spell you cast?"

"If you insist," he sighed, bored. "The spell was cast to weaken them. It was a tricky bit of magic with one annoying stipulation. It took time to reduce them to nothing. I had to give them sixteen years for them to dwindle. My patience has paid off."

"No, it was just enough time for me to find Arianna . . ."

"Or so you thought. The Princess will never know who she is and she'll never be able to fully control her power. I cursed you to fail."

"But I haven't. I reclaimed Bob and my sword."

"And yet the spell remains unbroken. Soon Bankhir and Garfel will be mine, and I will rule the galaxy."

"Not so fast. Three weeks remain. Your spell will not hold up to ancient magic."

"Ancient magic," Silivus snorted. "The unification of Deep Magic and Warrior Magic will never happen. No Warrior has ever loved a Magic Keeper. They are too opposite, too different, which is why the ancient magic is a mere myth."

"A myth that has you scared, because if I succeed, I will be stronger than you."

"I do not fear you, Quicksilver. I have had nearly sixteen years of sapping your worlds of glorious power and will continue to siphon the very heart out of your people. I will be unstoppable."

"But why drain them? Without magic, the worlds will be destroyed."

"Why not? They were strong, and I was weak. Now I am the strong one and they are nothing. It's not rocket science, boy," Silivus sneered. "I only need them alive to siphon magic. They don't need to function."

Angry heat scorched my insides. "Not while I am still breathing," I growled.

"Exactly," Silivus said. "Which is why I am giving you the option to die."

"You could ask me to quit," I said.

"You and I both know that'll never happen. Though I hardly think you will want dear, sweet Arianna now. She is only a husk of what she once was."

"I don't care."

"Glad to hear it," he said. "Which leaves me with one alternative: ordering your death. Last chance. Would you prefer to die first? Or would you like me to order the men I've hired to kill Corbin and the Princess while you watch? Your choice."

"Why not come after me yourself, Silivus," I challenged. "You and me, right here, right now."

"Because I'm not stupid," he said. "Even diminished as you are, you are still a Warrior with your own brand of magic. Magicians can't use magic to kill, and you are bred to do just that. I'd rather pay to have other men die in my place as they whittle you down to the bone. I even picked a particularly demented race of soldiers, just for you. They seem to prefer to peel the flesh off you while you live, before bleeding you to a painful death."

I already knew I had an attitude, but my sarcasm only escalated with Silivus's foul words. He made my teeth stand on edge.

"Coward!"

"Your words do not anger me," he said. "But I've grown

tired of your whining. Tell me, what is your stance on dying today?"

"I will not die, and if you harm one hair on Arianna's head, I will hunt you down and destroy you," I said.

"So," he said, grinning like Christmas came early. "That's a no?"

"It's a *beutchar* no," I snarled, swearing the worst Bankhirian word I knew.

"As you wish, Your Highness." Silivus snapped his fingers and disappeared as a horrified scream from Corbin ripped across the valley. Marvin ran out of the house with the mangy cat in tow.

"That didn't sound good," he said. "What's going on?"

"It's the beginning of our end," I said. "You might want to clear out until it's over."

"I don't run away, son. I'm a Marine. You tell me where to fight and I'll fight."

It was commendable, but still I said, "You're pushing eighty, Marvin."

"I can still shoot a gun."

The old vet had spirit. I could work with that.

"Fine. Get your gun and pray you can shoot straight," I said. Marvin saluted and ran back inside with the cat yowling in protest. I turned back to the desert valley, searching for Corbin, cursing that my eyesight was worthless. I strained to find them until I saw Bob running with his head down and his hooves kicking up clods of dirt. To my relief, Corbin was on his back.

"Sire!" he shouted. He pulled Bob up to a skidding halt. "We are being hunted."

"I know," I said. "Silivus sent them. He came to warn me."

"Warn you?" Corbin slid off Bob's back. "That was surprisingly noble of him."

"Not exactly. It was more like a grade school taunt from a bully. He came to let me choose the order of our deaths."

"Who's first?"

"You. Then Ari."

Corbin shook his head. "I can't fight this one alone and without magic. Silivus sent fifteen Horbryn mercenaries. They are the cruelest soldiers in the galaxy, and they don't kill clean."

"Let me guess, they like to peel the flesh off you first?"

"With a curved tool while you are still alive."

"Great. The bad guys sound better and better," I said. "How many can you handle?"

"I've never done more than four at once."

"You're a Warrior of the galaxy! That's not an even cut between the two of us."

"Which is why I say we should run. No offense, Your Highness, but you aren't exactly Warrior quality right now, and I have been without magic for fourteen years."

"And you think running will solve this?"

"It is wise to know when to retreat."

"Then I am not wise," I said, and grabbed the end of Bob's nose to turn his face to me. "Get it where I hid it."

Bob nodded once and ran straight south.

"It?" Corbin said.

"Danthis. I knew Silivus might look for it. I strapped it to one of Bob's old herd mares so it would always be on the move and out of town."

"That was clever."

"You sound surprised."

"I can sound however I like; we are about to die."

"Is it too late to join the party?" Marvin called as he burst out the back with two semiautomatic shotguns in hand and a Colt .45 under his belt. His pockets jingled with ammunition.

"Go inside, old-timer," Corbin said. "This isn't your fight."

"This is my planet." Marvin snapped. "It's my fight now."

Corbin opened his mouth to argue, but I held up my hand and stopped him.

"Let him be, Corbin. In this case we need all the help we can get."

Help.

I was struck with an idea. It was a long shot, but an idea. It took Bob ten minutes to return. We heard him long before we saw him. About fifty head of wild horses thundered around the house and through the yard. They didn't look left or right. With one determined purpose they ran out toward the open desert valley. The ground shook under their hooves as they formed a perfect V-shaped strike force.

"They're going after them?" I asked and Bob nodded. "They'll be killed!"

Corbin rotated slowly on his heel with his head bowed.

"Turn away, Sire. Do not disrespect their sacrifice."

I did as I was told, numb that this was becoming so real. Standing next to Bob was a doe-eyed, caramel-colored mare. I had picked her because she was sweet-tempered and had horse eyes for Bob, who studiously ignored her. She nudged his shoulder and nibbled at his mane while I unstrapped Danthis from her back. The sword was wrapped in a blanket, and try as I might, I could barely lift it.

Oh yeah, I needed help. Loads of it.

I handed Danthis to Corbin and scrambled on top of Bob. It was a whole lot more difficult to do when I was a scrawny shrimp again. Marvin gave me an added push.

"How long until the Horbryn get here?"

"They're on foot, so I'd say about ten minutes out."

"And how long can you hold them off?"

Corbin took a deep breath and thought about it good and hard. "With Marvin picking off the ones on the outside, I'd say I could keep them busy for a good ten minutes. Fifteen minutes tops."

"Can you make it twenty?"

"That's suicide, but I'll try."

That might be good enough. It had to. Bob danced in place, anxious to be off.

"My sword," I said, holding out my hand. Corbin paused, gripping the hilt.

"Where are you going?"

"How much magic would it take to get me back to normal?" I asked, ignoring his question.

"We don't have enough time for that," Corbin said.

"How much?"

"More than your body can handle in one go," Corbin said. He put his hand out on Bob's chest to stop me. "What do you plan to do?"

"What I should have done from the very beginning. Tell Ari the truth."

"And if she can't handle it?"

I ground down on my tongue. I didn't want to think about it. It was the big 'what if?' in this mess where we'd all end up dead. "I don't plan to die today," I said, and held out my hand.

This time, Corbin placed Danthis in my palm.

"Spoken like a true warrior, son," Marvin said. "You'd better be off."

Corbin scanned the valley. Even I didn't need his perfect vision to see the boil of dust and dirt on the horizon to know that the mercenaries were coming.

Corbin gripped my hand over the hilt, securing it to Danthis. When he lifted his face to mine, the pupils of his eyes had turned blood-red.

"What's with the eyes, Corbin?" I said.

"Battlelust," he said. "No Warrior can fight without it. I will hold them off and die honorably if I fail."

"Let's operate on the idea that you won't."

"I will fight. You are my King, and I obey none else," he said, solemnly. "I will follow you to the pits of hell if that is what you ask. This is my oath."

I almost didn't know what to say to that. I wasn't king yet. However, if I pointed that out to him, I had a feeling he'd behead me. Besides, I didn't know how to respond to an oath of fealty.

"I accept your oath," I said, but felt guilty that he swore over his life to me for so little in return. "But, uh, do me a favor, Corbin, and stay alive."

A grim crooked grin cracked on his tanned face. He stepped away from Bob and slapped his hand on his haunches. Bob broke into a run.

"I swear on my horse and my sword, I will live to see you crowned," he called after me, then filled his lungs and let loose with a terrifying war cry. Bob didn't need direction as he ran toward the center of town to Ari's house. Behind us, Corbin drew his sword. The last look I got was of him swinging his weapon in a graceful arc and laughing manically like a madman.

This had to work.

24

In theory, my grand plan of spilling my guts to Ari seemed childishly simple. It was easy as—go in, tell her the truth (hope she didn't freak out), then pray she had enough magic left in her to help me save Corbin's hide. It was a good plan, but it didn't stop my heart from thudding into my throat and my palms from sweating.

Bob trotted up the front walk and deposited me on the doorstep. Once I was there, my hand froze an inch shy of the doorbell, shaking like I had malaria. Bob huffed impatiently and pushed me forward with his nose.

"Would you knock it off?" I said, shoving his face away. "If you had the weight of two planets hanging on your next move, you'd be shaking too."

Bob gave me a horseish shrug and waited impatiently, stamping his hoof on the cement walk.

"Pushy fleabag," I muttered under my breath.

Bob grunted out an 'I heard that' whinny and glared at me. I pressed the doorbell.

When the door opened, a kind-faced older woman, who must have been Ari's adopted mother, answered. She had soft brown hair and a friendly smile, nothing like the monster I had cooked up in my head about her parents.

"Hi," I said, realizing a moment too late that I still had my sword in hand. Not exactly a good first impression. "Is Ari home?"

"Arianna isn't allowed any visitors right now," Mrs.

Hernfeld said, sweetly (to my annoyance). "She isn't feeling well."

"But we're friends, and I'd like to see if she is okay."

"Maybe another time."

She was straight sugar. It grated on my nerves. The door began to close and so did my chances. I walked in, stopping it with my body. There is nothing quite like a heavy wooden door slamming in on my leg to make my day better.

"Right now is the only time I have," I said, forcing the door open. Then, on second thought, I motioned for Bob. He leapt up onto the porch. "Keep an eye on her."

Bob muscled his way forward, pinning Mrs. Hernfeld to the doorjamb with his ears laid back and giving her one of his classic unblinking stares.

"It was . . . uh, nice to meet you," I said, apologetic. "I'll find my own way, thanks." I brushed past her to the stairs and took them two at a time. On the landing, Ari's door was shut. A sickly light shone under it. I walked in, checking my watch. Four minutes down, sixteen left.

What I saw made my stomach twist. Ari was laid out on her bed with her arm hanging limply over the side. A fat needle was shoved into her vein that was connected by tubing to a machine. It slowly pumped glowing bluish-green fluid out of her. My mind revolted.

Kicking the door shut, I tossed Danthis to the floor next to the bed and fell to my knees. There had to be a switch or something to turn the thing off—but there was only a blank panel. No cord connected the thing to an electrical outlet, which meant the machine was running on Ari juice. I'd have to pull out the needle.

Up to this point, I had no clue if I had issues with needles like some people did. I didn't have the time to think about it. I peeled off the medical tape, exposing her arm that was bruised black and blue, and in one yank tore out the needle. She didn't bleed. Regardless, I gently pressed some gauze I found on her bedside table into the hole and folded her arm over it. The motion woke her up.

"Is it finished?" she said, her voice cracking weakly.

"No. I stopped the machine. You don't have to do this anymore."

"Why?" Ari turned to look at me. My heart wrenched in my chest. Her eyes had turned pale and her skin was pasty white. Even her hair had streaks of gray and white in it. Only the smooth planes of her face gave any clue that she was young. It took her a long time to focus on my face.

"Ian?"

"Hey," I said, forcing a smile. "Long time no see."

"You look different," she said. She rolled to her side and reached out to trace her finger along my cheek. "More grown up."

I wasn't sure what she meant by that. Hopefully, that was a good thing. Not that I put too much thought into it, seeing as I was distracted by her touch. Ari traced the tip of her finger down my neck and into the opening of my jacket.

"You have scars," she said, confused. "You never used to have those."

Crud. In just a second, she was going to remember who I'd gotten them from. Hurriedly, I zipped my jacket closed.

"I did that." Ari's eyes got wide and she sat up. "I did that to you!"

"No, Ari, it's okay. I'm fine, see?" I took her hand and put it back on my cheek.

The second she touched my skin she ripped her hand away. "Get out!" She could barely shout, but she didn't need to. The hurt in her eyes said plenty. I checked my watch. Six minutes down, fourteen to go. I didn't have time to be sensitive.

"Sorry, Ari, but I'm not leaving."

I expected her to put up a fight. I half wanted her to, but her shoulders slumped in defeat. "Why are you doing this to me? Why are you hurting me?"

Well, this was it. It was go time, last minute, do or die. I took a deep breath and decided it was high time I just went for it.

"I am not the one hurting you, Ari. Silivus is the one hurting you, and I'm not going to take it anymore."

"Silivus?"

"Yes, Silivus. You know him as Mr. Churchill, but to me he is the magician named Silivus."

It took about a second and she said, "A magician? You're crazy."

"It'd be easier if I was," I said. "Just hear me out and I'll explain everything, okay?"

"Why should I?"

"Because you deserve to know who you are."

"Who I am?" she huffed out a weak laugh. "I am a freak, that's what I am. I am a freak who hurts people."

"No, you're special," I said. Ari finally looked at me, and in her milk-white eyes was a faint flicker of green.

"How?"

"You're going to think I'm crazy," I said, and then

amended it with, "or crazier than you already do, but I'm not human. And neither are you. We were sent here nearly sixteen years ago by a magician called Silivus."

"I wasn't sent anywhere. I was born in Reno."

I shook my head. "You were born on Garfel."

"But what about my parents? I wasn't adopted."

"I hate to sound harsh, but you are nothing like your parents. I just met your mom, and trust me, you are not her kid." I took a deep breath and said a prayer. "You are the Princess of Garfel."

"The who of what?" Ari said incredulously.

Time to jump down the rabbit hole. "Princess of Garfel. Garfel is the sister planet to Bankhir, which is the planet I am from."

Ari fixed me with a disbelieving blank stare. "Okay, now you're just making this up."

"Trust me, reality is stranger than fiction in this case."

"So, if I am the Princess, then who are you? Prince of the Bank? And I bet we are here to rule Earth together," Ari said, mocking me.

"Bankhir," I corrected. "And yes, I am the Prince."

Ari shook her head slowly, half dazed, with her mouth hanging open. "You're nuts."

"I don't care what you think about me," I said. "You can travel by magic, read minds, and communicate by text through your skin using your thoughts. And you think I am nuts? Have you ever sat down and wondered why there aren't more people out there like you in this world? Has it crossed your mind, at all?"

Ari's eyes narrowed. "That's different. What I have is a disease."

"That's a load of bull," I snapped. "You don't have anything out of the ordinary where we come from. Your planet, Garfel, it is teeming with magic, and all they do is use it and make lives better."

"No, I hurt people."

"You only hurt people because humans are weak. They have heart and spirit, but they can't handle magic. They aren't built for it like you and I are," I said, fighting the urge to check my watch again. "What you have is real. You were meant for something bigger than this, Ari. Your people need you."

"My people?" Ari said, rubbing wearily at her forehead. "Let's suspend reality for like a minute and say I believe you. If my people need me so much, then why am I here?"

I heaved out a heavy sigh. This was the tricky part.

"We are here because our planets are falling apart and our people are dying," I said, editing out as much as I dared under the circumstances. If we survived, I'd tell her the particulars later. "We were given sixteen years to find each other and return to save them."

"How are we going to do that?"

"Well," I said, stalling even though I didn't have the time. "It's kind of a long story."

"At this point I could deal with bullet points and be fine. It's not like I am going to believe you anyway."

Here goes.

"Our planets have been at war for a long time. It was agreed that if one kid was given from each planet to grow up away from the fighting and . . . uh, you know . . . 'find' each other, then we could make the fighting end."

"What do you mean by 'find,' exactly?" Ari said.

"Uh, you know, sort of like fall . . . for each other?"

"*What*?!"

Yeah, that didn't go over so well. Ari leapt off her bed and escaped across her room to get away from me.

"This is insane. You do realize that, right?"

Good thing I left out the part where we had to get married.

"Yes, I realize it's insane, but you don't understand what this means, for both of us. It means that our people can finally find peace. They can't live without each other," I said, and snapped my fingers when a brilliant idea popped into my head. "Remember when you first met me? What did I look like?"

"I don't know, just a regular kid. Why?"

"I was five inches shorter than you and barely weighed a hundred pounds."

"Okay. So?"

"Well, the more you got to know me, you started to notice that I was changing."

"You said it was just a growth spurt."

"Yeah, I had a massive growth spurt that had me shoot up to six-foot-five practically overnight. Don't you think that was a little odd?"

"Sure, it was weird."

"That is why our people need peace. Can't you see it? Bankhir and Garfel orbit each other, they need each other, because Garfel puts out the magic and Bankhir grows on it."

"So you *did* only use me for my magic," Ari said. "And here I thought Churchill was being the jerk."

Gah! I could have pulled my hair out. She wasn't getting it!

"No, well . . . and yes too," I fumbled in frustration. "Bankhirians are warriors; we live to protect Garfelians and the galaxy, and the Garfelians supply us with magic so we can do our job. You see? We need each other."

"Then why are we fighting?"

Finally, she was asking the right questions! I checked my watch and found that I didn't have the time to answer them. Telling her that Silivus started everything, duped our parents, and drained the magic from our worlds would take more time than I had available.

"Look, our lives are on the line here," I said, frustrated. "I need to know, is there any way you could believe me? Even a little? In fact, if you could like me a little too, that would really speed things up for me. I'm not talking right away or anything, but in the near future. It's kind of . . . no, it's a *really* big deal."

"I've always liked you, Ian. You are the only real friend I have."

Even when our lives depended on it, I was still stuck in the Friend Zone. Infuriating? That was an understatement. Despite that, three weeks of misery nearly exploded inside of me. I was on a time crunch and I was gearing up for a fight.

"Then how could you leave me like that? You just chucked me off like I meant nothing!"

"I had to," Ari's voice cracked. She swallowed hard to fight back tears. "I hurt you."

"Yeah, you did," I said, waspish. "But you could have stuck around."

"I—I couldn't. I couldn't stand to see you in pain like that and know that I caused it."

"But you didn't cause this. Churchill did. I was there. I watched him force you to use your magic. He made you to lose control. He wanted you to suffer," I said, shouting angrily. It was cruel, but I wanted Ari to fight back.

"I was the one that lost control," she said, half defeated.

"You know what it feels like to lose control," I said. "You can feel it build up inside of you."

Defeat changed slowly to barely recognizable conviction. There was a small glimmer of hope in her—so faint I could barely feel it. "I didn't have build up that day. I wasn't even wearing gloves."

"Exactly," I said. "So, in other words, I could have been there for you through all the hell Silivus put us through, but you wouldn't let me! Instead you just walked out on me and let me take it alone."

Ari's cheeks flushed a dull pink. Her milky white eyes flashed a dark green. "I was there," she said, her voice firm. Now she was back to fighting, but to me it felt like winning. "I was there every day from the second you got home from the hospital. I was there."

For a second, I thought my eyes were tricking me. A streak of gray hair disappeared and turned glossy black. Not only that, but her eyes, after a few blinks, were darkening to a deeper shade of green.

"You were there," I said. "Behind the shed."

Ari nodded. "Churchill would drain me, and most days I had only enough magic to travel down the block, but I was there. I couldn't stay away."

All the anger drained out of me. She had been there. I knew it! My lungs unclogged and my airways had free passage. "I didn't want you to stay away, Ari," I said.

This time it was unmistakable; color flooded into her face. Normal, healthy color. Here I thought it was just a one-way thing for me, when all along I was helping Ari strengthen her magic. No wonder our worlds were falling apart. The Magic Keepers needed the Warriors just as much as the Warriors needed the Magic Keepers. Magic couldn't thrive without either of us. Ari needed me. Which gave me an idea. It was a long shot, because I was pretty sure she was going to shut me down. However, prospective death made me plunge forward anyway.

"Look, I want you to not think about what I just told you for a minute," I said.

"How can I not? You basically told me I am an alien."

"Instead of focusing on that, think more about why we are here."

"You said we had to find each other."

My heart rate spiked. "And we did. Except it's always been different for me," I said, scrubbing nervously at my burning ears. "Remember the night I told you it was your magic that made me . . . you know," I stalled, sweating. "Uh, try and kiss you?"

"You said my magic made you irrational and do things you wouldn't normally do."

"Right," I said, inwardly cursing my cowardice. "I lied."

It took her about two seconds to process. "Oh no, Ian. I told you being with me wasn't a good idea. Look what being friends with me did to you." She stalked over and pulled down the neck of my shirt to uncover the scars snaking over my collarbone and shoulder. "I did that to you."

"I haven't forgotten," I said brushing her hand away. "And I don't care. I know you don't believe me, and soon it won't matter," I said. It all rested on me now. There was a reason I grew, and it wasn't all about the magic. It wasn't until I could see Ari for who she was—not a quest, but the girl who stole my heart—that I became the Warrior I was meant to be. She was the one that made me strong.

I was a love-soaked sap, baby. Bring it on!

"Ari, will you do something for me? I swear I won't bother you ever again." Literally, I couldn't; I'd be dead soon anyway.

"Like what?"

"I want you to forget everything that happened," I said stepping closer to her with my sword between us. "Forget about your magic. Forget what I told you about who you are. All of it. We're just two normal people, going to a normal high school."

"But I'm not normal," Ari said. "I will never be normal."

"No, you're not. You've always been more to me," I said, hoping beyond hope that she got my meaning, because I didn't think I could spell it out for her. Already my courage was running out.

"Ian?" she said, bemused and staring at me half-curious. "Are you falling in love with me?"

I wasn't sure if the idea grossed her out. In fact, I couldn't tell what she was thinking at all. Unfortunately, she had this lost look on her face, which made it hard to judge what she was feeling. But, thank the stars, she asked the right question, even though I was sure she had no clue why.

"Yes." I said it, and I couldn't believe my own ears.

"You?" she said, pointing to me in a daze. Then she pointed back and forth between the two of us. "You love me?"

"Yes."

"Are you sure?"

"Yep."

"Oh my go—"

She never got to finish. Out of her body came a blast of Deep Magic that collided into me in a spiral of rich blue-green. It filled me up better than a meal of meat and potatoes. I watched as muscle grew under my skin, the floor traveled farther away, and I got pecs. Nice. What was better than that was that my arms quadrupled in size, and I didn't stop until every inch of me was 100 percent Warrior. Then, if that wasn't enough, silvery tendrils of Warrior Magic snaked around my wrists and fingers.

Ari's mouth hung open so wide I could see her tonsils.

"Do you believe me now?" I said with a grin. Hooking my finger on the neck band of my shirt, I loosened my collar that was strangling around my new, thicker neck. The fabric gave way easily, and my fingers were wreathed in wisps of silvery smoke. My Warrior Magic was finally waking up.

"I think I believe you," Ari nodded. Her voice was a faint squeak.

"Thank you!" I said. In one lunge forward, I picked her up and hugged her. Relief was nothing close to what I felt as she tried to get her arms around my chest. My arms glowed bright silver as my magic seeped into Ari's bony frame and filled her in. When I let go of her, color drained back into her face and her eyes were a brilliant emerald green once again. Her grip definitely had some strength behind it.

"Well, I gotta go," I said.

"What? Why? You came here just to tell me a load of . . . stuff, I guess, and now you're going to run off?"

"Uh, yeah," I said. "About that—Silivus is doing this 'I want to take over the galaxy' thing with our planets and he's getting impatient about it. He sent some mercenaries to kill me. They're going to kill Corbin, and you too, if I don't hurry up."

"Corbin is a part of this?"

"Well, as you noticed, we look a lot alike, but yeah, he's not human either."

"Oh my gosh, is there anyone I know that isn't an alien?"

"Really, Ari, it's just us, I swear. Well, except for the alien assassins coming to kill us."

"And what am I supposed to do? Just sit here and wait to be killed?"

I didn't have time to argue. Bob whinnied shrilly. In two strides I was at the door. Down on the landing, Bob had the front half of his body in the house.

"What's happening, Bob?"

Bob's ears pricked forward in the direction of the vet clinic and he grunted irritably. He could hear something. I shut the door and ran to the window to look out toward the clinic. It was like my eyes went into telescope mode and zeroed in on a half circle of bad guys with swords drawn walking in unison as they closed in on Corbin and Marvin. It was seriously cool (the zoomed-in eyesight, not the bad guys).

Corbin kept his eyes on the threat, but I could hear him as if he were in Ari's room with me.

"Kid," he said. "If there is any chance you can hear me,

now is the time to get your Warrior boots on and get down here."

"You think he heard you?" Marvin said.

"If anyone has got the guts to do what he left to do, it's Ian. He'll hear me."

"I'm on my way," I said.

Corbin turned with a smirk and got a firmer grip on his sword. "Good work, Highness."

I slammed the window shut and headed for the door. "Really, I've got to go. If I survive, I'll be back, and you can ask me all the questions you want."

"Hold up," Ari said, grabbing my arm. "You're serious. There are a bunch of guys out there that are going to kill us?"

"How many times do I have to say it?" I said.

"Once was plenty, but if they're after me too, then I want to come."

"Not a chance," I barked. "Not with trained killers out there."

Ari nearly howled in frustration. "You are such a meat-head! I want in. If you fight, I fight with you."

Ah man! She had to lay the loyalty stuff on me. It got me every time and made my gut run cartwheels. I reached out and ran my fingers though her hair, not hesitating because, let's face it, I was probably going to die anyway.

"You're sure you want to come?" I said, and yes, I was considering it. She could ask for anything and I'd probably cave. "There will be a lot of blood and guts."

"I'm coming," she said stubbornly.

"Fine," I said. I grabbed her hand and bolted out into the hall and down the stairs. "Time to go, Bob."

Bob finally let the terrified Mrs. Hernfeld go with a satisfied grunt that he had done his job. I blew by her without a word and ran out the front door with Bob two steps behind us.

"Bye, Mom!" Ari called over her shoulder. "I'll be back later after we knock off some bad guys!"

25

Bob danced impatiently on the front lawn. He kept grumbling at me to hurry it up. I put my hand on his neck to calm him down.

"Make sure you hold on with your legs," I said to Ari. I turned her around, grabbed her at the waist, and tossed her up onto Bob's back. Ari got out a short "ha!" before I vaulted over Bob's haunches and kicked him into a run. Bob was in a bigger rush than normal, and Ari slammed into my chest. I had to hold her tight around the waist so she didn't fall off.

"What happened to holding on?" I said over the wind whistling in my ears.

"Well, Bob isn't exactly running at normal horse speed, now is he?"

He wasn't. Houses rushed by in a blur and Bob sailed over a car in the intersection to avoid collision. We had one more turn and then it was three blocks to the edge of town. When the clinic came into view, I could see the mercenaries clearly, as if they were standing an inch away from me. They seemed to know who I was. Instead of moving in to strike, they stopped, swords up in salute before the slaughter.

Bob skidded to a halt in a plume of desert dust. I jumped off and left Ari on his back. I may have been a sap to agree to bring her along, but I wasn't stupid.

"Bob, let her off your back and I'll turn you into glue," I said, ignoring Ari's protests. Bob nodded. I scratched him quickly under the chin. "You're a good horse," I whispered. "The second this battle goes sour, I want you to get Ari out of here. Run her to safety, got it?"

Bob struggled with the command. I could tell because his face turned stony like a regular horse. It took a few seconds, but he nodded again. I patted him on the nose and turned away to face death. Swinging Danthis in my hand, I gripped the gilded hilt until the weight of the sword felt comfortable.

"I thought you were going to hold them off?" I said, stopping at Corbin's side.

"I think they were waiting for the main attraction to show," Corbin said. "It's been a stare-down ever since. What took so long, anyway?"

"I had a lot to explain."

"Under the circumstances, son," Marvin said. "You could have stuck with 'I love you' and called it good."

Great, *now* I was getting courting advice.

The Horbryn soldiers stood like statues with their leather armor frozen in place and gray capes flapping in the wind. There were eleven of the original fifteen left, thanks to Bob's wild herd. And, to my satisfaction, most of them looked a little worse for wear. They didn't move, like they were waiting for the final command.

"Child of Bankhir," a soldier in the middle shouted. "Will you surrender to us?"

"Suck maggots, magician's puppet," I shouted back.

"You know, a straight 'no' would work," Corbin said out the corner of his mouth. "I wouldn't rile these guys up."

"Sorry."

"Today, you will meet Death," the soldier bellowed. The Horbryn rushed forward as one.

"Remember," Corbin said, bringing his sword up. "Strike hard, and if you go for the heart, strike twice!"

"Why twice?" Marvin said. He fitted his shotgun to his shoulder and aimed.

"Two hearts, old timer. Make those bullets count!"

There comes a moment in every Warrior's life where their training is put to the test. In my case, I had no training. I had a dozen efficient assassins running at me, ready to flay me into warrior steaks. The logical thing to do would be to turn tail and run.

And I did turn, sort of. I turned to glance back at Ari, who was gripping Bob's mane with all her might. Time stopped and clogged for a second. I couldn't help thinking that if I had to do it all again, I would do it, even the dying part. It lit a fire in me that spread through every inch of my body and turned my vision flaming red.

Battlelust.

A blast from Marvin's shotgun sped things up to high speed. Yelling at the top of my lungs, I spun around and swung Danthis with two hands. It was a good thing I did. Two halves of the soldier I sliced through fell to the ground. His companion leapt over the pieces with his sword over his head.

I barely had time to get Danthis up to block the bone-shattering blow. I pushed him off me, but not before ducking as another Horbryn struck from the side with a double-bladed ax. It was all I could do to defend myself as a third assailant swung in with a spear. I kept them at bay for another round of strikes. It became apparent that they weren't striking to kill, but to maim. They preferred slow death. Sick.

By shifting to my left, I opened up my right side to the spear. I lurched forward and parried a swipe at my chest from the ax. By then I could feel they had a rhythm. If I sprang forward at the middle man with the sword, I could offset the other two. It was suicide, but I lunged forward and buried my elbow into the swordsman's jaw. At the same time, the spearman overcorrected and jabbed the ax-man under the chin, making a clean entry into the skull. That was one down and two to go. With the spearman busy removing his weapon from his companion's head, I swung down with Danthis and chopped off his arm.

Even injured, the Horbryn stayed eerily silent. Which was a good thing. The hiss of metal swinging in the cold air was my only warning to duck. The angered swordsman screamed and swung wildly into his companion, severing his head completely. I plunged Danthis into his chest before he could recover and strike again. He stumbled, but laid into my face with the butt of his sword. Stars danced in my vision.

This double-heart thing was a beast. I readjusted my jaw and shook my head to stop the spinning. Half dazed, I squinted through blurred eyes as the Horbryn soldier swung for the kill.

I didn't have time to deflect.

BOOM!

"No time for dillydallying, son," Marvin yelled as he popped out an empty shell from his shotgun. The assassin stumbled backward and fell to the ground with a hole in his second heart. The old man's white hair was flying wild as he swung his empty shotgun into the head of another soldier. Corbin was taking on five at once and holding his own. He was amazing. I'd never seen anything like it as he smoothly went from striking to parrying in rapid fast-forward. Silvery Warrior Magic swirled around his arms, making his blade whistle in a blur.

I needed to get back into the fray. I retrieved Danthis out of the swordsman's chest and ran to meet two assassins who were bearing down on Marvin. I went in for the first strike and an amazing thing happened. Bluish mist spiraled down my arms and lit up my blade. Corbin was practically swimming in the stuff, and he bayed like a hound when he saw it. When Deep Magic mixed with the weaker Warrior Magic pouring out of our arms, we ignited in a fury of silver and bluish-green. It was intoxicating.

Nice touch, Ari. She kept it regulated at a low stream, which meant that Corbin easily outstripped their fastest assassin and made it look childishly easy. I thrust in through one Horbryn heart and Marvin shot out the other, and we were able to make short work of what was left over from Corbin. I felt invincible. Corbin had his battle in hand, and with a little help from Marvin and me, we broke into the assassin's tight fighting system, obliterating them. It didn't take long for the battle to end.

When we were done, the tendrils of Deep Magic retreated and I bent double, exhausted. Marvin's hands were shaking as he kicked away a pile of empty shotgun shells.

"Either I'm getting old or I am horribly out of shape," Corbin groaned. He rubbed at his lower back and hefted his sword over his shoulder. His spine cracked as he stretched.

"If that was out of shape, then I'd like to see what you're like at fully fit," I huffed. "You were amazing."

"Thanks, kid, but I am out of practice. Chasing after you for fourteen years made me rusty."

"Ah, it felt good. I like a fight when the lines are black and white. No guesswork with the enemy," Marvin said, and kicked the foot of one of the fallen. "How many of these guys were after you?"

"Fifteen," Corbin said. "The wild horses took out three. The other half of the herd survived and scattered."

"I counted eleven when I got here. What happened to the last . . . ?"

Ari screamed. We spun in unison to see her being ripped off the back of Bob, who reared in agony. The last Horbryn soldier had buried a dagger in the horse's haunches just before grabbing her. Bob tried to kick out, but he fell thrashing to the ground and couldn't get back up again.

"Marvin, get Bob," Corbin shouted as I ran for Ari.

Before, fighting against my attackers, I was in control. Even when in full battle-fury mode, I had control of my faculties. Now I was anything but cool, and my vision swam in red.

The Horbryn pulled Ari up by the throat, using her as a shield as I swung in for the first attack. I barely stopped Danthis in time to avoid slicing Ari's neck. I pulled away, but kept the sword up and at the ready.

"Let her go," I said.

"Or what? You'll kill me? This isn't a trade, Warrior. I was sent to kill or be killed."

"Then be killed," Corbin said, joining me at my side. "There are two of us against one of you."

"Too bad. It's the girl I want. The magician promised her to me, and I am here to collect. Besides, I revel in slowly defiling my victims," he said, nastier than an oil slick as he pressed his cheek into Ari's. "Let us go, and I'll assure you she will die cleanly. If not, one nick with my hook and she'll bleed out in a mess. Though, I have to admit, I will miss playing with her. She's such a pretty little thing."

The freak had a dented metal hook pressed on Ari's neck, right at the jugular. I leaped forward, but when the tip of the hook drew blood, I backed off.

"Careful," he taunted. "It won't take much. A hole in the jugular makes such a scene."

With great effort, I lowered Danthis. "What do you propose? You want to kill her, and we won't let you."

"I might let her live," the Horbryn smirked, clearly lying. "Either way, you'll back off. I've got the girl, and if you attack, she dies with me."

"Well," Corbin said, putting his sword away at his side. "It looks like we aren't getting anywhere with this, so maybe we should let you get on with it."

Was he out of his mind? An assassin had Ari by the throat and Corbin was chilling at my side, like nothing life-threatening was going down at all.

"No, we aren't going to let him get on with anything," I said. "What is wrong with you?"

"I've got plans to head north," Corbin said, almost flippant. "I hear the aurora borealis this time of year is pretty spectacular."

He flashed me a knowing grin.

It was embarrassing, but I got it after a minute. My head snapped back around to Ari, who was gulping back tears. "Lose it, Ari," I said. I had Danthis up again and ready to rush forward. "Lose control!"

Ari caught on faster than I did. She gripped the Horbryn's arm, scrunching her face in concentration. She was still too pale, and her hair was still gray, but her eyes had nearly reclaimed all their bright green color. Arcs of electricity and Deep Magic crackled down her arm and into her hands, and she dug her fingernails into the Horbryn's flesh. The air charged around us as she practically zapped the skin off him. The assassin yelled out in pain and his arms flew off Ari. Before he could recover, I switched my blade from front to back and slammed the hilt into his face, knocking him clean out. Not pausing, I swung Danthis back around in a deadly arc to finish him off—when Corbin grabbed my arm and stopped me.

"That is enough," he said.

"But . . ."

"Take a deep breath and let it pass."

I didn't know what got into him. Let what pass? All I wanted to do was lop this guy's head off.

Wait a sec. Listening to my own thoughts snapped me out of the fog. I didn't kill defenseless people, even if he was an assassin. The red in my vision cleared and I gasped. Danthis dropped out of my hand. "What have I done?"

Corbin put his arm around my neck. He buried my face in his thick shoulder so I couldn't look back at the carnage I had helped create. Instantly, I felt ill; my hands shook. I broke out in a cold sweat that made my muscles tense and my whole body shudder.

"The first time is always the worst, Highness," he said.

"Will I forget?"

"No," he said gently. "But you must learn when to stop."

My stomach churned so badly I wanted to throw up.

However, if I was struggling, I was sure Ari was in full-blown shock. I pushed away from Corbin and turned to her, keeping my eyes on her and nothing else. The cold air was ripe with death, the metallic smell of spilt blood and release of bowels.

Red marks streaked down Ari's cheeks where her fingers had dug into her face. She stared, unblinking. Every so often she would gasp as if she was trying to cry and couldn't. I held my hand out to her, but she flinched away like she expected me to strike her.

"It's okay," I said, putting my hands up where she could see them. "I'm not going to hurt you."

"Your eyes," she said. "They went red. You looked at me and I could see them turn red!"

"Yeah. Apparently the Warrior body comes with a funky eye color," I said. "I'm not human, remember? We talked about this."

"I know, but you didn't tell me you had a crazy kill switch."

"That was unexpected," I said. "I didn't know either."

Ari forced herself to take in a breath and exhale it. "I—I think I'm going to be sick."

"Hey, you volunteered to come," I said, trying to kid around to calm my own upset stomach. "Last I checked, vomiting wasn't allowed on the battlefield."

I probably should have kept to sympathy and left the sense of humor for another time. Ari swayed. I caught her before she fell.

"Careful," I said, brushing her hair out of her face. "It'll be okay. Come on, breathe, Ari. It's over. I promise you don't have to come with me to another battle. You don't have to see me fight ever again, I swear it."

Ari's arms came up and wrapped around my neck. It took a minute of her hanging on to me for her to breathe normally again. She was thin enough that I could have wound my arms twice around her waist, but I opted to stroke my fingers through her hair instead. The streaks of gray were disappearing. There was something about the blue-black sheen to it I found fascinating all of a sudden.

"I don't care what you swear," Ari said against my neck. "You're alive, and that is all that matters."

Now that felt pretty darn good. I turned to Corbin, who was grinning and nodding like everything was going to be okay. Still clinging to her, my eyes fell on Bob. Marvin was at his head soothing him. When he caught my gaze, he gave me a thumbs-up and a wan smile. Bob was going to be okay. When Ari finally let go of me, the color in her face had returned to its usual olive tone.

"Still need a barf bag?" I said.

Ari tried to laugh. "I'll be fine."

"Your Highness," Corbin interrupted. "The Horbryn psycho is coming around."

"You want to wait here?" I said to Ari. "Or back at the house? It's your call."

Ari took my hand and interlaced her fingers in mine. "You know, I think I want to stay with you," she said. "That is, if you don't do the funky eye thing again. It creeps me out."

"Okay. No red eye," I said. "I think I can handle that."

Frankly, I didn't think I could go back into battlelust if I tried with Ari hanging on to me. My gut was doing too many loops with the roller coaster.

Corbin stood over the Horbryn with his sword and mine leveled at his throat. He leaned forward, resting his foot heavily on the assassin's chest. There was a perfect C-shaped scar on his upper lip I hadn't noticed before. His blond hair was matted to his sweaty forehead and dirt from the Nevada desert caked to his neck and arms.

"Wake up, soldier," Corbin barked.

The assassin jolted awake and struggled to get out from under Corbin. "I will not die dishonorably," he spat. "Give me my sword and let me fight."

"We aren't going to kill you," I said.

"We aren't? I kind of liked the idea of giving him his sword back and taking this punk down one-on-one," Corbin said. "I need the practice."

"Another time," I said, and bent closer over the assassin. "You said you were sent to kill or be killed. Am I right?"

"That is my creed. I swore it with a blood oath."

"Yeah, well, that's a load of blah-blah-blah," I said, getting an idea. "So I think I'll send you back to the slimeball magician and let you duke it out with him."

"No!" the Horbryn shrieked. "You filthy Bankhir liar! Warriors were bred to kill. Now, kill me!"

"Tough break," I said. "And while you're there, give Silivus a message for me. You tell him that if he wants Bankhir and Garfel, he'll have to go through me. If that head case has any honor in him at all, tell him to bring it on, because he's going down. Nobody takes my planet without a fight."

The Horbryn assassin laughed. "You talk like a child. The Great Magician will burn you. He will burn the very heart out of you. He will . . ."

"Can I shut him up now?" Corbin asked as the Horbryn blathered on and on about how great Silivus was.

"Be my guest."

"Wait," Ari said. "I thought you said you weren't going to kill him."

"I'm not. You are going to send him to Silivus, postage-stamped with his dead buddies," Corbin said to Ari.

"I can't do that! I'd end up killing him. Besides, I have no idea where to send him."

"It's easy. You just need to calculate how many will be traveling, create a bridge in your mind, and send them there. It's simple, really."

"You've traveled by magic?" Ari said, dumbstruck.

"Erm . . . no. Not exactly," Corbin said. "I think the last Warrior to travel by Deep Magic was my great-uncle. He was a bit senile in the end, but he clued me in on the logistics."

"I don't think that's helpful, Corbin," I said.

"No time like the present to try it out," Corbin said, taking Ari's hand and placing it on the Horbryn's arm. "I'll give you the image of where to send them. You concentrate on controlling where they go."

"What will happen to him if I can't get it right?" Ari said nervously.

"Does it matter?" Corbin said. "Don't take pity on the Horbryn. They're the scum of the galaxy."

Ari closed her eyes, blocking out the Horbryn who was staring murderously at her. "Fine. Where am I sending him?"

"I'll show you." Corbin pressed his finger and thumb into the base of Ari's head, just as he had done with me when he showed me our home.

"Okay, I've got it," she said and stood up. "He's ready to go."

"Well," I said to the Horbryn, who was red in the face

and thrashing. "So long! And don't forget the message."

"Too bad I won't be there to see it," Corbin chuckled dryly. "Silivus is going to pitch a fit!"

"See you later," Ari said. She swiped her glowing hand through the air and the Horbryn and his dead kin disappeared. All of them, leaving only the imprint of their blood in the frosty, dry desert.

26

Over the next three days, there was a break in the cold snap that hung over the desert. Bob was healing well, though his backside was stitched up and wrapped in a big fat bandage. He wasn't happy about his injury. He would swing his head around and glare at it, as if the white gauze offended him personally.

Out in the barn, I brushed Bob down on Thursday afternoon, alone. Ari had asked me to give her time to process everything I threw at her. The wait was killing me. I wondered how far I could take it down to the wire before I asked Ari out or made a formal courtship offer. Neither option seemed likely to get a favorable answer.

"It's time you figured it out, son."

For a second, I thought my father had come up behind me, but it was only Marvin.

"I know," I said, leaning against Bob's wide shoulder.

"If I were your father, I'd want to hear from you sooner than the eleventh hour."

For an old guy, he was one nosy dude.

"Listening in at the door again?"

"Always," Marvin said, tapping at his hearing aid as he walked by and grabbed a bale of hay for the horses out in the corral. "And you've got a visitor."

I looked up. As Marvin walked out one end of the barn, Ari walked through the other, giving me a small, sheepish wave. She was back to normal. I should say she was back to the way I liked normal to be. Her eyes and general health were good except for one streak of dull gray hair that starkly contrasted against the glossy black.

She walked up to Bob and ran her hand along his back. She didn't have her gloves on or her compression suit. As she stood there in a bright yellow sundress and boots, I couldn't help but stare. She was gorgeous.

"You're looking better," I said, trying not to gape.

"Thanks, I feel better."

"You sure? Judging by the volume of your fight last night, it sounded like your parents aren't okay with you being this way." Superhuman hearing had its advantages, just not in this case. I didn't like hearing them yell at her like they did.

Ari shrugged. "They'll have to get used to it, because I'm not changing."

"Glad to hear it."

"Me too," she said as she scratched Bob's back. "Speaking of changes, what all do you have to live with? I already know about the crazy red eye, but what else is there?"

"Really good hearing," I said. "Especially if I don't tune it out. Sometimes I end up with what sounds like a hundred voices talking all at once."

"Which explains you knowing about the fight."

"Yep. And I have super sharp vision."

"How sharp? You can't see through clothes or anything?"

I snickered. "Nah, distance mostly. And I am really digging the superhuman strength. Can't beat that. Not to mention a photographic memory. Once it's in my head, I never forget."

"That and you are freakishly tall again."

"Six foot five isn't freakish."

"Try six foot six, and when you add on a ton of muscle, it's freakish," Ari said, playfully. I lost a snappy reply when I looked at her. Unconsciously, I reached out and loosely wound the grayish streak in her hair around my finger, letting her hair unwind itself in my palm.

"I'm not so sure I'll get used to this though," I said.

"Sorry, but I'm stuck with it," Ari said. "Believe me, I've tried, and no amount of magic will make it go away."

"You're still beautiful," I said. "It just reminds me of . . ."

It reminded me of worse times, and Silivus, and how he tortured both of us.

"Never mind," I said, and went back to brushing Bob.

"You're not getting off that easy," she said. "What does it remind you of?"

"Only of things I regret," I said. Ari looked away from me and gnawed on her bottom lip.

"About that," she said. "I got something for you. It won't make things better or anything, but I want you to have this back."

She pulled a long chain out of her dress pocket that had military dog tags strung onto it—and something else I thought I'd never see again. The tags shone dully in the sun. The pendant refracted a glint of white light off the polished silver disk. I scooped up the necklace and looked it over. "Ian Quicksilver: Super Human," I read.

"Alien didn't sound right. Do you like it? I was thinking since you are a Warrior and all, dog tags would be more fitting. Marvin helped me with it. One of his Marine buddies got them stamped out for me," she said in a nervous rush. "You don't have to wear them, I just thought that you might prefer it to carrying my pendant around in your pocket."

"Are you sure you want to do this? You know, that pendant is the only thing you have that comes from Garfel." I didn't really want to give it back, but I had to check.

"I still want you to have it."

In fifteen and a half years, I don't think anyone had gotten me a gift that was new or just mine that I didn't have to share. I tossed the chain over my head and dropped the tags and silver disk down the front of my shirt. I'd never worn dog tags before, but they fit.

"Does this mean you'll send me messages again?"

Ari nodded. "It was torture not to talk to you. I promise, I won't ever go silent like that again."

Grinning, I tossed a spare comb to Ari. She brushed Bob's back while I brushed his neck. The horse was strangely silent as he swished his tail and stared studiously out the barn door.

"Ian," Ari said. "What is Garfel like?"

"I don't know."

"Are you sure? Because you mentioned that you have a photographic memory and that you never forget."

"That's right, I don't forget, but I've never been to Garfel. I've seen it as a rising moon over the ocean on my world and that's about it."

"What about Bankhir?"

"Now that's different, though I'm sure my memory is jaded because I think it is an amazing place. I miss it. Besides, I gave that memory to you, remember?"

"Yes, but does that mean that you can't remember it now that you gave it to me?"

I thought about it long and hard. I attempted to recall the castle, the shoreline, and the smell of sea brine and salt, but the image wouldn't appear.

"Huh," I said. "I guess so."

"That's not fair," she said. "What if I gave it back to you? It's your home."

"It was worth it. I wouldn't take it back if you tried," I said. "I take it you are finally buying into the whole princess idea? It's about time."

"I haven't bought into anything just yet," Ari said, evasive. "I am reviewing my options."

"Right," I kidded. "You saw with your own eyes my transformation and helped fight off fifteen alien soldiers and you are reviewing your options?"

"It's a lot to swallow," she said. "I'm still trying to wrap my head around being from another planet and a princess and all that."

"You're not alone. I still get hung up on Silivus's curse, and I've had almost sixteen years to get a grip on it."

"Curse?"

Crud. I thought I'd explained that part. Reviewing years of history in the span of twenty minutes, under pressure of death, called for a load of editing. I was sure I'd left out plenty.

"Yeah, we were cursed," I said. "The guy really gets under my skin. He took away your memory, all of it, but made you deal with your magic without explanation or knowing how to cope with it."

"Which is handy when I think you're crazy and you tell me I'm royalty."

"Exactly. But I remembered everything. He took away Bob and Danthis and made me live here, weak and unprotected, and every second of my life I knew what I had lost."

"That's got to suck," Ari said.

"Understatement of the day," I said.

"But you got it back. Look at you. You look and act like a comic book superhero."

"Are you saying I'm channeling Superman? Because I definitely don't do capes or flying."

"What about spandex?" Ari kidded.

"Completely out of the question."

"Well, I wasn't thinking you were like Superman," Ari said. "I was thinking you are more like Captain America, and it's not fair."

"You want to be six foot and go ape-crazy on bad guys?" I teased.

"No, I'm saying it's not fair that your end of the curse was broken and mine wasn't. I want to remember who I am. I want to know that I came from another planet, not just believe it."

I had wondered about that. Theories were rolling around in my head and I had a pretty good idea why her end wasn't broken.

"I think—and this is just a guess—that my end was released because I fulfilled the requirements of my quest." Which was the lamest way to spill my guts again.

"Because you fell in love with me," Ari said. Thank the stars she didn't sound skeptical about it this time.

"Yeah," I said. Finally, Bob dropped the horse act, swung his big head around, and rolled his eyes at me. He nickered low and deep in his barrel chest, as if to say 'way to crush it.'

"So the curse isn't fully broken, right? Our planets will still be destroyed?"

"They will still be destroyed," I said, nodding.

"And to stop it, I have to . . . like you?"

"Way to cut a guy off where it counts," I said. "Don't worry, I won't force you into anything you don't want to do."

"But your people," Ari said. "*Our* people will die. I don't want that on my conscience."

"So you're saying you want me to force you?"

"No, I'm saying I want to try," Ari said. She paused as if the decision was difficult for her to formulate. "I want to try . . . for them."

"Try," I said. "Am I that bad?"

"You're not bad at all, it's just—" Ari stopped and thought about it while she picked aimlessly at Bob's hair. "It was hard for me to let you be close to me. I hate it when I hurt people, but when I took you down, that was a whole other level of . . ." She struggled to explain. "I don't want to do that again. I don't want to hurt you."

"Okay." It wasn't the most romantic reason, but heck, I'd take it.

"And," Ari added, "I want to do this for you."

"Me?"

Ari took her hand off Bob and pulled aside the collar of my shirt. She traced her fingers over the scars on my collarbone that snaked down my chest and wrapped around my back. Since I'd grown they had stretched out and faded a little, but they were still there as a reminder.

"Yes, you," she said. "I want to make what I did to you right."

I'd argue, but instead I took her hand and pressed it

over my heart. Now seemed a good time to make a complete idiot of myself.

"Arianna Hernfeld, will you accept my offer of courtship?"

Ari snort-laughed and covered it with a cough as she forced back a smile.

"Hey," I said. "Don't mock me. I don't want any loopholes."

"Sorry," she said. "But that was kind of cheesy. I couldn't help it."

"Granted, it was," I said, "but do you?"

Thankfully, she didn't keep me hanging.

"Yes, I accept."

I felt like a million bucks, and a weight lifted off my shoulders. *Father,* I thought, *if you can hear me at all . . .*

Ari's hand glowed a bright bluish-green against my shirt and I could feel her Deep Magic seep into my skin. A wisp of silver Warrior Magic joined it from my own hand as it passed through my ribs and over the bone plate to my heart. It took all of a minute, then a ball of light shot upward out of my chest, through the barn roof and into the sky.

I figured that would be the end of it and idly wondered how long it took for a message formed out of magic to travel clear across a solar system. Ari pulled her hand away, her cheeks a startling pink. I wasn't sure if that was a good response or not.

"Ian!" Marvin shouted, breaking into my thoughts. "Ian! You'd better come see this!"

I ran out the barn door with Ari and Bob trotting close behind. Marvin had dropped half the bale of hay he was carrying out to the pasture. He stared straight up.

It began with a muted boom, and then an explosion of blue and green lights, much like fireworks, if fireworks were colored bolts of lightning. Streaks of silvery electricity shot out in all directions in the clear blue sky, crackling with static charge.

"What is this?" Ari shouted over the racket. Bob whinnied a hearty laugh as Corbin stepped off the back porch and joined us in the yard.

"It's a celebration," Corbin said. "It's the King's display for the people when there is victory."

"It looks like he got my message," I said. Time was still ticking and, believe me, I felt the crunch. My father overdid it to celebrate right now.

I tried to shove my worry aside, but a nagging feeling at the base of my neck struck up, and it wouldn't go away. Rubbing the back of my neck, I turned away from the alien fireworks. That's when I saw him. Silivus was far out into the desert, draped in black robes and glaring poisoned daggers of hatred at me. My vision narrowed and zoomed in on him. When he spoke, I could barely hear him over the ruckus in the sky.

"Enjoy your victory, weakling prince," Silivus hissed. "After today I will only redouble my efforts. No one you know and care about will be safe. You have not seen the last of me."

Ice curled in around my heart. The chill came automatically as Silivus dissolved in a mist of filthy black smoke, leaving the dry valley deserted once again.

"Ian?" Ari said, jolting me back into the yard by slipping her hand in mine. "What are you looking at?"

"Nothing," I said, tearing my eyes away from the empty desert.

"Are you sure?"

"Yeah," I said, trying to work up a convincing smile. "There's nothing to worry about."

I lied. I wanted to forget all of it: Silivus, the quest, my deadline. I let go of Ari's hand and put my arm around her shoulders, convincing myself that the move was out of affection instead of overreacting. I pulled her protectively to my side and scanned the yard and desert. All was calm. For now. Even the warning system at the base of my neck quieted.

Between Silivus, my father, and the fate of two worlds, this was going to be the most dangerous courtship in the history of the planets.

Bring it on.

Discussion Questions

1 What is the first thing you would do if you found out that you came from another planet?

2 Would your reaction change if you discovered you had an impossible quest to complete to get back to your home planet?

3 Ian had his memories to help him. Would you be able to accept the truth if you, like Ari, had forgotten who you were?

4 Silivus is . . . formidable. Would you be able to stand up to someone who made your life difficult?

5 How far would you go to complete something as important as Ian's quest?

6 Would you be able to help a friend, no matter how dangerous the situation became?

7 How important is loyalty to a Warrior? Why do you think it is this way?

8 Do you think Ian would have been able to face Silivus and the Horbryn if Corbin and Ari weren't loyal friends?

9 In the end, would you have been able to show mercy as Ian did?

About the Author

Alyson Peterson lives in a mountainside gully (of all places) in northern Utah with her neurotic, shed-tastic dog, two ninja kids, and superhero husband. She spends her time painting, breaking bones at her martial arts class (mostly her own), and reading as many books as she can get her hands on.